In the Green Heart

ALSO BY RICHARD LLOYD PARRY

NON-FICTION

Ghosts of the Tsunami

People Who Eat Darkness

In the Time of Madness

In the Green Heart

RICHARD LLOYD PARRY

JONATHAN CAPE
LONDON

1 3 5 7 9 10 8 6 4 2

Jonathan Cape, an imprint of Vintage, is part of the
Penguin Random House group of companies

Vintage, Penguin Random House UK, One Embassy
Gardens, 8 Viaduct Gardens, London SW11 7BW

penguin.co.uk/vintage
global.penguinrandomhouse.com

First published by Jonathan Cape in 2025

Copyright © Richard Lloyd Parry 2025

The moral right of the author has been asserted

Penguin Random House values and supports copyright. Copyright fuels creativity, encourages diverse voices, promotes freedom of expression and supports a vibrant culture. Thank you for purchasing an authorised edition of this book and for respecting intellectual property laws by not reproducing, scanning or distributing any part of it by any means without permission. You are supporting authors and enabling Penguin Random House to continue to publish books for everyone. No part of this book may be used or reproduced in any manner for the purpose of training artificial intelligence technologies or systems. In accordance with Article 4(3) of the DSM Directive 2019/790, Penguin Random House expressly reserves this work from the text and data mining exception.

Typeset in 11.6/15.8pt Calluna by Six Red Marbles UK, Thetford, Norfolk
Printed and bound in Great Britain by Clays Ltd, Elcograf S.p.A.

The authorised representative in the EEA is Penguin Random House
Ireland, Morrison Chambers, 32 Nassau Street, Dublin D02 YH68

A CIP catalogue record for this book is available from the British Library

ISBN 9781787335097

Penguin Random House is committed to a sustainable future
for our business, our readers and our planet. This book is made
from Forest Stewardship Council® certified paper.

For my own Helen and Kit, and for Stella

1
BLOOD

I

Imps were waiting for Helen and Kit when they stepped out of the jungle. They had been there all afternoon, squatting beneath the bridge at the boundary between the village and the forest. Beneath the trees, daylight was filtered to a soupy dimness; beyond the stream, sun burned into the rising red ground. The children whooped at the sight of Helen's white bonnet, and ran behind and in front, laughing as Kit trod uncertainly across the bridge of logs and laboured up the slope to the village.

– He'len! He'len! shouted the children with the mud of the stream glittering on their ankles; strapped into the sling, Helen raised her right hand, and let it fall, as if in recognition.

– Good day, imps, said Kit, the words of the foreign language still clumsy in his mouth. – How do you fare?

– He'len! He'len! shouted the imps. – Toif! Toif!

Kit crouched down, panting, halfway through the climb, and Helen clucked and gurned while the imps took turns, peering into the baby's mouth with expressions of concentration and counting her teeth.

At the top of the hill, three of the boys skittered off among the palms and vanished into the dark hollows beneath the raised houses. Only the girl and her small brother kept up with Kit, so close on either side that their shoulders brushed against his shorts. Kit looked down at the girl, and her smiling, upward tilted face. A green ribbon tied up her black hair. He knew that she longed to carry Helen; he also recognised that at the age of nine or ten she had years more experience than him in the care of infants. But, at the thought of surrendering Helen, a barrier of anxiety loomed in his mind; however much he liked the girl, he could not give his baby daughter into her arms.

– Now we go to eat, he said, and the children smiled again and widened their eyes. – Thank you, imps.

He walked on to the house, elevated like the others on its platform of logs, and ducked into the shadowed gap beneath. The space was filled by a squat metal container, six feet high, with a door on one side. Its matt grey surface was at odds with the gloss and green of the tropical vegetation that trailed over and around it. From deep within, it gave out a low, barely audible hum.

Kit was rinsed with sweat. He opened the door of the Koolroom and stepped inside. The processed air was bracingly chilled and dry. He set Helen down on the bed, and pulled the damp T-shirt over his head. Then he removed Helen's bonnet and her one-piece cotton suit, long-armed and long-sleeved to ward off the sun, and wet from being pressed against him in the sling. He slid her small body across the quilt so that she lay beneath the buffeting jet of air from the ceiling. The paper nappy bulged between her legs. Lara could be heard behind the partition, rattling among the medical supplies.

'We're back,' he called, as he towelled the wetness of his chest and belly.

'Welcome home, team,' said Lara loudly. There were sounds of glass and metal being shuffled impatiently.

'What are you looking for in there?'

'Anti-parasitics.'

'D'you need a hand?'

'They're in here somewhere.'

A pile of pharmaceutical boxes had already been heaped up by Lara beside the bed. Kit considered the purpose of these preparations and what they meant for him and Helen.

There was a pause in the sounds on the other side of the partition, as if Lara was thinking too. She said, 'So what did you two get up to this afternoon?'

'We went into the forest. Not far, but far enough. We found that kind of tree house that they built in there, just found it by chance. I climbed with her a bit of the way up. D'you know, it's the first time I really listened to the jungle? At first, you're so struck with how it looks. I never noticed until today how loud it all is.'

'It is. It's amazing.' Lara resumed her clatter on the far side of the partition, pushing or pulling something heavy along the floor.

'The children were waiting for us when we came out. They counted her teeth again.'

'They love her teeth,' Lara said distractedly.

'They know the word "teeth" now. I taught them, and they remembered it. *Toif! Toif!*'

Lara made no reply.

'She loves it in the forest. There was a bird we could hear, although we couldn't see it. It could have been some kind of monkey, but I think it was a bird. She was pointing up towards the noise, and smiling. And it's cooler there, under the canopy. Humid, though, so it feels hot. The hardest part is that walk back up the hill.'

Kit's eyes settled on the photograph attached by a magnet to the inside of the Koolroom's metallic door: Helen in the white hospital gown, moments old, with spikes of wet hair and eyes still puffy with the journey from water to air.

On the bed, she executed a sequence of kicks and punches which slapped the dry surface of the quilt.

Toh! she shouted. Moy yoy yoy!

Kit smiled at himself: transported by the beauty of her image, he had forgotten that the actual Helen was lying in front of him. He raised the lid of the box by the bed and took out the rectangular changing mat. Beside it, he placed the wipes, the cream and a crisp new nappy. He pulled Helen gently towards him by her ankles, arrayed her on the cushion, tore the old nappy on each side of her hips, and tugged it free. There was nothing dark this time; the plumpness was all liquid. But a livid rash filled the fold between her buttocks, and reached the top of her thighs. Kit's heart flexed with the thought of how uncomfortable this must be. He stroked delicately with the wipes, and smeared the rash with coral-coloured cream.

Lara stepped out from behind the partition, brandishing two pharmaceutical boxes, the size and shape of cigarette cartons. 'Found them!' she said, leaning forward and waving them in front of Helen. She put her arm around Kit's shoulder and placed a kiss on the side of his head. Lara was as tall as Kit; with her emergence into the cramped sleeping space, the walls of the container seemed to contract around the small double bed and cot. Kit kissed her on the lips, and she stood back to give him room to dress the rash and fasten the adhesive tabs of the new nappy. A stock of them, scores of tight plastic packets, ferried for days upriver, formed a squat mound next to the Koolroom, covered by a weighted tarpaulin.

'Her poor skin,' said Kit. 'See how sore she is.' He put the top back on the tube of ointment, resealed the wipes, and restored them to their box. Then he folded up the soiled nappy, a dense brick of paper and urine, and dropped it into the burn bucket by the door.

'You missed a bit there,' said Lara. She was right: the nappy rash had spread beyond the continent of rawness surrounding Helen's loins and established a new colony, a small but angry island of red in the middle of the baby's left buttock.

After dinner they sat upstairs on the verandah with their legs dangling over the platform. Kit ate tinned peaches from a plastic bowl. Lara inhaled on a small joint, its tip the last source of light visible in the village. The cooking fires had flickered and faltered, and the meal-time murmur from the other houses was dying away. Even in the deep of night the village was never silent, for there were always muffled coughs, indistinct and unknowable groans, relays of barking from wakeful dogs, the voluntaries of untimely cockerels and the plash of pissing from the platforms. The Koolroom, where Helen slept, emitted a profound throbbing hum close to the outer threshold of hearing; the faint white noise of the baby monitor was more intrusive. Without being conscious of it, Kit and Lara spoke almost in whispers.

'When will you be back?' he asked.

'It'll take a week. Eight, nine days max. If the people we need to talk to aren't there – if someone is out hunting, say, who we need to see to complete the surveys. Or some dire medical situation, that kind of thing. Which won't happen, by the way, because they have a midwife there and she is really good.'

The sound from the monitor altered suddenly in texture, suggesting movement in the Koolroom below. Kit and Lara both stopped speaking and angled their heads. But the rustling faded back into hiss.

She put her arm around his shoulder. 'I'm sorry, baby,' she said. It was an endearment that she only ever used when she was mildly stoned. 'You'll be OK, right?'

'It's your work,' he said, and squeezed her in return. 'It's why we're here. But it's a long way.'

'It's the next village.'

'It's two days' walk.'

'A day and a half. At the very most.'

'You have a daughter.'

'And she will be with her father, who loves her and will look after her as well as anyone in the world.'

Kit thought: she speaks so honestly. It would have been obvious to say 'better than anyone', just as it would have been simple to pretend that the work would be done in six days, rather than a week. But Lara never flattered or exaggerated to ease the passage of an awkward moment. She would leave tomorrow, and she would come back again, as quickly as her work allowed. He and Helen had all they needed. The time would pass quickly.

He said, 'She misses you when you go away.'

'Strictly – she doesn't, you know. The baby books make out like she does, but she won't develop the capacity for that kind of identification for a while. If anything, she'd miss you, because you hold the bottle. But really, it's the bottle she's dependent on. I don't mean to sound cold – of course, she'll feel love and attachment when the time comes. But right now, this is the little creature she is. She's a survival machine.'

'If you say so, doc.' He took the joint from her fingers, and held it. The thin end was wet with Lara's saliva; the smoke was sweet and acrid. It would be easy to take a few drags; the ease that they brought would bring Lara and the world closer. But it was unthinkable that both of them should be stupefied with Helen in their care. He passed back the joint.

She said, 'It's going to be a whole lot easier when the rains start, and then we can take the river all the way. It's already starting to rain upcountry. Ten days – maybe even in time for me when I come back – the river will fill up and we'll be zipping down it by boat.'

'I thought the rain made the tracks impassable?'

'Those tracks are terrible at the best of times.'

'I just don't like the idea of having nowhere to go, by road. Of being trapped by land.'

'You get over thinking like that. The rivers are the roads once the level rises – they're the highway. But until the rains start, they're closed.'

This was the pattern of so many of their conversations; they were like games of chess between players with radically different styles. Lara advanced her point of view with bold, factual statements. Kit responded obliquely, without offering direct contradiction. He edged sideways then back, and found himself agreeing with what she said as if it had been his own thought. But he could not reach the state of agreement without going through that volley of opening moves. The pieces had to be set up; the game had to begin.

'We'll be fine,' he said. 'Of course. I can give some more lessons to the imps. I'll work on the Tongue. What else do I need to do?'

'Just remember to check in with Kay by radio at nine and six. When the radio starts working again. Because I'll be taking the satphone. You won't be lonely, by the way. You're going to have company from tomorrow.'

'Is it tomorrow? You think he'll really come.'

'Most definitely.' She relit the joint. 'He got through on the phone when you two were out. He's on his way back now.'

'Oh, God.'

'And I'm sure he's looking forward to seeing you too.'

'It's not me he's interested in,' said Kit, and they smiled at one another. 'What else did he say?'

'He's still convinced that something's going down on the border, but sounds like he's not found so much. Just the usual wild talk.'

'So nothing to worry about then?'

'Oh, *he's* worried. He sounded paranoid. He has something to show us, but he couldn't say what it was' – she made quotation marks with her raised fingers – '"on an open line".'

Kit smiled without answering. Moments passed, and kept passing. The sound of the forest rose in his ears, the treble of birds above the seething of the insects. Time going by in the jungle way, without ticking of clock.

Then Lara was speaking. 'Kit,' she said. 'You're doing it again. You're drifting off – don't drift off on me.'

The monitor rustled, and once again fell silent.

Lara and Kit's house was built on hardwood columns and covered by a sloping roof of thatch. The floor was made from lengths of split bamboo, flattened out and held down with wooden nails to form a springy plane. At the centre was a square hearth, a deep box of fire-hardened wood containing ash and sand. Lara would have liked to use this as the villagers did, with logs constantly burning, the smoke creating a billowing, companionable fug. In consideration of Helen's small lungs, she compromised with a small fire burning low in the hearth's corner.

'How can people sit round a fire when it's thirty-six degrees?' Kit asked.

'It's not about the heat,' said Lara. 'People say that a house is empty without a fire – it's like living in some place with bare walls or a concrete floor. And they mean that it's haunted too. The fire keeps out the spirits, not just the mosquitoes.'

'Keeps out imps?' The word for children, Kit had learned, in his early studies in the Tongue, was the same as a category of mischievous jungle fairies.

'Worse than imps. The bad ones.'

The house was old and solid, its inner surfaces seasoned with a sooty patina. It had been the home of a childless widow who had died the previous year. Its position, on a rise on the edge of the village, secure from floods and predators, suggested that she had been a woman of rank; the loan of it, Kit knew, was a mark of the esteem that Lara had earned in the months before his arrival. Nailed high up on the central pillar was a shrine, an open-fronted box containing carved forms of men and beasts, and ribbons of yellowed animal skin. Above it, in the topmost reaches of the eaves, almost unrecognisable behind the dried grass that curled out of their noses and eyes, was a cluster of skulls. They were the war trophies of the widow's ancestors. They appeared not to have been disturbed since the house was built, and had about them an air of serene antiquity. Most of the houses contained such relics. Once a month, the face of an ancient lady, the widow's sister or niece, would appear at the top of the notched log which served as a staircase connecting platform and ground; wordlessly, she would enter the house, nod to Lara and Kit, and stand before the pillar, intoning a low song, before nodding and leaving again. Far from being disturbed by the skulls, Kit found he was comforted by their presence. On the day they moved in, it was Lara who pulled a face as she looked up.

'It's what they represent,' he tried to explain. 'This place, this environment – so extreme and fragile. The sun dries everything up, then the water comes and washes it all away. Mothers die in childbirth. Kids die of simple illnesses. Parasites, snake bites, failed crops. But then you see these artefacts, which are older than anyone here, older than the parents, probably, of the oldest person here – and you understand that this is an ancient place, and that life goes on, despite everything.'

'Honey, they're trophies of war,' said Lara. 'They're

symbols of continuity like any other captured loot. So they look quaint now, all dried out and grizzly in the eaves. When they were fresh they wouldn't have been so pretty, mounted on a spike with the flies buzzing in and out. It's the kind of continuity that says, "We defeated you – we continue. But you lost – so we chop your head off, and eat your heart. No continuity for you."'

'They didn't eat their hearts.'

'Most certainly they did.'

Kit shook his head and smiled. 'But think about when Helen is grown up,' he said, 'and we can tell her that when she was a baby she lived in a house with severed heads on the ceiling.'

'She certainly is a privileged little girl,' Lara had said, and pulled another face.

Tonight, the heads were all but invisible in the glow of the camping lamp. Kit lay beneath the mosquito net, his head supported by an elbow. He was leafing through the dense ring-bound file, a block of tatty sheets dense with Lara's handwriting. In a few months, alone and unguided, she had recorded the rudiments of the local language, the Tongue.

Lara was arranging cartons of pharmaceuticals and polythene-encased documents on the floor.

'When I say this,' Kit asked through the mesh of the mosquito net, 'have I got it right? *Thank you, imps. Now we go to eat.*' The interior of the house was covered on four sides, and once within it they no longer felt the need to whisper.

Lara smiled. 'You've got it right.'

'Because whenever I say it, I feel as if they're laughing at me.'

Lara was trying to stifle laughter of her own, as she sucked on the spliff.

'What's so funny?'

'It's because – because, you speak like a woman!'

'What?'

'*Now we go to eat*. That's the woman's form. A man says – something else.'

'Like what?'

'I don't know! I mean I recognize it when I hear it, but it doesn't stick with me, because I don't need it.'

'Is it the pronunciation?'

'It's intonation, but it's also a completely different verb, another word altogether.'

'You mean I talk like a woman?'

'Yes, you do. But a married woman, and a mother. Don't worry – you don't talk like a virgin. That's a different register.'

Kit sat up beneath the net. 'And you've known this all along?'

Lara nodded, her mouth pursed with restrained laughter.

'So you let me make a fool of myself. Why didn't you say something?'

'Don't get mad,' Lara said, no longer smiling now. 'I just – you worked so hard at it, and I hadn't known how hard you'd been working, and I was touched by how much you'd done, all the progress you'd made. We came here, and you had nothing, and then one day, you were talking, really communicating, and it felt like that was the important thing, not the exact words you were using.'

'But it does matter, in fact?'

'That was something else I didn't realize,' she said. 'That it made such a difference in practice.'

'They must think I'm a freak.'

'But, honey – you're unusual to them anyway, right?' She was standing over him and looking down through the net. 'We both are. Our roles here – we've got to accept that we're freaks. Freaks, but decent, sympathetic, helpful freaks. Unthreatening, non-judgmental, consistent freaks. Isn't that the beauty of our position? We can live with these people, these remarkable people, we can observe their lives, their society, we can help them, and we can even fit in to a certain extent, get included in things that people from the outside never see. But we're still apart, and that's fine by us. We can take it on our own terms, without being bound by all the rules and conventions.'

'That's all very nice, in theory,' said Kit. 'But I'm the one being laughed at. It must be a bit confusing for everyone – no? – me talking as if I'm gay.'

'That's the thing – you don't. I asked about that, and it's really interesting: gay men and women use other registers altogether. So you do sound like a woman, but a straight woman – respectable. A good wife and mom.'

The words unlocked the laughter Lara had been holding in. Her features crumpled in a pink mask of tears. She sank on to her knees, then sat down on the bamboo.

'I'm sorry,' she said eventually, when she had stopped hooting. 'It's not that funny.'

'You're stoned,' said Kit, but his annoyance had passed. 'It's just – you've got to tell me these things. You've done the study – I have to rely on you.'

'Oh man, it took me long enough for my own purposes. I haven't got time to go over it all again for the male language.'

'I rely on you for everything here,' Kit said, from inside the net. 'Even the words I speak.'

'Oh, baby,' she said, and laughed again.

Lara objected on principle to the artificiality of infant formula, but from the beginning she had also ruled out breast feeding. 'The milk is hers,' she said. 'My tits are my own.' Kit did not feel in a position to question this; he kept to himself the observation that the alternative, repeatedly pumping her breasts, seemed several times more troublesome. Before going to sleep in the Koolroom, he fed Helen with the milk that Lara had expressed that afternoon. He woke twice again in the night to feed her. The first time, she drank hungrily, belched, and slumped immediately on his shoulder. The second bottle went down with difficulty. After a few minutes of sucking, Helen's mouth would grow slack, and the teat would slither out from between her gums, provoking angry cries. It took Kit most of an hour to coax her back to sleep. He paced up and down the narrow space between the bed and partition, counting his steps, and murmuring songs and rhymes into Helen's ear until her head slackened and her breathing slowed.

Lara had finished her packing late, and slept in the house above to avoid disturbing them with the bustle of the early start. But soon after dawn, she opened the container door and slipped behind the partition to retrieve the vials of vaccine which she transferred to an insulated pouch. Helen woke, gasped, cried briefly, gasped again, then fetched up a happy shouting. Kit lifted her out of the cot, pushed on her bonnet, and carried her outside to see Lara off.

Paulus, the young health worker, was there with the two village men who would travel with them. Overseeing their departure was Obson, the village militia man. He wore a dusty camouflage jacket over a green T-shirt bearing the face of Mochtar Mohamad, the new prime minister; his old bolt-action rifle was slung over his shoulder. Paulus and the two men were dividing up the packets of food and drugs that they would carry along the trail, sealing them in waterproof plastic, and squeezing them into rucksacks.

– Good morning, Mr Obson, said Kit, in the words he had learned from Lara's file.

'Good morning, Mister Kristian,' said Obson in English. 'Good morning, Miss He'len.'

Bouwh, said Helen in a tone of earnestness. Then, with quiet sarcasm: Bauwh.

The two porters put down their bags and peered at Helen as she kicked and gesticulated. Kit was fairly sure that they were father and son. The younger man had short dense hair that glistened as if dressed with oil. His skin was deep black, and the tattoos trailed from beneath his T-shirt and shorts, up his neck and down along his arms and calves. The people of this place were celebrated for these tattoos, the charcoal patterns on aubergine skin thrillingly obscure and mysterious, like shadows in darkness.

The older man might have been any age between forty and eighty. His hair, which was longer and bristled up on his head, was completely white. He looked – and Kit shrank in shame from the thought which, he suspected, encoded racist notions on his part – like the photographic negative of a dark-haired white man. His skin too was intensely dark, but some change had occurred with ageing, a mottling and lightening, or a slow change in the composition of the ink, making the figures of the tattoos clearer and less enigmatic: fish, snakes, birds, spears, shields.

The men were talking with animation as they peered at Helen. Kit could follow little of what they said, but knew that it was to do with her teeth.

'For our people,' said Obson, 'child's teeth is like a fortune telling in your country.'

'Like this,' said Paulus. He pointed to his open hand and sketched lines across it with a finger.

'Like palm reading? You mean they can read her future in her teeth?'

'Why not?' said Paulus.

'It is against Islam,' said Obson gravely, 'but they like it.' He flapped his hand at the father and son. 'I am not so good at the reading, but they know well.'

'So – tooth-reading. Now it makes sense.' Kit took satisfaction in having uncovered this ethnographic titbit for himself, without having it pointed out to him by Lara. 'And what is Helen's future?'

Obson put the question to the village men, who peered in at her mouth, and engaged in a lively dialogue. Two teeth, tiny but scintillatingly white, emerged from the gums of Helen's lower jaw. The older man appeared to be describing them, as a dentist might describe the condition of a patient's mouth to an annotating assistant. He frowned and corrected himself as he struggled for the appropriate words. Kit looked at the limbs of the men, which were slim, but flawlessly muscular and defined. Despite their animation, their heads and hands remained still.

The tooth readers agreed on their assessment which was conveyed lengthily to Obson.

He frowned with concentration as they spoke, then turned to Kit. 'They said she will go on a long journey.'

He waited for more, but Obson nodded conclusively.

Kit smiled. 'That's the kind of thing that fortune tellers in my country say too.' In the Tongue, he added – Thank you for teaching me, Mr Obson.

The two porters looked at one another, then at Kit, and broke into guffaws. Paulus was trying not to laugh.

'Is it wrong, Obson, what I said?' Kit was careful to maintain his own smile. 'Did I make a mistake?'

'It is right, it is right,' Obson said, with his eyes laughing and downcast. 'It is because it is . . . cute, this way you say it.'

A moment passed and prolonged itself into a silence. It was broken by the appearance of Lara, who was climbing down the notched log from the platform of the house. Her body looked supple and powerful as it held itself against the log. Her hair was held in a high band.

'Time to go, my darlings,' she said, kissing the faces of Helen and Kit. 'Look after one another, OK?'

Kit nodded and stroked a globe of sweat from her cheek. He was never entirely comfortable exchanging physical intimacies in public – wasn't there a taboo about such displays? But Lara was unselfconscious about them.

She surveyed the tightly packed bags on the red earth. 'All OK, Paulus?' she asked.

To the father and son, she addressed a series of formal-sounding phrases, of which Kit understood only, – Let us travel. She lifted the pack on to her back, and as she leaned forward the convexity of her belly became visible, the residue of the pregnancy.

'Goodbye, my loves,' she said. 'See you in a week.' Then she, Paulus and the two men began to walk quickly towards the forest.

Obson raised his arm in farewell. Kit held up Helen's hand and waved it towards her mother. But the child resisted, and began to grumble and arch her back.

'Bye-bye!' Kit said, on behalf of both of them. 'Come back soon.' And then he called out, – Travel in safety.

The father and son spluttered with laughter again, and repeated the words to one another in unmistakably mincing tones. Helen began to cry.

2

Court Hardy walked out of the jungle late the following afternoon.

Helen and Kit were on the verandah of the house, where Helen was feeding. The girl with the green ribbon was there, crouched on the bamboo with her brother, watching the fast rhythmic movement of Helen's mouth around the rubber nipple. The boy fidgeted, scratched, and flicked at columns of trundling ants. But the girl was still. Kit watched her face, as she watched Helen's. From time to time, at some small alteration in the pattern of the child's sucking, she pursed her lips. When Helen broke off from the bottle, her eyes widened; her head nodded gently to the vacuum clicks of the fluid passing through the eye of the teat. Only at the end, when Kit eased the sated Helen on to his shoulder and patted from her a climactic, baritone burp, did the little girl smile. He could feel her yearning to hold and nuzzle the soft, drowsing baby, so strong it was almost a physical force. His reluctance to hand her over was like a constraint around him, a girdle of confused and guilty anxiety about contagion, pollution, darkness and dirt. He was ashamed of these thoughts; he knew that they were irrational; but he also understood that they could not be overcome, and that all he could do, for the time being, was to meet the girl's tenderness with his own.

Her brother stirred and looked out from the verandah. A band of imps was approaching with shrill calls and whistles, accompanied by the strutting figure of Obson. Among them, staggering in long, exhausted steps, was Court.

Kit sat with Helen on his lap, looking down as he tottered to the bottom of the notched log followed by his small company of guides and bearers. Court's thin, straw-coloured hair was glued to his scalp with sweat. His spectacles were grimed with droplets which had rolled down the glass and dried off, leaving fine salty tracks. His face was grey beneath several days of beard.

'Good afternoon,' said Kit, with an attempt at warmth. 'You must be tired.'

Court gave an ironic smile. 'Good day to you.' He nodded beneath the platform of the house towards the Koolroom. 'You haven't got anything cold and fizzy in that big fridge of yours, have you?'

'Come up.'

The tripod strapped to Court's back wobbled as he ascended the log. His boots, which wore a sheath of drying mud, were too big for its notches; twice they slipped out, leaving him kicking the air and gripping the log between both arms. He was panting as he manoeuvred himself on to the platform.

'Fuck me,' said Court, wheezing. 'Fuckadilla and Cunticula.'

Kit stood. From his arms Helen flapped hands towards the visitor. Bah, she said, declaratively.

'Hello, little girl,' said Court, still breathing heavily, as he wriggled out of his pack.

'I'll just put her down,' said Kit. 'Give me a moment. Help yourself to water. The stuff in the jar is from the well, and it's clean.' With a smile of his own he said, 'I don't have beer or champagne, I'm afraid.'

There was more grunting. By the time Kit had balanced the sleeping Helen in the hammock, Court was slumped on his elbow beside the ceramic jar, slurping water from the coconut shell that was attached to it by a cord.

'Fuckaroo,' he said eventually. 'Thank you for that, my friend. Thank you.' He placed a hand over his heart as if to reckon its beating. 'My friend – you don't, do you, have a cigarette?'

Kit removed from its place in the thatch the packet that Lara used to make up her joints, and handed it to him. 'My thanks,' said Court. 'I ran out two days ago.'

He flicked a steel lighter, and sucked hungrily on the cigarette. After a few noisy exhalations, Kit said, 'You had a tough trip? You must sleep here tonight, of course.'

'I had a remarkable trip. And thank you. I would be very glad to stay here. I might even lie down now, if I may. Feeling a bit seedy.'

'Make yourself comfortable. Take that mat in the corner.'

'The mat,' said Court in a level voice.

Kit knew that Court wanted to go below and to sleep in the Koolroom. He knew that if Lara had been here, she would have suggested it. But he would not be making the suggestion; and if Court asked, he would give an excuse.

Without standing up, Court crawled on to the mat. He lit another cigarette and smoked it, as he lay on his side.

Kit felt the pressure of the silence, the awkwardness of the favour which had not been asked and which had been silently refused. To relieve it, he said, 'So you had an interesting trip?'

Court nodded, horizontally, one side of his head on the mat. 'Interesting, yes. Terrifying.' He pulled himself up and rummaged in one of the pockets of his sodden shirt. 'What it all means – well what it all means is that you and your wife and kiddy have got to go. You can't stay here any longer. I've got to go too. I've got to get my images out, I've got to get this story out. Here—'

His hand emerged from his pocket, and he flicked it towards Kit. A small, heavy object flew from his palm, and fell short, skimming across the bamboo. Instinctively, Kit darted after it, picked it up, and found that it was a bullet, still encased in its brass cartridge.

It was three weeks since he had first appeared in the village, heralded by a radio message from the capital. The distinguished journalist Court Hardy was in the city; he was travelling in their direction to investigate rumours from the border.

Eight days later he had appeared at the bottom of the notched log. He was in late middle age; stout, towering and ebullient. 'Lara! Kristian!' he boomed, as they climbed down from the platform. 'I have heard much about you.'

Kit knew all about Hardy too, or rather his reputation: the fearless radical, indignant witness to violence, repression and injustice. His work – in the boiling, churning places of the world – had been much talked of when Kit was a university student; he had even been to a lecture that Court had given in a packed theatre.

Lara was just as excited to meet this dashing and subversive figure. They talked nervously of his imminent arrival; they welcomed him with shy enthusiasm. For Kit, the process of disillusionment had taken three days.

At first, he wondered if he was being unfair. In the confusion of greeting Court, and heaving on to the platform his heavy bags, neither he nor Lara had explained that shoes were worn only on the outer verandah – that it was, in fact, a minor village taboo to bring them inside. But it must have occurred to him that everyone else who entered the house went barefoot, and that his boots alone were printing tracks of mud across the shiny bamboo. It was the same with the sleeping arrangements. When the time came to retire on the first evening, Kit brought out mats on which the guest could arrange himself on the platform. But Court was already halfway down the log, and following Lara into the confines of the Koolroom. A space was cleared for him at the foot of the bed, with much disturbance to the grumbling Helen. He took his place there every night, grunting and snorting inches below Kit and Lara's feet.

'It's only for a few days,' Lara said the next morning, after Court had trudged out to the latrine. 'And he's remarkable, right? How often d'you get to meet someone like him?'

That night, over flasks of rice wine, Court talked long and late. He spoke in sweeping soliloquies, charged with historical reference, anecdote and invective, enamelled with quotations from literature and philosophy. To much of Court's thinking, Kit gave his instinctive assent: that international politics and business was configured in the interests of a small group of powerful and wealthy people, to whom the well-being of the majority was of only incidental concern; that journalists lied, for much of the time, or remained silent upon matters of the greatest importance; that war was an atrocity, in which people who should know better had been conned into finding glory and nobility. He found himself stirred by Court's presence, and by the atmosphere of the evening. The deep, passionate voice, with its booming rhythms, rolled on across the hours, in talk of massacres, coups and invasions. The sour tingle of the rice wine, the creaking of the house's settling timbers, the glimmering of the hearth, and Court's jowly, commanding face shadowed in its light brought out in their lives an unrealised glamour. At one point, in listening to Court, he became aware of something that startled him – for the first time since her birth, he had gone for five minutes or longer without thinking about Helen.

It was the next day when he noticed Court's habit of referring to himself in the third person. The first time, Kit had been confused by references to 'Mr C.'; then he understood. 'Have you read much Hardy?' Court asked Lara, who smiled, hesitated, then launched into a chatty reminiscence about studying *Tess* as a sophomore. 'The other Hardy,' said Court, interrupting her.

At the same time, one of the attractive things about Court, the flattering directness of his gaze, the sense of being singled out by the brilliant beam of his attention, gave way to its opposite. The longer he talked, the more often Kit recognised observations, anecdotes, and entire paragraphs from the lecture he had attended years earlier. Fervent with eloquence, Court would pause, his glance abstracted, in the attitude of one dragging new insight from the depths of his intelligence, before repeating something that he had said, in the headiness of wine, only the evening before.

It was when he spoke of local politics that Kit experienced the biggest jolt – the realisation that Court was not only opinionated but poorly informed.

He was talking about what had brought him to the village, the rumours of murky goings-on across the border. It lay in the uplands, several days' journey west of the village, a straight line ruled from north to south across mountain, cliff and elevated jungle. On this side was what the people of the village referred to simply as the Country; beyond it lay the Christian Neighbour or the Jesus Place. For most of its history, the border had been an arbitrary division of people who spoke similar languages, worshipped common gods and lived as they had always done, on dry rice, wild pig and fruits and tubers foraged from the jungle. Four things had transformed the fortunes of the Neighbour: logging, mining, missionaries and the friendship of the Superpower. Nowadays, on the far side of the border, lorries loaded with ore rumbled down fast roads cut through the bush; river barges carried timber to the sawmills on the coast. The towns through which they passed had cement churches and airfields with advanced radar systems. At the river's mouth was a city with banks and ministries, a cathedral, a brothel quarter, a lane of embassies, a ragged skirt of slums and the warships of the Superpower in the deep-water port.

When the Country had elected Mochtar Mohamad

the previous year, it had caused alarm across the world, nowhere more than in the Neighbour and the Superpower.

Out had gone the old prime minister, the unsmiling, grey-suited friend of the West; in came the fiery, witty, English-speaking Muslim. Within weeks, he was redrafting the constitution and nationalising banks; within months, he was revoking the Superpower's lease on a naval jetty in the capital, and sending home its detachment of marines. Listening to the short-wave radio late at night, with Helen in his arms and the bottle in his hand, Kit would digest the latest news with amazement. Even when she was not stoned, Lara took giddy unpatriotic pleasure in the discomfiture of her government.

'You don't know how happy this makes me,' she said. 'They have had it so long coming. Finally – finally! – someone has the guts to say no to Uncle Fuckface.'

'CSF!' she shouted, after a joint. 'CSF! Confederated States of Fuckface!'

Ever since the election, there had been dark stories about the transit of infiltrators across the border.

Lara would hear them on her travels between the villages. In some accounts, the interlopers were Christian missionaries; in others, they were armed thugs or trained paramilitaries, bent on undermining the new government; or even regular troops belonging to the Neighbour's large and well-equipped army. In the most alarming stories, they were accompanied by soldiers of the Superpower itself. Local hunters had spied them in the jungle, it was said; others, who had gone to investigate, had vanished and never come back. The rumours were told and retold, and passed among the remote villages, never in quite the same form. They lacked names, places, detail; they were vague, inconsistent and impossible to check. Court had swallowed them whole.

'They can't let it stand, you see,' he said. 'Mochtar's victory – it's intolerable to them. A Muslim – worse than that, a Muslim *socialist*. Worst of all, a profoundly well educated – Western educated – intellectual. He is the nightmare for those people. He's come from within their system, nurtured on their scholarships and in their institutions. Then he's turned round to say, "Sorry – no. We can do better than this." Then he's won – won an election, fair and square, and by a landslide, against all the predictions of the think-tankers and special correspondents and the punditocracy. It's beyond their comprehension. They will act, as they always do. They will act with violence, manipulation and illegality to restore the *status quo ante*. They are acting already.'

Lara, who was rolling a spliff, said, 'All that is true, Court, OK? Anyone who knows history understands that's the kind of things they do. But these stories from the border – couldn't they be just that, stories? In this kind of place, there's always talk like this. These are pre-literate societies, right? It's an oral culture. You tell stories as a way of understanding an environment that is dangerous, often frightening and where tragic things happen all the time.'

Court, who was by nature an interrupter, was nodding silently as she spoke. He smiled with indulgent respect.

'So, OK,' Lara went on. 'The first time I came here, last year, before this election, a hunter went missing in a village right up by the border. All the men went out looking for him. So, they searched and searched. No sign. And then the elders all got together, and they announced what had happened to him. It was a badger bear, a talking, man-eating, twenty-foot-high badger bear with red eyes that was rampaging through the forest. Don't ask me how they knew, but they were absolutely certain. They were holding ceremonies for a week – killing pigs, burning teeth, sending menstruating women out into the forest. Then the story changed. The hunter had been found – but turned to stone. He'd come across one of the nomads in the forest, they said, and he'd pissed the guy off somehow, and this nomad had turned him to stone. There's a guy here who swears he's seen the petrified dude in the forest. Promises he'll take me there some day. And this is culture – right? – and culture is a beautiful thing. I respect these beliefs – it's not for me to judge how these people choose to understand the world they live in. But when it comes to making important decisions about your own life, you've got to look at what lies at the bottom of these stories. You don't want to go chasing badger bears.'

'My dear Lara,' said Court, with more nods and smiles. 'It's not just me who believes this. People in the capital, serious people at the highest level, have been following this closely. There's something very nasty going on, and people from your country are behind it.'

'Those people are evil fuckers, and I'm the first to admit it,' she said. 'But what would they have to gain? This country means nothing to people back home. If it sank into the sea, folks back in the place I grew up wouldn't even notice.'

Court elaborated on the case that would be made for armed intervention. The Country's geographical position, close to crucial straits and sea lanes. Access to minerals newly discovered in the eastern province. 'When they justify it to themselves,' he said, 'they'll talk about the strategic picture and counter-terrorism, and how this country has become a base for bomb making or training camps. But what it really comes down to is fear – fear of blackness, fear of the dark. And the need for an enemy. And the impossibility of accepting the existence of people with a different conception of the way that the world should be.'

Lara was smiling, but Kit, who had been silent, was prompted to speak up. 'It's not the Cold War anymore,' he said. 'If the—'

'It's worse,' said Court. 'Then you had a clearly defined enemy. Now they're just running from bogeymen, shooting at shadows.'

'But hang on, where's the army that's going to—'

'Right there, just over the border – the "Jesus Men".' Court chuckled mirthlessly. 'Well trained, well equipped – by guess who? They don't need to send in the Marine Corps – your "Christian neighbour" already has one of its own. Jet fighters, napalm. Special forces with silver crosses round their necks. They'll come up with an excuse. Terrorism. Or drugs. Or they'll stage an incident, claim that the other side crossed the border first.'

'It just doesn't sound very likely to—'

'My friend, my friend,' said Court. 'Stop for a moment. Think about it. Has it occurred to you why you are so reluctant to accept this? That there is perhaps an element of denial? Because if I am right about this, then your life here is going to change, and drastically. You're going to have to take your little baby, and leave, with dispatch. And that must be hard to accept.'

There was a silence. Lara poured the rice wine. The languid smile returned to Court's face. 'What is a badger bear, anyway?' he said.

'Small, stripy jungle bear,' said Lara. 'They're shy generally, but if you corner one they can give a nasty bite. Only the supernatural ones are twenty feet high.'

'Well, bogey bears or no bogey bears, Mr C. is going to go and find out.' He smiled delightedly, and there was another pause. 'My dear Lara,' Court said next. 'Could I trouble you for a touch more of that remarkable marijuana?'

Lara reached over and proffered the wet end of the spliff.

'It's all yours, baby.'

By the third day, Court's flirting with Lara was undisguised. Kit did not feel threatened by it in the conventional way. Lara, he could see, found it as absurd as he did, signalling to him with raised eyebrows and covert grimaces of mock agony. What infuriated him was the way that Court, in his own home, had manoeuvred him into roles that he refused to accept – the reactionary defender of the Superpower, the jealous lover and cuckold-in-waiting. In the few moments during the day when Court was not within earshot, it was all that Kit could talk about.

'Apart from anything else, he's a hypocrite,' he said. 'All that crap about how much he loves children, and the dead one that he found in the refugee camp. He's been living off that story for thirty years. But have you seen the way he looks at a living child – at Helen? At her dirty nappies? Suddenly the great war reporter isn't so brave.'

'He can be a bit much,' said Lara.

'You notice that he's never actually lived among any of these afflicted people that he claims to love so much? He parachutes in for a few days, tops up on moral outrage, and then jets home again.'

'I hadn't thought of that, but you're right.'

'And he's only interested in war. When you're talking about parasites and dirty water, the small, unspectacular, unglamorous things which kill far more people, he glazes over.'

They were sitting in the house. Lara was expressing milk with the plastic pump. Kit was giving Helen her afternoon bottle. Court's voice could be heard outside, speaking loudly to the village schoolmaster, a silent and anxious man named Justus whom he was engaging as guide and interpreter. They had left for the border the following morning; Kit's irritation had lifted, and his life had returned to its routine. And now Court was back.

'Your splendid wife,' Court said suddenly. It was late in the evening, and they faced one another on the mats in the declining glow from the hearth. Court had awoken from his nap much refreshed and eaten heartily from a pot of chicken stew. 'Your magnificent wife,' he said. 'Or your partner – I'm not sure what you prefer. She's not actually a doctor, is she?'

He was toying with the bullet, which he tossed into the air, and caught as it fell. Kit had resolved, as part of his revenge, that he would wait as long as possible before asking about it.

'Well, she has a doctorate.'

'But not in medicine.'

'No,' he said. 'Not quite. I mean she began medical school—'

'But didn't finish. And she's not . . . affiliated with anyone these days, is she?'

'The agency in the capital – the people you met there, who put you in touch with us—'

'But this isn't their project anymore, is it? It was, but then they pulled out.'

'It was cancelled, yes. And Lara disagreed with that decision. The drugs and refrigeration were all here, and it wasn't worth their while to transport them all out again. So—'

'So she stayed on, and carried on, all on her own. Well – with you.'

'She doesn't like to give up on something that she started.'

'But you're unsupported here? No one's responsible for you?'

'Lara's ex-colleagues – the couple she worked with here – we radio in, they radio us, when they can get a signal.'

'And with baby in tow.'

The curves of the cartridge caught the light of the fire as Court flicked it into the air.

'We are here to work,' Kit said. 'Lara does important work here, work that saves lives. Helen is our daughter: where else would she be? She has everything that she needs.'

'For God's sake – there's a thousand things that could harm a kiddy out here. Put aside malaria – the other day, I squashed a scorpion. Big bloody scorpion, next to your kettle. I've been to some isolated places, but this is extreme. It's a jungle. You're a week away from any help at all.'

'The jungle – the forest – is a challenging environment, but we're equipped for those challenges. Extremely well equipped.'

'Because you sleep in a fridge.'

'The Koolroom is a useful piece of technology, which has benefits for everyone in the village.'

Court laughed, as if Kit had said something authentically witty. 'Listen,' he said. 'Listen to how you're talking. You're sounding like one of them.'

'Court,' said Kit, trying hard to sound bored rather than cross. 'Are you honestly in a position to lecture people about risks? Isn't that the whole point of you? A bit of discomfort and danger for the greater good?'

'I certainly have imperilled myself from time to time. But only myself. I try to keep infants out of it.'

How dull it must be to be Court Hardy, Kit thought – to wake up every morning, knowing exactly what you were going to think about everything that happened, not only to you, but to everyone else. He smiled in the relief and exhilaration of anger. Court had taken the first step, had crossed the line into outright rudeness. Kit's way was open. The words that he had been rehearsing, cool words of unanswerable reproach, rose in him like a flush to the cheeks. He pulled his knees up against him on the mat, and looked across the fire at Court.

'In what version of reality,' he began, 'do you have the right—'

Through the baby monitor came the sound of Helen's screams.

Kit jumped up.

'You should probably see to that,' said Court.

By the time Kit emerged from the Koolroom, Court was no longer alone. Obson was sitting beside him on the platform with the worried-looking Justus. Unfurled before them was a densely detailed map; beside it lay Obson's rifle. Court was holding his small black video camera and showing the two men something on its screen.

'Mr C.,' said Obson, looking up at Kit. 'He find a bullet.'

Without waiting for Kit to reply, Court said: 'I have to get down the river. Walking is too slow. It's agony. I have to get back to the capital and get my pictures out. I asked Mr Obson here to discuss ways that could be accomplished.'

'The river's not passable,' said Kit. 'There's still no rain. The water's too low.'

'Everyone is thirsty,' said Obson. 'Waiting for a change.'

Court looked at him, awaiting further utterance. When none came, he turned to Kit again. 'There's always a way,' he told him. 'It's a river, for Christ's sake.'

'Not at the moment,' said Kit. 'Until you reach the trading town, it's just trickles across rocks. You'd be carrying the boat for miles. It's quicker on the path.'

Obson said: 'It's a big bullet. Christian bullet. Not like the bullet for my gun.' He reached over and touched the wooden stock of the old weapon.

'I can't face that fucking path,' said Court. 'What about a horse? A donkey?'

Kit gave a snort. 'Have you seen many donkeys around here?'

Obson said: 'The mountain people, they tell him that they see the Christian soldiers.' He pointed towards the camera. 'He made the film of them saying so.'

'Then I need to use that phone of yours,' said Court. 'Or the radio.'

'Lara's got the phone,' said Kit. 'The radio's not working for now.'

Court smiled bitterly. 'The fuckers have gone and jammed the frequency.'

'Now, you're being paranoid.'

'Kristian – wake up!'

'It's one thing being paranoid yourself,' said Kit. 'But you've got no right to scare other people.'

'Kristian, they are up there. Their numbers are increasing. They're going to invade.'

'You haven't seen them. You haven't found anything. You heard a lot of rumours. You shoved your camera in the faces of people who are half-terrified of you and your booming voice, and who will tell you whatever they think you want to hear.'

'They gave me *this*! They found it.'

'It's a bullet. The world is riddled with them. What does it prove?'

'Oh, Kristian, how little you know.'

Obson spoke to Justus in his own language. – Show to Mr Kristian the bird.

Justus stood and rooted in one of Court's bulging bags. He pulled out a muddy green bundle, and unfurled it before them. It was a shirt in camouflage material. On its right sleeve was the emblem of a stylised eagle, and on the other was the embroidered rectangle of the famous flag, as bright and familiar as a face. On the chest, black letters spelled out a name.

'Muck Pug,' read Obson.

'McPugh,' said Kit.

'Poor McPugh,' said Court, 'What was he doing up there? Not, I suspect, hunting badger bears. And not alone.' He bared his teeth mirthlessly again. 'They didn't even take off their uniforms.'

Obson took the shirt, and looked closely at it. 'The bird is holding arrows,' he said, then muttered something in the Tongue.

'They told us the story of the owner of this shirt,' said Court. 'Army Specialist McPugh and his unit were up there, miles over the border, doing whatever it was that they were doing, when he slipped into rapids and broke his neck and his body ended up a good way along the river.'

'It is high, up there,' said Obson. 'The rivers are steep.'

Court went on. 'The people we spoke to heard soldiers looking for him. They were shouting at one another, hacking through the forest. They were afraid. They were very clear that there were two kinds of soldiers – those of our Christian neighbour—'

'They have black faces too, people look like us,' said Justus, unexpectedly speaking up.

'—and the soldiers of the Superpower.'

'Some of them have white faces and some of them have black faces,' said Justus.

'After three days his comrades gave up. So much for leaving no man behind. But the day after that, the local hunters found the body in the water. It was in a poor condition by then. So they burned it and buried it. They kept the shirt, which they gave to me. They had the dog tags, but they placed them with the bones. They showed me the place. I could have dug them up. I couldn't bring myself to do it.' He shook his head. 'But there isn't much doubt, is there, Kristian? It's not the bullet. It's the uniform.'

'This is difficult,' Kit said. 'This is difficult to explain.'

There was a silence. The noises of the insects rang out in the trees outside the house. The baby monitor gave out one of its rustles and each of the four men on the platform cocked an ear. Justus took the green shirt, rolled it up and restored it to Court's bag.

'There is a way, down the river,' said Obson. 'My friend can take you. You go in a small boat, you carry the small boat sometimes over the stones. You can carry your camera, and photograph, and movie, and take them to the city.'

Court nodded as if proved right. 'It's easy to explain,' he said to Kit, 'if you're prepared to face up to what's happening. There's going to be a war here, and you're going to be in the middle of it. You've got to come with me tomorrow.'

'I can't leave without Lara.'

'I will go now,' said Obson. 'I will talk to my friend.'

'Lara can look after herself,' Court said. 'She has guides who know what they are doing. She can find her own way. You have to take your child to safety.'

Obson and Justus were standing up.

'We have to go, Kristian,' Court said gently. 'We have to go.'

He picked up his camera, opened it delicately and removed the tiny rectangular memory card. He laid a hand fleetingly on Kit's shoulder, then followed Obson and Justus down the notched log.

3

Kit lay flat on the bamboo, looking up at the skulls in the eaves, then sat up and poked with a stick at the embers in the fire. He stood up and then sat down again, thinking about Lara, wishing that she was close; then he retreated to the Koolroom. Its cramped colourless interior, the texture of its processed air, soothed his inflamed feelings. What did Court Hardy matter anyway? In here, the temperature was never more or less than 25 degrees. Helen was at rest in her cot, where she would peacefully remain for another two hours at least. He took down the photograph of her as a newborn and held it up beside the living child.

In sleep, beneath the caress of the Koolroom's fans, Helen smiled to herself. The first time that this had happened, Kit had made an effort to be unsentimental. It was wind, he told himself, or a chance flexing of the muscles of the face. But over the days he became aware that something more complicated was happening within Helen's eyes. His daughter, Kit saw, was acquiring self. Smiling was not its only component. She became capable of recognising and then sustaining a gaze. Her eyes tracked the commotion of a rattle. She began to hit on the bells and mirrors suspended above her mat. Self crept in stealthily, although in an approach that was also, Kit thought, like a retreat. The image came into his mind of a moving sea, alive with light and depth, pregnant with hidden life, withdrawing to expose a beach and, lying on it, glistening in the sunlight, a gold ring.

There was no moment at which she emerged irrevocably from the impersonality of infanthood. The sea could rush back in as quickly as it had withdrawn. At the bottle's teat, on Kit's shoulder, even at play, a stillness would overtake her. Her eyes and limbs were quelled. She was awake, and seeing, but very far, it seemed, into the distance.

'She's just like you,' Lara would say, as they contemplated Helen in her trance. 'That's you, when you zone out.'

In those moments, Kit felt connected to something that was both bright and dark, something deep in the past but also a part of the future. Helen had come from this place; and, at times, she was still there. Her father, her mother, the world and everything in it, were nudging and tugging and dragging her out. It was impossible that she could remain behind for much longer.

She had been born at the bleakest moment of winter. As the day had drawn closer, Kit, like a child at Christmas, had willed the sky to snow in his child's honour. Instead, there was drizzle and a bitter, humid wind. Lara's labour had lasted an entire night; in the strip-lit maternity unit, Kit lost all sense of time. When Lara and Helen were wheeled out, the sun was rising. In the ward, blinds dimmed a tall window; peeping between them, Kit looked on to brick terraces, the spires of churches and gardens of naked trees.

Lara had arrived in the city fifteen days earlier, at the

last moment she could have boarded an aircraft. It was the end of weeks of anxious indecision. Until the moment that she emerged, pale-faced behind her luggage trolley, Kit had not been sure that he would ever see her again. Almost immediately, she was restless to leave.

He was teaching in a language school near the river, the same place where they had first met two years earlier. Even back then, Lara had been impatient and unsettled: bored and embarrassed by her job, for which she was overqualified, and stifled by the sprawl and impenetrability of the city. Kit's expectations had long ago been lamed by experience, but Lara, tipsy with the excitement of living abroad for the first time, had found herself on a long downward slide of disappointment and isolation. It was not enough, as it was for him, to stay afloat on the city's surface: to achieve adequacy in income, friendships, and diversions, enough of each to sustain the sensation of forward motion through life. Lara needed more. She wanted to break inside and penetrate beneath and, although she could not have explained exactly what this meant, she knew when she was failing.

It had something to do with the people she encountered, who were either dull or cold. The other teachers at the school were friendly enough but embedded in their own lives; the crowd of cheery language students changed every week. Lara did make friends, but they were foreigners more or less like her – educated, untethered, of affluent professional stock. Their transience repelled her and made her feel more transient herself. The better Lara got to know the city and the more people she met, the sadder she became.

Kit, who carried his own burden of loneliness and reserve, had been dazzled by her arrival at the school. Her accent, her height, and her glow of thwarted ambition made other women seem tepid by comparison. His hesitant displays of interest were returned with a speed and directness that took him aback. Lara was flirting with him, then sleeping with him, then living with him, before Kit fully recognised what had happened – that, faster and more deeply than at any time in his life, he had fallen in love. Her hungry energy jolted and enlarged his existence. To Lara, he revealed himself in ways that he had never done before, with inklings of panic, as well as relief. Lying beside her in bed after hours of talk, and sex, and self-analysis, Kit felt sometimes as if he had been prised open like an oyster. 'I have a habit of doing this to people,' she told him, not without pride. 'Is it too much? I come into someone's life, and sit myself down, and turn everything over. Not everyone likes that. I get that it's scary. Do you like it?'

Within weeks of meeting, they had moved into a flat above a kebab shop, with a dribbling shower and groaning radiators. The noise of buses and the smell of roasting meat were unbearable to Lara. Through one of the other teachers, they found a small house in a semi-rural suburb, within reach of meadows and country pubs. But the long journey to work, and the deeper sense of isolation, were worse; soon, they had moved back again. A home, Kit came to understand, was not in itself going to soothe Lara's restlessness. The pain of lost opportunity, symbolised by the medical degree that she had begun and abandoned, reared up before her wherever she turned. Towards Kit, it expressed itself in alternating ardour and coolness, punctuated by bouts of despair.

'Lara, Lara,' he would say, when she became distraught. 'Stop. Look at yourself. Look at what you have. You are one of the lucky ones. You have an advanced degree in linguist—'

'I'm bored by fucking linguistics!'

'—and you have an excellent medical training—'

'Training? Kit, I didn't finish! I fucked up. I flunked out.'

'—you have a decent job, teaching students who like and respect you—'

'I have a witless job, Kit. I have a null, repetitive, pointless job.'

'—and you live, comfortably, in one of the great cities of the world—'

'I live in the capital of fucking . . . Rainland!'

'—you are in the prime of your life—'

'Is this the fucking Samaritans? Because now I really do feel like killing myself.'

'—and you have me, who loves you, and would do anything for you.'

She looked up at him from her cross-legged position on the carpet. In a smaller voice, she said, 'But you leave me sometimes.'

'Lara, I have never left you.'

'I don't mean like that. I mean you drift off, you zone out, you disappear from yourself.' She looked away from him. 'I feel like I'm alone those times. It scares me.'

He put his arm around her shoulder. 'You are one of the lucky ones,' said Kit. 'We are lucky.'

Lara shook free of his arm, sighed and stretched her arms above her head. At least she was indignant now, rather than frenzied.

'Well, lucky you,' she said, 'for being so goddamn lucky.'

Kit bought tickets for plays and musicals and made reservations at fashionable restaurants. Lara fiddled with her phone during the acts, and toyed with her food. He took her one Friday to a cavernous night club, where the air vibrated with amplified sound. They stood side by side, watching the dancing from the edge of the room, then left after an hour and took the night bus home. Among her students, she was calm and kind; outside the classroom, a nagging unhappiness possessed her. In the early days, it had been thrilling to share a workplace with Lara, to kiss and touch over lunch. Steadily, these had become gloomy interludes. One evening, after a few days of sour silence, Kit returned early from a cancelled class to find her slumped on the sofa beside an open bottle of wine. Scattered across the floor were the printed pages of what looked like a contract.

'Hello,' he said.

Lara did not meet his eye.

'What are these?'

She said nothing, but made no effort to stop him picking up the documents.

'Who is this? What is LifeShots?'

In a blank, defensive voice, she said, 'They vaccinate people.'

'Where is this place they're talking about?'

Lara told him. He repeated the name of the Country. He had heard of it, of course, but was not completely certain which continent it was on.

'I took a job with them.'

The contract, Kit now saw, had been signed and dated the previous week.

'What kind of a job?'

'Nursing, I guess. I can pass for a nurse, even if I'm not a doctor.'

'But when?'

'Soon.'

'And what about me?'

He sat down. She poured him a glass of wine, and he took a sip and then put it down. Time passed. He remained sitting. He was aware of the taste of the wine in his mouth and the appearance of the room – the spongy armchair on which Lara slumped, the wear in the thin carpet. But he became unconscious of noise. It was not that he had lost his hearing, but he was detached from it. Lara was speaking to him, he could see that – her lips were moving. When sound returned to itself, she was shouting.

'—because this is it, Kit. This is exactly what I'm talking about.'

'Lara. I'm here. I'm sorry, Lara. I just drifted off.'

'It's like talking to someone through a pane of glass.'

'I'm sorry – it happens. I don't mean anything.'

'This is your life, a day of your life, and it requires your presence.'

'You don't have to – go.'

Lara shook her head intensely. 'I've tried, and I'm sick of

trying. I'm going to do this. What choice do I have? I have to try something else.'

After months of chill and drizzle, the weeks before Lara's departure were warm and long. The atmosphere in the flat was eased by the marijuana that Lara had been given by a departing student. Relieved of a future in the city, she opened herself up to its possibilities. There were evenings at the pub with the other teachers, and picnics in the ripening parks. At weekends they rose early and went running by the river, before meeting with friends for brunch. On the Saturday before her flight, they even held a party in the flat, where people danced, and marvelled at Lara's intrepidity and self-sacrifice.

'I couldn't do that. I could not do what she's doing,' said a friend of Lara, a woman from the north. 'She's so free. You're free too. You're quite the couple, aren't you?'

'What do you mean?' asked Kit.

'So exotic, in a way. So mysterious. You're aloof but friendly. It's attractive.'

'Am I?' said Kit. 'Are we?'

On the train to the airport, after contemplating various ways of putting it, he said to Lara, 'Are we together?'

'Oh, Kit, I don't know. Let's see, can we? It's not like I'm going to meet anyone out there. I'm going to be living with quasi-Muslim animists for a year. It's not a single girl's paradise.'

After she had gone, there was a fortnight's silence into which he read the worst. He sat at his laptop in the evenings, tapping out ever shorter and more impatient messages, and reckoning his loss. After a week, he made a conscious effort to feel relieved. He smoked the remnants of marijuana. He accepted an invitation from his students and ended up drunk and self-conscious, croaking pop songs in an airless pub. He called the girl from the north, met her in a bar and failed to catch the last train home. The following morning, beneath the jet of her scalding shower, his head slumped.

He hurried back across the city and sat for a long time in front of the glowing screen that separated him from Lara. There must be words – he only had to find them – that could pierce it, and connect him to her. He started on a knockabout account of the karaoke night, but only succeeded in conveying how bored he had been. He considered a confession of his adventure last night: would that jolt Lara out of her silence? After two days of hunched composition he was on the point of sending it when the laptop began to ping, and ping again. It was a rush of messages, all from Lara, dating back two weeks. They had been written, sent, and held up, first by the unreliable satellite phone in the village and then by the server in the distant capital, which had released them in a flood. They were garbled and out of sequence; they overflowed with excitement and emotion. Lara's work was fascinating; her colleagues, Jim and Kay, a married nurse and doctor, had at once become friends. The place and its people were extraordinary; she was already working on a grammar and vocabulary of the local language. Lara in the jungle was a different woman from the one he had known in the city. Deprived of her presence, he found himself falling in love with her as if for the first time.

After three months, Lara travelled back to the Country's

capital with Jim and Dr Kay. Kit took a long flight, she took a shorter one, and they met in a hotel by a beach of shining sand. Encountering Lara again felt like being winded; he had never been so glad to see another person. They spent a week there, lying beneath parasols and in a teak four-poster bed. The sun and greenness made Kit feel as if he was waking from a cold, grey sleep. Lara was transfigured by them. Her skin, against which Kit rested his head, was tanned, and she seemed taller, somehow, and grander in presence, as if tropical heat and light had penetrated inside her, and planted her with confidence and calm. Moments of delight imprinted themselves upon Kit: Lara naked in the bedroom, her hair wrapped in a white towel; swimming long-limbed in the sea, powerful with health. They stayed up all night talking. Lara apologised for her ranting and rages. Kit promised to stop retreating from the world. They extended their stay by a day, then by another; and then they could extend no longer. At the airport, they held one another as they parted, and Kit flew home jumpy with love and optimism.

Soon after Lara returned to the village, the vaccination programme began to fail. A source of promised funding was abruptly withdrawn. A local employee in the capital disappeared under suspicion of embezzlement. Lara's colleagues quarrelled bitterly. Even the satellite connection, the channel of Kit's emotional sustenance, failed for a week. When the messages from Lara resumed, the chatty exuberance had gone. They were erratic and perfunctory, and often gave the impression of having being written while stoned.

From: lara.lee@LifeShots.org
To: krabone@paramail.com
Subject: Pork!

Hi Baby!

Just a quick one because the sat is up and it may not stay up allthatlong. Thimngs much better here today. There was a rally for the election which cheered everyone up, even Kay. Big men coming in from the capital, including a beardy imam. Buffalo had its throat cut, so meat for everyone and lots of the rice brew. Too much! Even the imam is drinking it, and the men are all eating pig too, passing it round semi-openly. They're so flexible and prabgmitc about that kind of stuff. This is the kind of religion I love! Oops gotta go now. More soon more tomorrow. Love you, miss you. L x

---

From: lara.lee@LifeShots.org
To: krabone@paramail.com
Subject: Bad shit

Dearest K,

I don't know where to begin. Such intense shit here today. According to Jim, there's basically half a million dollars just walked out the accounts somehow. Only person who can explain it is Abdul back in the capital, and he's walked too. Kay is so angry with Jim it's frightening me. I think she hit him today. I came back and he had this red mark on his face and she was crying. At least the fucking sat is up again, though now the radio's down. There's something weird about it. I'm getting sick of this tension and uncertainty. Feeling weird in myself too. Not the rice brew this time. Lots more to tell you, but I gotta lie down for a bit now.

I love you, Kit.

L xxxxx

PS Wrote this 24 hours ago, but the sat flipped out so just sending it now. They were voting today. Amazing sight, amazing excitement. The skinny Muslim doctor is going to own it, at least round here.

From: lara.lee@LifeShots.org
To: krabone@paramail.com
Subject: (None)

Oh baby it's late here, but theyve been on the connection all day trying to sort out this shit over the money and I'm writing this in the koolroom just to get away from them and only got a few moments. Atmos so bad today, Kay blaming jim and Jim blaming Abdul. No one inthe village is noticing thank god – theyre so crazy happy over this election. Also today I took one of the kits from the stock and yup I'm pregnant.

Gotta go.

Love you so much.

L xxxxxxx

Kit struggled to understand how it had happened. But this quickly ceased to matter. For a week and a half, Lara was silent; it was as if Kit's messages were falling into a void. The she began writing again, as chatty and casual as before, but without any reference to the only thing that he was interested in hearing about. His insistent questions were ignored. His next message carried the subject line, Elephant in the Room! The one that followed was written entirely in capital letters. He considered, and abandoned, the idea of seeking out Lara's parents, a grim-sounding pair of small-town doctors, with whom she maintained jittery contact.

'Dear Kay and Jim,' he wrote, after a brief rummage in the pages of LifeShots.org. 'You don't know me, and I apologise for this message out of the blue. I know that you have much else to deal with at the moment, but there's something that you may not know about.'

But it was another ten days before Lara finally wrote to him. They spoke once a week after that on the fractured line. She was chirpy and bright, in a way that left Kit feeling slightly sick. Even allowing for the distortions and delays of the satellite connection, there was a strained and unnatural air about her; it was as if an actor was performing a skilful impersonation of the real Lara, who had vanished in sinister circumstances.

'So, we need to talk about some things,' Kit would say,

after ten minutes of airy banter. 'Don't we? We need to make some decisions.'

'So serious, Kit! Worrying about all the big decisions.'

'Well, but. Yes, I am a bit worried about some things. We need to decide what to do.'

'It's late here now, I'm pretty tired. Let's talk about it all later. Tell me what you've been doing.'

He learned more about Lara's thinking from Dr Kay, who wrote with anxious frequency. It was almost as if she felt guilty. At first, Kay told him, Lara had resolved to fly back home to her parents. But weeks passed, and she remained in the capital. The crisis over the missing money was continuing; the police had become involved and everyone, including Lara, had to answer questions. At some point, she decided to stay in the city, and to give birth in the missionary hospital; assuming that Kay avoided prosecution, she would supervise the delivery. But with less than two months to go Lara changed her mind.

'She's been real confused,' Kay wrote. 'There's been a lot of stress and anger for all of us here, and we're each of us trying to work out what is the best thing to do. But she's made up her mind now. She wants to come back to where you are. Is that going to be possible, do you think? Can she get a place in a hospital over there? She knows that she's been making things difficult, and she's sorry. She says that she wants to come home.'

It was in the delivery room that Lara made her announcement. They had been at the hospital all day and most of the night. A nurse appeared every half hour to peer beneath

Lara's gown. She shifted about uncomfortably, from stool to bed to beanbag, while Kit fiddled with the compilation of songs, soothing in tempo, that he had carefully compiled for the occasion. After the latest check, the nurse hurried out and returned quickly with a doctor. And then Lara was on a trolley, being rolled down corridors of shining linoleum, as Kit jogged to catch up.

The doctor was walking rapidly alongside, and Lara was nodding at her as she spoke.

'What's going on?' Kit asked.

'It's not working out, and the baby's in distress,' said Lara, without obvious anxiety. 'They've got to do a C-section.'

'But you said you didn't want that?'

'It'll be fine, my love.'

'So this is an emergency?'

'Don't worry. Look on the bright side – you won't have to hear me mooing like a cow.'

'But is this, is this what we want?'

'There isn't any choice.'

Now they were inside a brightly lit room. Lara was arrayed on a wide bed. People in purple and green were going about technical tasks with calm urgency.

'You'll be awake right?'

'It's an emergency. Got to be a general. Hey, Kit – it's OK. It's all fine. They've just got to move fast.'

Needles were being readied next to them. Covers were placed on Kit's head, face and shoes.

'Stay with me, OK. You'll have to tell me all about it later.'

'OK.'

'And Kit – we've got to go back to the village. I can't

live in this city. I can't live in fucking Rainland. There's still work to be done over there. You can come with me. We can all go.'

'But I thought that was all over?'

'It's over for Kay and Jim. But they said that if I want, I can go back. The drugs are all still there. The Koolroom is still there.'

'Lara, Lara – we can't take a baby to a jungle.'

'I was pregnant in the forest. How much harder can it be to look after a child there?'

The needle was in her arm.

'I have to go back, Kit. I can't *not* go back. I only feel myself when I'm there.'

She was immediately unconscious. A hundred seconds later, Helen was born.

By the time she woke up, Lara was more determined than ever. It had become an element of the protective instinct: she had to get Helen away. Without understanding when exactly it had happened, this also became what Kit wanted. The most important thing, he recognised, was to make the decision irrevocable before anyone had the chance to talk them out of it. The practical arrangements were surprisingly straightforward. But ten days before they were due to fly, the bell of the flat rang. Standing outside, furious and distraught, were Lara's parents.

It wasn't only that they had never met Kit; it became clear that they had been told almost nothing about him. When he first walked into the small living room, Kit had been fairly sure that Lara's father – handsome, powerful, with a parade-ground strut – was about to punch him.

Only the presence of Helen, newly fed, profoundly at peace, made this impossible. After an hour of cooing, the reproaches gave way to tears. It was agreed that the new grandparents would rest and come back the next day. As soon as they had left, Lara was packing a bag.

'Lara, you can't just run away from this. They love you. They are concerned.'

'Do not question my judgement on this, Kit. I know these people. They are ruthless. Tonight we sleep in a hotel.'

They came back for the rest of their things in the middle of the night. Three days later, they slipped in again to find an envelope containing a letter from a solicitor. Kit scanned it with dazed detachment: *Dr Hueffer-Lee's intention to seek custody . . . Ms Lee's history of mental instability . . . pending the order of the court . . . do not, under any circumstances, seek to remove . . .*

'You see?' said Lara. 'They're bluffing, but . . . those fuckers.'

She called the airline and brought the flights forward. In the taxi and the check-in queue, she glanced repeatedly behind her. After they had taken their seats on the plane, as Kit was fiddling with the infant seat belt, Lara grasped his hand. A man was stalking down the aisle, a stocky, short-haired man with a briefcase, and an expression of unhappy determination. Lara's eyes were fixed on him. The man walked past them without pausing. She exhaled. The engine note rose. The aircraft ran its race along the tarmac, and finally came the moment of upward tilt and sudden suspension, the feeling of being neither on the ground nor in the air, and then the sensation of lightness and of lift.

Lara turned to Kit, who was hugging Helen against him. She smiled, with tears on her face. 'So we're on our way.'

'It's OK, Lara.'

'Are we mad?'

'I don't think so. I don't know anymore.'

Lara ran a hand across her own cheek, and reached out to stroke Helen's. 'Now the real ordeal begins, right?'

Kit nodded: Helen was weeks old, and an entire day of flying lay ahead of them. But she hardly cried, hardly stirred, for the whole journey.

On the night of his return to the village, Court Hardy slept upstairs. But after Kit had gone to sleep, he came down and knocked gently on the door of the Koolroom.

'It's arranged,' he said, standing respectfully outside. 'There's a small, light boat, with a fibreglass bottom. It won't be easy, but there's always a way. We leave tomorrow morning. We need to leave early. You and Helen have to come with us.' It was the first time that Kit had heard him whisper.

Hours later, he woke into a tumult of din and confusion. He looked immediately to Helen, who was visible through the mesh of the cot. Her face was contorted in the light of the lamp; her limbs were thrashing in protest. But the sound of her cries was overwhelmed by a pulsing throb in which Kit struggled to distinguish between sensation and sound.

The Koolroom was buzzing like an alarm clock. The air itself was stricken with vibration; Kit's eyes took in the glass of water beside the bed, whose surface was a pattern of outward-racing ripples. He picked up the howling Helen, strapped her to him in the sling, wriggled his toes into rubber sandals and stepped through the metal door.

Outside the sun was beginning to rise. The quaking of the Koolroom gave way to a rhythmic thumping in the air. Kit pressed his hands protectively over Helen's ears and stumbled towards the noise. In the open centre of the village, people were milling with oil lamps and electric torches. He saw the tottering figure of the old chief and his two sons. Obson was there with his rifle. Their heads were turned up towards the source of the uproar, a hulking shape hovering against the blue-black sky. Thrashing rotors picked up the earliest glimmers of daylight and spun it on their blades; the wind from them churned up leaves, twigs and clods of earth. The surface of the thing was smooth, with stubby wings and blunt-nosed projections; its black windows seemed to absorb rather than reflect light. It moved with a throb, first over the trees at the edge of the village, then across the houses, until it was directly above the open space where the crowd had gathered. People were gesticulating and shouting to one another. Their hair rippled under the battering attack of air. Suddenly, the beam of a spotlight blazed out from the machine, a cone of illumination so well defined as to appear solid. The people on the ground scattered, as if from a gunshot. A few stood their ground, and the moving circumference of light bathed their dark faces in radiance. Then the thing was moving purposefully over the village, and its light was searching out the roofs. It played over the ridge of Kit and Lara's house, and the flat solar panels, source of energy to the Koolroom, flashed beneath it. It lingered in this position, rotors beating, unmoving. And then, all at once, the search-light cut out, and the shape surged higher into the sky and juddered away.

In the falling off of wind and tumult, Obson, who had been fiddling twitchily with his rifle, raised it towards the sky and fired a single shot.

The machine halted in the air. Then it was turning, rushing back, and dipping low, the searchlight on again, stabbing into the corners of the village. Everyone ran for shelter. They cowered beneath the platforms of the houses, the dust and leaf litter in their mouths and noses. One figure was still out in the open: Court Hardy, his camera held aloft, its red light blinking. The beam of the spotlight shone down directly upon him. He did not flinch. The tiny light of the camera met the blaze of the spotlight and held its ground as the black thing beat its rotors close above.

4

'It's called the Siskin,' said Court. 'The Siskin Ferox. Also known as the Bird of Paradise. It's very new, very secret. Like a plane and helicopter in one. That noise—'

'That noise that isn't a noise.'

'Yes, that. Infrasonic or megasonic, or something. I don't know – I don't follow these things in any detail: they disgust me. From a distance, it makes no sound at all. Close up like that, it causes disorientation, deafness, nausea. I don't think it's been deployed anywhere else before now. It's got—'

'It was filming you, as you were filming it. One of those things sticking out of the bottom had a lens. It was a camera.'

'That's highly likely. Either way, the fact that it's been here, the fact that it's here now – you see how serious this is, don't you, Kit?'

They were sitting on the platform, drinking tea that Court had made while Kit was in the Koolroom. It had taken an hour to soothe the frantic Helen. At times, she had screamed so hard it was difficult to believe that she could also be effectively breathing. The idea of waking her up again now was unbearable.

Court looked at him anxiously over the rim of the plastic mug. Aggression and self-assurance had melted away; his expression was kind, unhappy, almost pleading. He said, 'They're bound to come back now. They've got to, now that they've been seen. But how long? It could be days. Hours. How long have we got?'

By the time they went out again, after Helen had woken and been fed, the village was in uproar. The sun had risen and it was hot, but everyone was outside. People sat in front of their houses on colourful mats; many were touching and examining one another's ears. There were queues at the latrines and splashes of sick at intervals along the paths. One man was stalking the margins of the village with his bow drawn taut, looking up at the sky.

'The boat has gone,' Court said after a huddled conversation with Obson. 'The small fibreglass boat. It left early, to take a message for the capital. They didn't come for me. Obson said that I would have slowed them down. I suppose that is true. But they could have taken the memory card. They could have taken my story for me.' He sighed. 'I asked for a guide to take me on the path. It'd be hopeless alone. But no one will come.'

Like everyone else, he kept glancing up at the sky. 'It's beginning to look as if we are fucked.' He smiled. 'Well, Mr C. declines to be fucked.'

They were standing on the open space of grass and earth that served as market and meeting place. The hunters were counting out arrows between them and placing them in bamboo quivers. A buffalo was being slowly dragged out towards the centre. Kit recognised the man who was responsible for village ceremonies, holding a heavy blade.

Obson approached, chuckling, spry, almost jaunty, gripping his old rifle, and twirling it like the baton of a majorette. The fact of having fired it at an enemy had added greatly to his gaiety.

'Mr Kristian!'

'Mr Obson. What is happening?'

'We are defending.'

'You know, Obson – you know that it is difficult to defend against an army. They are very strong. Their guns are very strong.'

'We can do what else?'

'You could leave. People could pack up a few things, go into the forest. They could hide out. Like you told me, when there's been fever in the village. The women and children, at least. Just for a few days. Until we know.'

Obson smiled and saluted, then strolled over to supervise the death of the buffalo. Court stood nearby, holding to his ear a small battery-powered short-wave radio. Through the static, Kit could hear the sound of a clock chiming, thousands of miles away.

'Nothing,' said Court, after the news had ended. 'Nothing about here at all.'

It was time to feed Helen again. They walked back to the house.

'Are you noticing it too?' Court asked. 'In your hearing?'

Kit nodded. Sound was out of kilter still; noises had lost their familiar proportions. The shout of one hunter to another was dull and muted; but his fingers on the fletching of the arrows rustled like the wind.

They walked on, and Court said, 'It's what people like us want, secretly, isn't it – for people to flee? Obediently flee from the violence that we release on them. Then we solve the problem that we've caused, with refugee camps and latrines and bags of rice, and we prove to ourselves how compassionate we are. And so the violence is encouraged, made possible really, by the aid. Those saintly humanitarians in their white jeeps – they're just another branch of the Marine Corps.'

'I thought you wanted to flee yourself,' said Kit.

'I want to get this out.' He held up the plastic memory card with its strips of shining copper, as small and shiny as a bead. 'Nothing matters more.'

An uneasy torpor settled over the village. In the forest beyond the houses the birds cried and the insects whined. From the centre came the thwacking of the stone knife and the groans of the dying buffalo, massive and bloated in the strange new hierarchy of sounds.

Having been thwarted in the idea of escape, Court had sunk into lethargy. He sat on the edge of the platform, prodding listlessly at the keys of his laptop. Even Helen was absent and subdued on her mat, withdrawn into that mysterious state of abstraction. Only Kit was restless and active. In the Koolroom, he opened the freezer and counted the remaining pouches of Lara's milk. From inside his bag of clothes, he pulled out the single tin of infant formula that he had hidden in defiance of her wishes. He placed it in a rucksack, along with the changing mat, the skin ointment, a small camping stove and billy can, an electric torch, biscuits, dried noodles, a compass, a penknife, a tube of liquid soap, hand-cleansing gel, and a first-aid kit. He stuffed the rest of the available space with disposable nappies and wet wipes. Then he pulled some of them out again to make room, when the time came, for the frozen milk.

There was a knock at the door of the Koolroom; beyond it, he heard small voices and laughter. He opened the door to find half a dozen of the imps. Their faces and thin bodies were wet and shiny, and a sharp metallic tang rose about them. The little girl with the green ribbon stood in front, in her hands a basin slopping with dense dark buffalo blood.

– For He'len, she said. – To make her strong.

Back on the platform, he found Court hunched over the radio, reading aloud from the screen of his laptop.

'It's working,' he laughed. 'They got through. What a fucking relief. I'm dictating. It's almost done.'

Helen lay on her stomach, punching and kicking the bamboo.

'Are you still there?' Court boomed into the microphone.

'Still here, Mr Hardy,' said an indistinct female voice.

'OK, so: full stop and paragraph. Now I'll continue. You're ready? Stop me if I'm going too fast.'

'Ready, Mr Hardy,' said the voice.

He read from the computer's rectangular screen.

'The incontrovertible evidence.'

'Check.'

'Of military intervention comma.'

'Check.'

Court went on. 'Despite repeated denials of superpower presence in the country comma. Will provoke international uproar full stop paragraph. Open quotation we are a peaceful democratic country comma. And it is outrageous that a foreign army. Is violating our sovereignty in this manner. Comma close quotation said capital S Sergeant Obson, I'll spell that. Of the Volunteer Defence Force, initial capitals, defence spelled with a C. Open quotation we call on the governments. Of the world to denounce this. Aggression and bring its perpetrators. To account full stop close quotation story ends.'

Court removed his finger from the button on the microphone, releasing its hiss. There was a pause. He pressed it again.

'Did you get that?'

'I believe I got it, sir.'

'And I gave you that address. Please send it as soon as possible. As soon as possible. From Court Hardy. Can you send it now?'

'Sending it now, sir.'

'Thank you. You type very fast. Thank you very much.'

'Glad to be of service, sir.'

Court turned from the radio and reached into the eaves for the last of Lara's cigarettes.

'Fuck-a-doodle-doo,' he said, and Kit saw that his hands were trembling.

'Did Obson actually say that?' he asked. 'That stuff you had him saying?'

'Oh Christ, Kit,' said Court, smiling as he exhaled. 'It really doesn't matter, my friend. What matters is that I got the story out. That'll be up and online in an hour. And after that, we're safe. The world will know we're here, and they can't lay a finger on us. You're in the copy too, and Lara, and your baby girl. By name. Everyone named in that story is protected now. It's the best fucking insurance policy in the world.'

'And who was that?'

'On the radio? That was Kay. At the charity – your wife's colleague, Kay. It finally came to life while you were downstairs, she was checking in. So I told her that we're stuck here, and she took the dictation.'

Kit felt a hollowness in his stomach. He had spoken to Kay often and at length. That had not been the voice of Kay.

He took the microphone and spoke into it. But the connection was broken again, and in every direction he turned the dial it gave out only hiss.

Lara had left yesterday, but already she belonged to another place and time. He cast about for mementoes of her, but he knew that there were none. Lara left few traces as she passed through life. She wore no perfume or make-up. The soap and shampoo that they used to wash in the river, the small collection of paperback novels, were shared between them without distinction of ownership. There was a spare pair of trainers; a bathing costume; a drawer of plain and practical underwear, but almost nothing else personal to her – because Lara was so tall, they even shared T-shirts and socks. In the bottom of the Koolroom's narrow cupboard, she kept a small wooden box which Kit now opened. It contained photographs of Lara as a child, her doctoral diploma, folded and creased, a valentine's card given to her by Kit, leaves of marijuana. There was also a small notebook of drawings, carefully sketched in pencil: Helen, lying in her cot; smiling upwards; and being fed from a bottle. When had Lara made these? Kit had never seen them before. Carefully and in secret, she had filled the notebook, hiding it here in this box. The drawings were touchingly clumsy and artless, painful in their inept sincerity. Kit's eyes pricked as he looked at them. He put them back in the box. Then he took them out and squeezed them into the rucksack.

Where was Lara now? What did she know of what was happening? The villages towards which she had been walking were downriver, in the direction of the trading town and the distant capital. If she understood what was going on, Kit knew that she would try to come back to him and to Helen. But did she know? And what if she was prevented? In her absence, should he take Helen away from the village and into the forest? But out there, without guide or destination, would they be any safer than they were here? What, after all, was the worst that could happen if they stayed? The questions rotated in his mind, leading nowhere. Walls were narrowing around him and Helen. Lara, safe or not, was outside them.

If it starts, Kit said to himself, I'm going to go to the tree house. I'm going to take Helen there.

When he climbed back to the platform, Court was holding Helen awkwardly in his arms. His back was turned to Kit, and he was cooing and muttering at her, and seemed to be stroking her face. Helen was spluttering, almost choking.

'Little girl, little girl – here's Daddy!' said Court, handing over Helen, who wore a look of affronted surprise. 'She started to complain, so we had a cuddle. But, oh dear, I'm not a natural with the kiddies, I'm afraid.'

The Koolroom sealed off the outside world, but what had been a sanctuary had come to feel like a trap. After thinking about it for a long time, Kit put Helen to rest down there, and made up his own bed on the platform, where he could hear and see what was happening outside. Court lay across from him. Hours later, in the deep of the night, they both woke at the same moment. A sound could be heard, distant but distinct, a flat rattling coming from the forest.

'Automatic rifles,' said Court. He smiled.

Kit had wondered how he would feel, when the moment came. It was close to relief.

Court pulled up his knees, and sighed. He said, 'It's in scrapes like this – and I've been in a few of them – that you start to wish you had a gun of your own. Just a little pistol, to give the fuckers something to think about. You have to guard against that impulse. Once you start wanting your own gun, once you start wanting to kill, you're becoming one of them.'

Kit said, 'You were right, Court, about everything that was happening. We – I – we were wrong.'

'I dislike being proved right about such things.'

There was more firing, and then a flat explosion.

'I despise the kind of journalist who can immediately identify every shell or firearm,' said Court. 'But that may have been a grenade.'

Someone screamed in one of the nearby houses. The

screaming stopped, and people were running past just outside the platform, pelting out of the jungle and into the village. Kit went to look out from the verandah.

'Wait,' said Court.

'It's alright,' Kit said. 'They're ours – that was Obson's voice.' But by the time he stepped outside, they had disappeared. There was a thin moon high above the trees. Its light was glimmering on their leaves. Kit climbed down the log and went into the Koolroom. He hesitated over the frozen pouches of milk, took four of them, pulled the rucksack on to his back and carried Helen back up on to the platform in her basket, willing her to remain asleep.

More shouts could be heard from within the village, and more running feet, followed by the trundling of engines, which grew louder, then cut out.

'That sounds to me like some kind of tracked vehicle,' Court said. 'Please don't tell me they've brought their fucking—'

Both of them flinched, as a grating screech pierced the air. It took a few moments to understand that it was an amplified human voice. It was rasping out words of the Tongue, over the shriek of feedback. It seemed to be only a few yards away.

'What's it saying?' whispered Court.

Helen had opened her eyes and was about to cry.

Dogs had begun barking all over the village. Suddenly, without pause or interruption, the voice was gabbling in English. It spoke in a jerky declamatory style and a dense accent, as if reading words without understanding them.

'This! Is the Western Command! Of the Transitional Committee for National Salvation!'

Court's face had taken on an expression of mirthless satisfaction. 'Ha!' he said, nodding.

'This is a police action! In response to criminal activity and gangsterism! In the Western Sector!'

Kit lifted the wailing Helen out of the basket, and patted her on his shoulder.

'In the name of! The Transitional Committee! It is demanded that the drug smugglers! Foreign and native! Surrender themselves immediately for arrest and criminal processing!'

'This is even more stupid than I imagined,' said Court.

'All foreign nationals! And their native hirelings! Are required to come forward! With hands raised! All those bearing firearms! Or traditional weapons! Must surrender them!'

There was a pause, and a percussive sound, as if a hand was being placed over a microphone, and muted voices. Then the rasping resumed.

'You have five minutes! To comply! This warning will not! Be repeated!'

There was further scuffling and scratching, then a new amplified sound.

'Is that what I think it is?' said Court.

The words were those of the Tongue, but the tune was unmistakable.

'It's a hymn,' said Kit. Helen stopped crying, as if soothed by the plonking piano chords.

Court chuckled and shook his head. 'Kumba-fucking-ya.'

For a while, neither of them spoke. Kit unscrewed Helen's bottle, and squeezed the melting milk into it from the plastic pouch. Then Court made a throat-clearing noise.

'Well,' he said. 'It's a pretty clear choice.'

'We can't surrender.'

'But we can't refuse to surrender either, if we want to live.'

'They must be bluffing.'

'"Killed in crossfire." They would love to be able to say that. Now that I've got that story out, it's the only way for them.'

'Are you sure?'

'If we walk out now, hands held politely aloft, there'll be all kinds of snarling and arsing around, but they won't kill us.'

'Your article, Court.'

'What about it?'

Kit lifted the kettle of hot water off the fire, removed the lid and placed the bottle of white slush in it. 'Court, that wasn't Kay on the radio.'

Confusion, embarrassment and resignation registered on Court's features in rapid sequence.

'Ah,' he said, nodding. 'I missed that. I should have thought of it.'

He screwed up his temples in a tight frown as if fending off painful thoughts. 'Buggeranthus. Well, the choice is still the choice. Life or death?'

There was a pause, and the hymn came to an end. Then it began to play from the beginning once again.

Court stood and strapped on his pack. He looked down into the basket at Helen. 'Time to go, little girl.' He turned to Kit. 'We walk to them together, baby in arms, heads up, very humble and unthreatening. Please – get the things you need from downstairs.'

Kit stood up. He said, 'People think I'm weak, a failure. You think I'm a failure, sitting here looking after a baby while her mother goes into the forest. But it's none of your business, or theirs. It's what I chose.'

Court clapped both hands on his shoulders and shook them, smiling into his face with warmth and humility.

Outside the moonlight still lay on the leaves. But in the forest, powerful lamps were blazing, red and sodium yellow, harshly artificial, their illumination broken up by the trees. There it was, Kit thought – the place of surrender. It was no more than a few paces away – of all the houses in the village, this one was the closest to it. He went into the Koolroom and retrieved the rest of the frozen milk. He took a last look behind the partition, at the fridges with their stock of expensive and life-saving drugs. At the back of the container, behind a plastic panel, was a fat red switch. He pushed it and the lights of the Koolroom shut down with a final click; the air conditioner trailed into silence.

The clunk of the door as he closed it behind him was disturbingly loud. Through the filter of the leaves, the lamps seemed to be even closer. Kit wanted more than anything to shield Helen from injury and from death. He knew that he was going to walk towards the lights.

As he stepped up the log, he became aware of a scuffling above his head. Looking up, he saw hunched shapes, climbing over the steep thatch of the house. A face turned down towards him: Obson. Across his shoulder was the ancient rifle. Ahead of him, clambering confidently towards the peak of the roof, were two of the hunters, encumbered with bows and quivers. Obson's eyes met his. He smiled and lifted a hand in salute.

'Obson!' Kit hissed. 'Stop!' But now the three figures had reached the roof's narrow ridge and were edging along it towards the end closest to the jungle and the lights. Precariously but confidently perched, the men raised their bows, and loosed them silently. Obson, sitting astride the roof like a man on horseback, braced the gun to his shoulder and fired.

Kit heard the explosion, and the clunking of the bolt as he reloaded. There were voices and shouts from the forest, and the noise of an engine. The archers moved in a fluent rhythm: hands dipping into quivers, the settling of the arrow on its string, a pull, a pause, and then release. Obson fired again, and Kit heard a cry from the direction of the lights in the trees. The recorded hymn cut out in mid-verse. Then came the flat rattling of one automatic rifle, then another, and splintering thwacks above Kit's head. Fragments of wood and tufts of thatch were exploding off the house. On the platform above, Helen began to cry.

Kit dropped the bag of frozen packets, flattened himself on the ground, then jumped up again. Court was coming down the notched log backwards at speed, shoulders festooned with bags and straps. With one hand he held on, with the other he pressed Helen to the front of his body. She was screaming, and Court was shouting, but the rattling of bullets made it impossible to hear either.

They cringed beneath the platform. The din of shooting fell away. Court had carried down with him Kit's rucksack, and the baby sling. He helped Kit to wrap it around Helen and himself. Then he took his camera out of its bag, and pressed the button that illuminated its glowing lights. The two of them craned their necks from beneath the platform and looked up at the roof: Obson and the hunters were no longer there.

At that moment, there was a large explosion from somewhere near the centre of the village, followed immediately by a second one further off.

Court screwed up his eyes. 'Mortars,' he said with contempt. 'In a forest. These people are amateurs.'

He patted Helen on the head, shook Kit's hand and disappeared into the darkness in a crouching run. A moment later, he reappeared.

'Forgot to give you this,' he said, reaching into one of his pockets. It was Helen's bottle, warm from the kettle.

Bombs, Kit recognised in part of his mind, were exploding on to the village every few seconds. But all that he could hear was Helen's crying. He retreated deeper beneath the platform of the house, into the dark and narrow gap between the back of the silent Koolroom and the tethered heap of nappies. He loosened the sling, and applied the bottle to the child's lips. Usually, when her crying had reached this pitch, Helen would angrily reject the teat. This time, she took it hungrily. The flush faded from her face; the juddering vibrations of her body yielded to a calm rhythm of sucks; and the languor of relief overcame Kit. He knew that he had to think, with concentration and detachment, to assess the situation, and consider the next step.

But Helen was in his arms, feeding vigorously on a full, warm bottle. Her eyes were closed; her brow was clenched in a frown of hungry concentration. Kit could hear cries, shots and explosions, but it was as if they were reaching him from a separate realm, where time passed on a different clock. A mortar exploded close enough for him to be aware of the flash on the periphery of his vision. But beneath the platform, up against the Koolroom, he felt untouchably safe and secure.

He became aware of movement. Several sets of feet were walking along the track out of the jungle. They moved stealthily along the path, crunching lightly on its surface. Now the owners of the feet were standing next to the house, and speaking to one another in low voices. An electric torch flashed, alien and unnatural in the warm darkness; all at once, its beam was being directed below the platform. It darted over the log pillars and the outer wall of the container. Kit stilled his breathing; the light passed within inches of his face. Then it was gone, and he could hear the door of the Koolroom opening, and someone inside; and the sound of boots on the platform above, and more murmurs.

The words were in a language that he did not understand. They were not words of the Tongue. A walkie-talkie fizzed and crackled, and a voice spoke indistinctly from it.

Helen broke off from the bottle with a sigh. Kit knew that she needed to burp. Before she did so, the pressure in her stomach would make her cry.

Within the Koolroom, on the other side of the thin

metal wall against which he crouched, were sounds of lurching, impatient movement. He heard the refrigerator doors opening and the tinkle of breaking glass. Muffled bangs and crashes came from the platform above.

Helen's head was on his shoulder, and he was softly patting her back, coaxing out of her the trapped wind. She was twisting and snuffling with the discomfort of it.

'Please don't cry, Helen,' whispered Kit. He knew that she could not understand him, that she was about to start wailing loudly, that they would be heard and discovered, and that this was part of the natural course of things.

Helen belched, and gave a murmur of satisfaction. Kit exhaled, and lowered her head into the crook of his arm, and pushed the teat into her mouth for the second half of the bottle.

The intruders stamped out of the Koolroom; the feet on the platform descended the notched log. The darkness was beginning to glow with the first light of morning. From his hiding place, Kit could make out human outlines in front of the house. They were conferring again in low voices. 'Negative, negative,' replied the walkie-talkie in English. The torch flashed on, then off again. The outlines disappeared.

The mortar explosions had stopped. The teat of the empty bottle fell from Helen's slackening mouth; she was asleep. The bombs had set off fires that were casting an upward illumination as they spread between the houses. Smoke and embers were discolouring the moon. Having carried out their bombardment, Kit realised, the only thing left for the soldiers was to enter the village and start shooting.

5

All of the delight that Kit took in Helen, his fascination with her growing form, his pride in her beauty and uniqueness, were balanced by the understanding that they had been won through an immense gamble with his own happiness. Kit's love for her was helpless, without walls or will. And if the object of that love were to be removed – if Helen died, that is – he knew that his heart would collapse in an instant into bitterness and horror.

The brilliant fact of his daughter's existence was eclipsed by fear of its extinction. Kit came to recognise it as a marker of his mood. On his best days, the sounds of her snuffling breath, the heat of her soft head against his chin, chased away thoughts of death. But when he was tired or anxious, they would crowd in, stubborn and hectoring, as he was eating, reading or sinking into sleep, and send him in panic to Helen's basket, searching out her breath. With clenched teeth, he read and re-read the section of the baby book about cot death. He knew exactly the age at which the risk was greatest, and the point at which it fell away. In the small flat in the city where she had spent the first few weeks of her life, he had enacted the scene in his mind. He could not stop himself, and he did not try; it was as if he relished the pain, as an injured man fingers a wound.

Sometimes it began with Lara – a shocked scream from the bedroom that told him in an instant that there was no hope. Sometimes it was he who entered the room. He would know immediately from the silence, from the shape huddled in the basket. He imagined the pinched face and cold limbs; Lara's frenzied attempts at resuscitation; the frowning ambulancemen and police; the tiny coffin; the months, years, decades of clammy grief. All of this could throb through his mind in the time it took to lift his fork from plate to mouth; and he would have to stand up, and mumble an excuse, and look in on the darkened room; and half an hour later, the same thing would happen again, not because the thoughts were uncontrollable, but because he invited them in.

The fantasies of the baby's death had ceased as soon as he and Lara took Helen to the village.

The space beneath the house was dark and obscure. The soldiers were not likely to look here again. Kit rested his head against the metal wall of the Koolroom. Helen drowsed against him, strapped tight in the sling. The familiar membrane, the barrier of glass that had so enraged Lara, had risen once again around Kit's senses. Part of him longed to remain here under its protection. But he knew that for Helen's sake he had to get away, across the stream and into the forest beyond; and that the only way to do so was to walk out through the village.

He stepped from beneath the rear of the platform into thickets of grass and heaps of coconut shells at the backs of other elevated houses. He walked between them; he could smell burning and see ahead of him columns of smoke. The glass began to shimmer and to thin. By an effort of will, he prevented it. There were things that he did not want to see and hear. He knew that Helen's survival, and his, depended on his reactions in the next few minutes. He made a bargain with himself: that he would see all of it, but feel nothing.

Many people were outside. Some of them were running, some shouting.

There were bodies on the ground, and holes where shells had fallen, with smoke or dust drifting out of them.

Several of the houses were on fire, as well as the school.

People were sitting, walking or crawling on injured limbs. In the early light, it was difficult to tell whether the blood on them was their own or the dried gore of the buffalo killed the day before.

Close to the well, Kit registered the sight of a muscular arm, severed from its owner; deprived of pumping blood, the tattoos on it – a fish and a monkey – were visible.

He saw Court Hardy, stepping quickly from place to place, with his camera raised. Kit watched him moving it slowly over the bodies of three children, covered with dust and blood. A woman crouched beside them, crying.

Kit made an effort to walk steadily, and not to run. He didn't want Helen to wake up.

The sun was rising, and colour began to resolve out of the scene. Dark-skinned soldiers were walking into the open area at its centre. They wore uniforms in a camouflage pattern, but in shades of grey, not green; they walked with rifles held in front of their bodies.

Kit understood that now, at last, he was looking at the soldiers of the Neighbour. There was nothing obviously malign about them. They held their guns loosely; they gave the impression of being slightly lost, and baffled by the scene before them.

A woman, whom Kit recognised as the village midwife, broke off from the bleeding man to whom she had been tending. She ran up to the soldiers and screamed at them in the Tongue. She shoved one of them, a very young man, with both hands, and grabbed at his rifle. The soldiers looked embarrassed, rather than angry. The young man pulled back on his gun; the others looked on confused. An officer barked words at her, which she ignored. Then he removed a handgun from a holster at his waist, and fiddled with it while the woman roared and gesticulated. The officer had a dark birthmark on his face; it spread from beneath his chin and over his left cheek. Eventually, satisfied that all was in working order, he held the gun in his right hand and with his left pushed at the woman. She shouted louder. Kit placed his hands gently over Helen's ears. The soldier kicked the woman between the legs, and kicked her hard again. She fell on the ground and he shot her in the face.

The chief's son ran up. He stretched his hands out in front of him, as if to say: stop. The officer shot him too. And then there were more groups of grey-uniformed soldiers in the square, and they were all shouting angrily, and pushing people up against the houses, and separating them into lines. Kit broke into a trot, and slipped into an alley between the houses on the far side.

Ahead of him, a group of six soldiers were coming up

the alley. Kit walked rapidly towards them. It was as if time was both slowed and speeded up. The soldiers stopped, and gazed at the man and baby. They were young, with clear eyes and flawless childlike skin. They stepped back respectfully to make space in the narrow lane for Helen and Kit to pass. Kit gave a small nod of acknowledgement as he strode purposefully on. He glanced behind him and saw that they were still staring, talking quietly among themselves. One of them was pointing at Kit, and raising his voice. As soon as the angle of the houses shielded him from their sight, Kit starting running.

Helen bounced in the sling, but did not wake up. They had reached the top of the slope that led down to the stream. Kit could see the bridge of logs where the imps used to hide. Beyond it was the forest. He felt his legs lurching out of control as he careered downwards. He was breathing heavily, and sweating; he was afraid of stumbling forward and on to Helen. Then he was over the logs and across the stream. He looked back and saw the young soldiers staring down at him. One of them was speaking into a walkie-talkie. But they did not follow.

The jungle closed over Helen and Kit, like water over the head of a diver. The sun had risen and green light filtered through the leaves, but on the ground it was as dim as twilight. A narrow track led away from the village; the tree house was off this, somewhere to the left. Four days ago, he had found it quickly, but now he was no longer sure where to break off the path. From the direction of the village, gunshots could be heard, and human cries. The scale and din of the forest made it easier not to think about them. Kit focused his hearing on the rattling of the insects, the calls of the birds. Helen woke up, in good spirits, and looked about alertly.

Kit paused, sat on a fallen tree, and filled the plastic bottle from one of the pouches of milk. Inside the rucksack, the other pouches were quickly melting; in a few hours all of them would be spoiled. He had forgotten, he realised, to bring anything for himself to drink. After feeding Helen, he licked drops of water from the glossy leaves of a palm.

Beneath the towering trees it was impossible to judge the angle of the sun. Kit dithered, ambling back along the track in the direction of the village, then retreated again. He heard voices of women and children, scuffling through the jungle on some other track, parallel to this one. He picked his way in their direction, through the thicket of trunks and bushes. Vines snared his ankles and webs broke on his face. Then came a different and heavier kind of scuffling, and a rally of automatic fire, and he stumbled back to where he had started, panting and soaked through with sweat.

The sling on his shoulders was digging into his back. He sucked more water off the leaves, sat down and looked around.

An invisible bird gave out a great whooping cry close at hand, with a strangled cough at the end.

'Where's your mummy?' he asked Helen. 'Where is she, do you think? What is she doing now?' There was more distant shooting, although from which direction it was difficult to know.

Kit began to feel overwhelmingly tired. He propped himself against a tree trunk, and allowed his head to nod into sleep.

He was woken by the sound of running. He rose to his feet. Two of the village hunters were pelting along the path. On seeing Kit, they stopped and gaped at him. Both were bleeding; one was limping. They still carried their bows.

– Help me, said Kit, in the Tongue. – Help us.

The hunters looked at one another, and then ran on.

– Where is the tree house? Kit called after them.

One of them stopped and looked back, and gestured broadly into the jungle before disappearing.

Kit's throat was dry again. His body ached. He sat down on a log, but slipped off it and landed awkwardly, jarring the sling and Helen against the ground. She began to cry.

Someone else was approaching along the path. Kit considered running into the trees again, but the thought filled him with exhaustion. He stood, facing the footsteps, singing softly to Helen.

It was the girl with the green ribbon.

The tree house was close to the track, but invisible from it. Helen and Kit had passed the place repeatedly as he had paced back and forth.

The girl took them there silently. She wore a frayed yellow dress and was barefoot. She had no obvious injuries, but she responded to none of Kit's halting questions. Her smile was replaced by a frown that made her look even younger than she was.

– Where is your brother? Kit asked. – Where are your parents?

He wanted to know her name. Such an obvious and simple question, but he had never asked it before. He had come close. But something – the girl's love and need – had prevented him. Names, he sensed, made things too near, and near things are dangerous. He felt the girdle of shame tightening around his guts again. He thought: being a parent makes you mad. You con yourself into thinking that care of a baby makes your heart wider, deeper and richer, connects you in compassion, imparts a generalised love. The truth is that you shrink and brace and tighten. You become an extremist, a fanatic for your own small bundle of genes and cells. You become a brute.

The girl said nothing as she slipped between the bushes and creepers.

The tree house consisted of a platform of lashed bamboo ten feet up, reached by a rough wooden ladder; here, Kit and Helen had spent the afternoon listening to the birds. He climbed up first with the sling, then reached down to help the girl. There was a jar of stale-tasting water, from which he drank, and a ladder of vine rope that extended above the platform into the tree's higher reaches. By now, Helen was giving out grumbling cries. He opened his bag, laid out the mat, the plastic wipes and the ointment, and broached and replaced her very full nappy.

The little girl, who usually took such an interest in Helen, sat on the edge and looked out into the trees.

There was no more shooting.

Kit drank again, and took off his sodden shirt. It felt

cooler in the branches than on the ground, and a weak breeze washed over his chest. At some mysterious cue transmitted by the temperature of the air or the angle of the light, the insects had fallen silent. Helen lay on her back looking up into the sky of leaves.

As his mind idled, Kit felt it drifting back towards what had happened that morning, and all that he had seen.

He nudged it back on course. Life was liveable now only as a sequence of episodes, loosely attached. There was no story to be told.

He rested his head on the rucksack and fell into a dense sleep.

He woke from it fugged with confusion about where he was, and why he was there. It felt as if hours had passed, and that the day was almost over. Helen had manoeuvred herself on to her belly, and was grizzling, her face pressed into a puddle of her own saliva. The little girl had gone. The forest was animated with noise again, of people running, branches breaking, cries of pursuit and alarm, and now, once again, gunfire. It was all around, and close, and getting closer. There was a crackling of leaves and branches immediately below the tree, and small voices. The head of an imp, a boy of five or six, appeared at the top of the ladder. He shot a glance at Helen and Kit, and then leaped on to the vine ladder and began pulling himself higher up the tree. Three more imps followed him. One of them had blood on her face. Last of all came the little girl.

– Child, how are you? said Kit, his mouth gummed with the thickness of sleep.

– Teacher, said the girl. – Men are coming. You must go up the tree.

She picked up Helen and handed her to Kit. He hated precipitous heights, but the ascent was made easy by the fact that he had no choice at all. The knotty ladder was well made, but coated with a mossy slime. At intervals, rough planks in the branches formed smaller platforms on which he was able to rebalance Helen in the sling. The branches closed up below him as he climbed; to look down was to see not a gaping abyss but a crosshatching of green. One hand, one foot above the other, and then repeat the action. Kit was afraid, he observed with detachment, more afraid than he could ever remember being; but the terror of what lay on the ground was greater than the fear of falling.

When the burning in his muscles became too much, he paused on the planks. At points on the way up, he passed the imps, who had sidled off the ladder and along the tree's larger branches. Hand over hand Kit climbed, losing the sense of time as well as distance from the ground. There were more shouts and shooting below. Then he was pushing through a narrow hole in another platform, a crow's nest of hardwood and bamboo, where the little girl was sitting.

Its parts were bound tightly together with vines and wooden pegs. Thicker vines lashed it to the tree's trunk and to the proliferating branches above and below. It rocked and shook with Kit's shifting weight, but it felt secure.

What beautiful work someone had done here, he thought – the hours of perilous labour that must have gone into it. And so here he was at the point to which life had led him – with Helen, a hundred feet in the air, trapped in a tree full of children.

There were voices in the branches below. The little girl disappeared below the crow's nest to confirm the well-being, Kit assumed, of the younger imps. As he listened for her return, he became aware of the sound of a much larger creature climbing up the rope, and getting closer. He peered through the hole, and into the face of Obson. It was the first time Kit had seen him without his gun.

When Obson was lodged alongside him on the platform, Kit opened his pack. The plastic bags of milk were flaccid and liquid. They were as warm as the air, the perfect temperature for Helen. He opened one and sniffed; it was sweet and uncorrupted. At the sight and smell of the bottle in preparation, Helen flapped her hands in excited anticipation.

Gowh! Gowh! she said.

When she had fed, he laid her down in the sling, loosely bound to the planks; even if she rolled, she could not roll off. Then he opened the first-aid kit and tended to Obson. He had twisted his leg after jumping from his sniping position on the roof, and scraped the skin on his back; he flinched as Kit painted it with antiseptic. His left eye was glued almost shut by swelling, and the skin on his nose and cheek was split and bleeding.

Pain and shock had robbed Obson of his English, and much of what he said was in the Tongue. It was not clear to Kit how he had got away from the village. He talked of being seized, and of standing with others in a line. Then he was taken somewhere else, where he was beaten, but from where he escaped. He talked about the

'Jesus men' in the grey uniforms. But there were others there. 'There were white soldiers and black soldiers,' Obson said. 'But not a black man like us. A black man without tattoo. A black man speaking English like a white man.'

Obson said, 'They were shouting through the . . .' With a flourish of the hand he made the shape of a trumpet.

'The megaphone.'

'They were shouting that we are selling, that we are making—'

'Drugs? Like, bad pills?'

'Bad pills, bad pills.'

He went on, 'They chase the children into the forest. They were shooting after them, they were laughing. The imps were crying. Some people ran away. I ran away. Everyone else they were killing.'

Obson started to cry and went on for a long time. Eventually he spoke. 'Mr Court,' Obson said. 'He's dead.'

'He's dead?' said Kit. 'What – what happened to him?'

'They want to know where is his movie. They hit him, but he does not tell them. They ask me and hit me. But I cannot tell where is the movie. Then they cut him. They cut it off. The Jesus soldiers. They cut him off. They – they – him in his mouth. They are laughing.'

His broad back shook.

Helen began crying loudly. An obnoxious smell rose from her. Kit's heart quailed. He had only just changed her; already, after a few brief hours in the forest, her stomach was sickening. He took out the mat, the wipes and the new nappy, and gently tore open the old one. It was stained an evil shade of yellow, and stank sulphurously. And in it, gleaming metallically even under the emulsion of shit, was an object that Kit immediately recognised. Obson saw it there too, and laughed. It was one of the tiny memory cards from Court Hardy's camera.

'Mr C.'s movie,' he said. 'He'len ate it.'

The shooting from the ground below had fallen away now, to be replaced by new sounds from the direction of the village. Obson pointed upwards. A knotted vine climbed the narrowing trunk of the tree, with bamboo pegs driven into it to assist in the ascent. Twelve feet above was the uppermost platform, as broad and solid as the one below. Standing on it, Kit realised with a tremor how very high up he was, close to the top of one of the tallest trees in the forest. From here, the village was laid out below, frighteningly close at hand. He could make out the schoolhouse, and his own house, on its detached elevation, with the solar panels glimmering in the evening light. Above was a familiar shape – the bristling black hulk of the Bird of Paradise. From this distance the machine itself was completely silent; all that could be heard was the tearing of the rockets that it was firing into the village. The missiles arced out in a parabola of fire and vapour, followed by a pluming inferno. The thatch burned in fierce sparks, followed by an outpouring of steady black smoke. No people were visible. Kit thought of the ancient skulls lodged in those eaves, their yellow jaws splintering into fragments.

Finally the black shape was hovering in front of Kit and Lara's house. It paused for a moment, as if in contemplation. The rockets when they came were multiple, and of a larger and more potent type. Rather than collapsing in on itself, the house exploded outwards and upwards, expelling fragments into the air. Bulky glowing particles shot high above the village and dispersed over the jungle like miniature parachutes, carried by the evening breeze. They floated clumsily down on to the trees, twirling and burning as they descended. Dozens of them were coming down into the forest around the tree house, slapping into the leaves.

Obson looked at Kit with an expression of horror.

'This is something terrible,' he said. 'This is something I have never seen. This is a new kind of weapon.'

One of the will-o'-the-wisps struck the platform on which they were standing. A second landed a few moments later. They still glowed with flame, and much of their exterior was singed black. Obson shrank back, as if from something dirty. But Kit reached gingerly down and picked one up, and shook out the burning, and recognised in his hand the charred carcass of a disposable nappy.

11
TREE

6

The shelling had stopped; the Bird of Paradise had lunged noiselessly into the distance and dipped beyond the horizon of trees. A drifting black column rose into the air high above the village, a cable of smoke knitted from the ropes of lesser fires. The occupants of the tree clambered cautiously to the forest floor. There were at least a dozen of them: Kit, Helen, Obson, the little girl and a darting band of imps who had taken refuge in the branches. They spoke in whispers, the older ones marshalling the younger. There was an hour of daylight left; it was obvious that, having razed the village, the invaders would turn next to the forest.

'They know how many foreigners in the village,' said Obson. 'They know you are not there. They want you. And they want Mr C.'s movie.' He held up the small black and copper rectangle that had issued from Helen's insides. 'This is the movie of the truth. I must take it to the city, to Dr Mochtar. For Mr C.'

Obson led the way along indistinct trails between the looming trees. Twice they glimpsed the Bird of Paradise through the high canopy of leaves, and Kit felt in his temples the pulse of its soundless aura. Once they heard the metallic bark of a megaphone from high above, but its words were impossible to make out.

They spent the first night in a shelter built for the village hunters, a rough platform of branches beside a fast-flowing stream. Obson and the imps were asleep as soon as they lay down. Kit was stricken by an exhaustion so intense that it was close to fever. He lifted the sling off his shoulders, lowered Helen on to the platform and unzipped his pack. He split the last of the plastic pouches; within it, Lara's milk had soured into curd. He delved into the tightly stuffed pack for the gas stove and the baby formula. He filled the billy can, brought it to a boil and let it bubble for five minutes. He scalded the bottle and when the water had cooled he mixed in the powder and pressed it to Helen's mouth. At first, she grimaced at the strangeness of the new mixture, and Kit's heart twisted with anxiety; but after a few tentative slurps and dribbles, she settled into a rhythmic sucking. With less than half the bottle drunk, she burped, and her head lolled against him. Kit fell asleep with his head on the pack and the baby on his chest.

He came to in soupy darkness, his head gluey and his mouth dry. In the garble of waking, he recognised two terrifying facts: everyone in the village was dead, murdered by agents of the Superpower; and Helen was not with him. He jerked upright, and found Obson and the imps sitting on the edges of the platform. Helen was in the arms of the little girl, with the bottle at her lips. The stove and billy can were undisturbed. He hurried over and put his hand to the unheated bottle. Helen, who had been feeding contentedly, opened her eyes as he pulled it from her lips, and began to cry.

'That water – you have to boil it. It's dirty. What are you doing? You have to kill the germs.'

He snatched up the wailing Helen from the arms of the girl. She screamed more loudly still.

The little girl's face was blank with surprise. Obson stood up and held his arms wide. It was the same gesture made by the chief's son, the moment before he was shot.

'She wants to help you,' Obson said. 'She sees you sleeping and wants to help you. The baby woke. She gives her the milk.'

'It's dirty!' shouted Kit.

'It is not dirty,' said Obson. 'It is good, the water of the river. Mr Kristian, we are not in the village now. It has changed. This is the cleanness of the forest.'

Distant lights had been sighted overnight through the trees: the searchlight of the Siskin Ferox. The soldiers could not be far away. They set off again along new paths; Obson walked ahead. Shamed by his outburst over the bottle, Kit extracted from his pack the hiking compass that he had bought weeks earlier from a camping shop in the city. He knew that he could not guide the party through the forest, but he wanted to re-establish himself as a responsible senior member: counsellor, if not pathfinder. He caught up with Obson, and walked beside him, peering at the glassy instrument in his hands. For much of the time the needle spun and twitched, crazed by hidden ores in the rocks. Even when it was steady, the meandering paths and absence of landmarks made it useless. Obson looked on patiently.

'It's OK, Mr Kristian,' he said. 'I know a way.'

Even by river, he told Kit, the journey to the capital took five days. The closest place of sanctuary – with its garrison, its telephone connections, its cars and its motorboats – was the trading town, a four-day walk from the village. But their escape had taken them in the opposite direction – further and deeper into the jungle highlands, towards the border with the Christian Neighbour.

'What happens in the rest of our country?' said Obson. 'How many soldiers come in? Where are they? How do our soldiers fight them? We cannot know.'

The only safe course was to continue on their path, then to loop round and back towards the trading town in the hope that they would outflank danger. It would take them far out of the territory familiar to Obson.

'It is a strange country,' he said. 'Forest, mountain, few villages. That is the place where the nomads live. They are dirty people. Disgusting people. But we can do what else?'

Kit had considered himself to be on close terms with the jungle. He had walked in its margins on most of the mornings that he had spent in the village; during the journey from the capital, it had loomed on both banks of the river. But he was unprepared for the experience of being constantly enclosed by forest. It dominated and overwhelmed each of the senses, with noise, colour, heat, soursweetness and stink. He felt like a man swimming in the shallows, who suddenly finds himself above a trench of ocean miles deep.

Kit knew none of the names of the trees or forest plants. He could find no pattern in their forms and distribution; each square yard of jungle was different from the next. The loftiest trees, like the one that he had climbed, were two hundred feet high, with trunks as thick as a man was tall. Some bore an even distribution of branches and leaves; on others, greenness burst outwards at the top of an almost bare trunk, and the shade below was pierced by angled blades of sunlight, like the interior of a stained-glass cathedral. The air on the forest floor was thick and unstirring; the heat of the sun was quelled to a clammy stillness. Kit felt himself to be inside something, rather than in the open; enfolded, without the sensation of being protected.

Time itself was muffled and distorted. The day's walking began each morning in what felt like the deepest night; it took hours for the sun to penetrate the high cover of leaves. The course of the day was marked by sound rather than changing light, and by alterations in the jungle music. Beneath it all was the buzz, creak, cheep, saw, rattle and sneer of insects, a din so loud and constant that he noticed it only by its absence; after crossing a clearing, or the openness above a stream, the noise reared up ahead, so that entering the forest was like stepping into the mechanism of a huge, violently electrical machine. Overlaying this were ensembles of birds and monkeys that cackled and tootled throughout the day. Occasionally, there were heavy scuffles in the vegetation above; once a lurid pheasant-like creature tumbled across the path immediately in front of Kit. But much of the life of the forest was invisible, except in its smallest manifestations – beetles glinting on twigs, strings of shining ants. Even in this dry season, the boggier sections of the path were booby-trapped with leeches, which clung to the undersides of leaves. The imps would stop as a group, and pluck the dark festoons from one another's necks and temples. Kit found one on the underside of his wrist, a gob of bloated mucus marked by delicate yellow stripes. Obson applied the tip of his smouldering cheroot, and Kit watched the creature writhe and fall to the earth, as his blood boiled inside it.

The sun was still high when they stopped and settled on a place of rest. Kit watched as the children curled on to fallen trunks and into the crooks of heavy branches. It was difficult to look at them. His heart, he recognised, was trying to keep at bay the village, its people and the fact of their destruction; these survivors were the living evidence of it. He had tried to think of them as a gang of imps, a jolly, piping rabble, as indistinct and uncountable as birds. But there was no getting round the arduous facts.

There were nine children.

The oldest was a muscular boy of about sixteen with a machete slung across his shoulder and the air of an experienced hunter. Then there were three sisters, who always remained close to each other, arm on shoulder, hand in hand. The girl with the green ribbon was next in age. The other four, the smallest of whom was little more than a toddler, were all boys. Within a few hours, Kit knew each of them by his voice.

The tiny boy was shy and prone to tears; he wore a blue T-shirt with the image of a clock. His slightly older companion, who raced about in a pair of dirty shorts, was laughing and exuberant, with a gift for clambering up trees and across boulders. The third boy had been born with a harelip, which had been corrected by Dr Kay – faint scars still marked him. He had a fine high voice, and was usually singing. The oldest of the four was quiet and smiling, and skilled at catching fish and laying a fire; he carried over his shoulder a woven bag, in which he kept fruit and roots gathered along the way. Kit watched as the little boys shaped nests for themselves on the forest floor, and the oldest girl unrolled the reed mat that she carried for her two small sisters. It occurred to him that all of them had simultaneously become orphans, and that none of them seemed surprised.

Kit laid Helen on the changing mat, and removed another of the nappies from his bag. Their texture was consoling; they were as crisp as wafers, the opposite of the forest with its wet and profusion, its endlessly ramifying life. The folded nappies opened like paper shells; Helen's loins were clasped in their sterile jaws. They kept at bay the air and water and all the teeming invisible creatures that lived within.

The first full day of walking had taken them along more or less distinct tracks, which crossed and recrossed shallow streams; on the following day, they began to ascend. Kit thought of himself as healthy, if not especially fit. But the climb through the jungle was the hardest walking he had ever done. Rather than a steady upward gradient, it was a relentless up and down across a switchback of low ridges. The path was little more than a thinning of the undergrowth, littered with fallen trunks, which had to be climbed over or scrambled under, and invisible low-strung vines that snatched at the ankles. The imps bounded back and forth, barefoot or in rubber sandals. Kit fell behind; soon, he was gasping and drooling, and stumbling breathlessly to a stop every few hundred yards. The oldest boy hung back to offer him a hand up the muddier slopes. Wordlessly, he eased Kit's rucksack off his shoulders; now he returned with a branch hacked into a walking stick. His outburst over the bottle, Kit saw, had made it impossible for anyone to offer to carry Helen; but he was staggering and slipping, and her head was bouncing around the confines of the sling, provoking her to screams of protest. As he sat on a log giving her the mid-morning feed, Kit became aware of the little girl doing elaborate work with a cat's cradle of vines. She was fashioning a sling of her own. After her milk, Kit lifted the drowsing Helen into it. With a few knotted strands, her bottom, back, neck and head were held firmly against the chest of the little girl who stood smiling at Kit, as if inviting apology and approval.

He smiled back. – Thank you, he said. Then – What is your name?

The girl told him. He knew the meaning of the word in the Tongue: Moon Moth.

She held Helen close to her, and called out, laughing, to the older boy, to tell him what Kit had just asked her. The boy laughed too, and pronounced his own name, shaking Kit's hand as he did so. He went into a long explanation of what it meant, accompanied by miming and actions. Soon Kit understood: Eagle.

Word spread among the children. They came forward one by one. First the sisters, then the boys. Obson looked on smiling. Some of their names had a meaning and some did not. Kit repeated them, as the children called them out, laughing.

Raila, Tayla, Silk Mouse, Ridwan, Jusley, Jefy, Frog.

Kit and Moon Moth passed Helen between them, and the walking soon became easier. The girl stayed close to him; Helen was never out of his sight. The easing of the physical burden imparted a surge of energy that woke up his senses. He became aware again of the whooping invisible birds, and the brightness of the leaves, and the primary colours of the T-shirts and dresses worn by the imps. The children called to him and Helen as they ran between the trees, and he called back and told them to take care. It was becoming impossible not to think about what had happened to them, and to their fathers and mothers, brothers and sisters, friends. Knowing their names, sharing Helen with them, made the world larger and greener, and more difficult to bear.

The biscuits and noodles had been used up on the first day. Obson and the imps ate as they moved, plucking up nuts and hairy jungle fruit. After choosing a sleeping place, the boys went foraging and returned with yam-like roots, a pheasant and a nest of white grubs, which they grilled on skewers of twigs. For Kit, they brought shiny fish plucked from the stream, which he boiled into a bony stew.

 Before going to sleep, Obson and the imps emptied their pockets and made a reckoning of their possessions. Apart from the contents of Kit's rucksack, they had the machete, the sleeping mat, the memory card, two sets of prayer beads, three straw dolls, two pocket knives, a deerskin water bottle, two pouches of tobacco, a broken pair of spectacles without lenses, a broken wristwatch and three half-empty plastic lighters. Obson examined the objects carefully, and redistributed them among the imps so that everyone had something.

 The climb continued the following day. The higher jungle was different in character from the lower: graver and more dignified, less frothing and antic. The undergrowth of weeds and bushes thinned; the trees were taller and more widely spaced. Limestone thrust itself from the bed of the forest, rising in abrupt cliffs and extending in horizontal planes of stone, some rough and pocked, others smooth and slippery, or crazed with fissures out of which sprouted pitcher plants and ancient-looking ferns. In places, the stone had been worn into natural sculptures in which the imps saw the forms of monkeys, bears and cats. Instead of the lazy meanders of the lower forest, the river gushed in noisy torrents through stone-sided ravines. The bridges across them were no more than parallel lengths of wobbly bamboo, one for the feet and one for the hands. Even the imps hesitated in front of them; Kit refused to contemplate the idea of carrying Helen across. They spent half an hour picking their way down a low stone cliff, across the shallow gush of the river, and up a higher ascent on the far side.

It brought them to an elevated clearing in the jungle. The limestone displaced the trees to create a platform of rock open to the sky. For the first time, Kit looked down over the forest in panorama. The sky was a blue expanse filled with immense white clouds; below, individual trees were visible as tiny dimpled tufts, monotonous as a carpet of moss. In the centre of the clearing of rock was an upright stone that resembled the hunched head and shoulders of a cowering man. The imps stood in front of it, sweating and panting from the climb, and shielding their eyes from the sun. Kit retreated to the shade of the trees and dealt with Helen's nappy and bottle. Obson approached; there was an air of exhilaration about him.

'This is a famous place,' he said. 'Beautiful place. This is the furthest I have ever come. From here we go down and we go back.'

'We're going down?' said Kit. He mixed the cooling water with the powdered formula.

'Tomorrow. We go down, and soon we come to the big path. There are villages where we can have food. And from there is the path down to the trading town.'

The oldest boy came up and spoke to Obson, who followed him to the edge of the stone platform. The imps were looking down and pointing at three distinct columns of smoke rising from the forest in the middle distance.

The peace of the sky was broken by a whipcrack of sound. They looked up to see the shapes of black fighter jets high above.

'Supersonic,' said Kit.

Obson raised the imaginary form of his lost rifle as the jets disappeared beyond the horizon, pursued by their roar.

The descent the following morning was as exhausting as the climb. Trees rose out of the steeply angled slope; Kit used them as buffers and handholds to slow his lurching progress. The children moved lightly and steadily, passing Helen from one to the other. Kit ached in joint and foot; his nerves were brittle with lack of sleep. But even as he staggered down the slope, he marvelled at his own lack of trepidation. The situation in which he and Helen found themselves was stunning in its extremity: marooned in a tropical jungle, in war, with children for his protectors. Horror had padded into their lives and laid its paw upon them. But then the horror had stalked on; and life was continuing, with one bottle, one nappy, one sleep following another. Helen cried when she was hungry or tired, but no more often than usual. Released from the sling, handed between the imps, she was happier than ever. Her colour was fresh; she was feeding and filling her nappy. The tin of formula was hardly begun.

The slope gave way to a straight and level path through thick trees. It wound uncertainly, with multiple forks and branches, and its narrowness forced them to walk in file. They passed through a dense stand of bamboo that blocked out the light, as impenetrable as the walls of an alley. Beyond, the track became faint and ill-defined. In places, Obson took the machete from the oldest boy and hacked his own path; twice, he gave this up, and led them back the way they had come.

'We look for a village,' he said, a little defensively, as they stopped for Helen's bottle. 'It is close.'

Late in the morning, when it had become obvious that they were lost, an acrid smokiness manifested in the air. At first, the smell renewed Obson's confidence and sense of direction; he picked up his pace, smiling and gesturing ahead. The smoke became thicker as they walked. Its haze drifted in the beams of sunlight that broke the canopy; and Obson slowed his pace again, and took on an air of watchfulness and caution. They came out of the forest at a stream, with a well-worn path beside it, and patches of cultivated vegetables. It was obvious before they reached it that the village had been burned.

It was a small place, no more than twenty homes, all of them reduced to greyed and blackened spars. Several were actively smouldering; in one or two, dimly glowing embers could be made out. Ash had drifted over the gaps in between the houses, but beneath it Kit could make out the marks of violent activity – broken spears and wooden-handled machetes heaped in a pile, patches of what looked like dried blood, and around them a concentration of prints, of bare and booted feet.

Kit looked about and realised that he and Helen were ahead of the rest of the party. Obson was some way behind, the machete hanging loosely from his hand. The imps stood in a tight group on the perimeter of the destruction. Then the oldest of the girls, Raila, ran forward. Tayla and Silk Mouse, in a panic at being left behind, rushed after her, and the rest of the imps followed. They moved from one burned house to the next, standing close and peering in intently, as if over the lip of a dark well.

Between the collapsed beams, protruding from the pools of ash, were familiar objects, made strange by the fire. A tin kettle, turned almost inside out by heat; a collection of charred cooking pots; and the fragments of an old-fashioned pedal-operated sewing machine. A split metal chest contained singed scraps of clothes. In one of the ruins, emerging from beneath a blackened pole, was a curved spinal column with its splay of ribs, as delicate as the leaves of a jungle plant. In other places, there was a sweet roasted quality in the stench of burning from bodies that had been incompletely digested by the fire; and at these the imps stopped and stared.

Two of them gave shouts from the trees on the far side of the clearing where flies were buzzing. Obson emerged from the same spot.

'Many dead people over there,' he said. 'Do not come.'

The imps all ran over anyway.

Something was happening to them, Kit understood; the smoke, the ash and the garish cadavers had prised loose the thing that had been locked down. Grief, that had been held at bay by the thrill of survival, was stirring and uncoiling in their hearts. The smallest of the boys, whose face was grey with soot, was spinning around and around and shouting. Raila was hunched over her knees on the ground, crying. Her two sisters stood by, helpless and panicked by her distress. The young boys sat slumped in the drifting ash. Even the proud young hunter stood with clenched fists and tear-streaked face.

'The little boy, Frog, he does not understand,' said Obson, whose hands were shaking. 'He thinks this is his village, our village. He thinks his father and mother are here.'

Kit, who had been leading, fell back to the margins of the burned village and turned away from it. He looked back towards the green panels of the jungle. Helen was wriggling in the sling; he would soon have to boil the water for her again. He laid out the changing mat on a patch of untainted ground, and settled down to the routine of boiling, scalding, mixing. Looking back at the weeping children, he was no longer sure of their names.

They each took a blade from the heap of junked machetes. The imps found baskets and filled them at the vegetable patch. They slept by the river and started up again early the next morning. After an hour of walking they were in a thicket of bamboo. To Kit it looked like the same one that they had passed through the day before. Ahead, Obson and Eagle were conferring, and the boy was shaking his head.

'Obson,' said Kit, catching up. 'What's up? Are we lost?'

Obson was looking away from him, towards the end of the shadowy bamboo alley. People had come into view. They were standing at the edges of the path: two men with bare torsos, pale faces and cropped fringes of black hair. They had sheathed machetes on their belts and long poles in their hands; they stood as still as forest trees. Obson was looking at them, as if waiting for something. They regarded him motionlessly. Obson took two steps forward with his hands held out.

– Good day, he said in the Tongue.

The two men walked towards him. The older of them was speaking, but so quietly that Kit could not hear him. Obson was talking, slowly and loudly, in the Tongue, and then in another language that Kit did not recognise. The men had plugs of bone in their ears, and necklaces of what looked like animal teeth. They were small, no taller than Kit's shoulder. The poles, he now saw, were blowpipes, each tipped with a spear of sharpened wood. One of them carried a dead bird and monkey on his back, knotted with vine to a woven basket.

The imps were smiling at one another as if embarrassed. Kit bent his ear to Moon Moth. She whispered the name that the people of the village used for the forest nomads, which was also the word for filth.

'The nomads,' Lara had said to him one day, as she sat expressing milk in the Koolroom. 'Everyone hates the nomads.'

'But why?' he asked.

'Lots of societies have someone like that, right? They're the Jews or the gypsies or the untouchables – the people you despise so that you can feel better about yourself. They say that they're dirty. Also, they don't like the way that they use poison in their blowpipe arrows – unfair to the pigs and monkeys. And they creep people out – get this – because they're pale. "White filth, skin very white!" the chief said to me once. "Like grubs. Very disgusting, very poor."' She smiled, and attached the pump to her other breast. 'The real problem is that they don't have a place of their own.'

Groups of nomads inhabited loose territories of jungle, within which they built shelters, hunted and harvested fruit, then moved on every few months. There was a rare and fragrant wood, and a stone found in the guts of the monkeys, that they bartered with the traders in exchange for blades and metal pots. 'And they make great baskets,' Lara said. 'But they don't grow anything. They're extractors, not cultivators, and that freaks people out. I guess it's because they can't be controlled. So, Dr Mochtar and his guys want to settle them. Build them villages, give them schools and clinics. But they melt away, they slip between your fingers, they won't play along. We had Paulus try to do a primary survey once, just the simplest data – numbers of mothers and children, ages, that kind of stuff. It was impossible.'

Later, she said, 'They're closer to the forest than anyone else. They're the outside of the outside of the outside. They're a reminder that humans are just creatures, that we're animals of the jungle like all the rest. That scares people. It is scary, right?'

The men led them out of the bamboo alley and off the path. To Kit's eyes it was an impenetrable thicket, but in the company of the two nomads the jungle became flexible and yielding; gaps and tunnels opened up in the green. After twenty minutes, Kit smelled smoke again. The trees thinned out, the dimness eased, and they found themselves in a narrow clearing where the nomads had built their homes.

The word hut was too grand for them. Each consisted of an unwalled platform of slender tree trunks, lashed together with vines, and raised on poles with a roof of fraying tarpaulin. Cooking fires smouldered, and dogs skulked beneath the shelters, along with snickering monkeys on the ends of chains. Small pale-skinned children stared at them as they approached, their black hair cut straight across the forehead like their parents'.

Since the burned village a transformation had overcome Obson and the imps. Their energy and self-possession had drained away; now, among the nomads, they looked more vulnerable than ever. The nomad children chased their skinny dogs, but the imps, who looked big and ungainly next to them, made no attempt to join in. They stood before the shelters uncomfortable and subdued. They glanced around, and whispered to one another, but there was no laughter. They held their limbs awkwardly; it was as if they were trying not to touch anything, even the ground.

The nomad men squatted as they talked; Obson

remained upright. Kit saw that it was a strained conversation, marked by long pauses of incomprehension, conducted in some crude pidgin in which none of the speakers was fluent. Obson mimed and gesticulated extravagantly: a raised rifle, a booming explosion and an aeroplane. He smiled a lot, in a way that suggested both unease and disgust. The hands of the nomads remained motionless at their sides or rested lightly on their blowpipes; their voices never rose above a murmur. Unable to follow the words, Kit studied their faces. Their hair, short at the front, extended below the shoulders; their eyebrows were plucked bare. Most wore dingy shorts; the older man had a loincloth of folded drapery. On their wrists and below their knees were black bracelets of rattan.

A stink rose from Helen's nappy and she began to twist restlessly in the sling. The smell, so familiar to Kit, had altered in the shift from breast milk to powder, becoming dryer and less sweet. He stepped away from the group and unfurled the changing mat on the rough grass. The nomad children formed a ring around it, staring down at the spread-eagled baby, and laughing when Kit met their eyes. After Helen was clean, they led them to the edge of the settlement, where three toy shelters stood, perfect miniatures of the real thing, containing child-sized baskets, a child-sized cooking bowl and a stack of child-sized firewood. From the roof hung a tiny cradle and inside it was a doll, a tiny poppet of rags and sticks.

In one of the full-sized shelters a mother was feeding her baby. The child sucked listlessly; it was very small, its spine and shoulder blades sawing under the transparent skin. Helen was coarsely pink and robust by comparison.

The children who had led him there were pointing from one infant to the other, comparing them point by point.

The other women covered themselves with T-shirts or dirty bras. But the mother sat unselfconsciously exposed, coaxing the child with difficulty on to her breast. Her puffy nipple was pearled with drops of milk. The sight aroused a painful longing in Kit – he felt it physically, as a weakness in his knees and thighs. The nomad woman's breasts were full of milk. He needed the milk in her breasts; Helen needed it, to live.

The baby's face was hollow and cadaverous, like that of an old man. When the mother raised her head, he saw that she was scarcely out of childhood herself.

The parley between Obson and the nomads continued for a long time, and ended with an exchange of goods: ten painkillers from the first-aid kit, half a pouch of tobacco, one of the lighters, Kit's plastic ballpoint pen, and the broken watch and spectacles in return for a small dead boar, two baskets and a heap of leaf-wrapped packets of sago. To Kit, it seemed an unequal transaction, but the nomads gave the impression of being satisfied with their acquisitions, especially the watch, which was passed between them and carefully scrutinised.

There were no farewells. Obson simply walked away from the settlement and led the imps straight to the stream, where they washed themselves vigorously.

'What did they say, Obson?' Kit asked. 'What have they seen here?'

His fraternisation with the nomad children seemed to have annoyed Obson, who did not immediately answer. 'It is difficult to understand their words,' he said eventually, 'but they said some things. They said that many soldiers have been through here, and many aeroplanes in the sky. The village, the first one we see, was burned two days ago, but the soldiers still come. They say that the soldiers are white men, as well as the black men of the Neighbour.'

'They saw them? Did they talk to them?'

'They run away. They run away and hide in the forest. They are good at hiding. They watch the soldiers from the trees. They see them going past. This is what they say.'

'You don't believe them?'

Obson smiled. 'They are strange people. Dirty people. You cannot trust. They have no side. They are their own side. I think perhaps they know the soldiers. Perhaps they help them.'

'They help the Christian Neighbour?'

'They do not like Dr Mochtar. He sends people here to give them houses. They don't want that. They like to live like monkeys.'

'So the soldiers are in front of us.'

'In front. Behind. In the sky.'

'Where do we go from here?'

'They tell me how to go to the river. From there we find a boat.' He nodded, as if he had just been persuaded of the idea himself. 'The rain starts soon.'

'But we have no boat. We have no money.'

'You are a foreigner, Mr Kristian. Someone gives you a boat.'

Kit tried to imagine stepping with Helen on to a wobbly

raft on a rocky river, crashing into banks and boulders, spinning down rapids without life jackets or helmets. The vision of surrender came to him again. If they did have ambiguous loyalties, then the nomads could escort him and Helen to the soldiers. The two of them were an encumbrance to Obson and the imps, who could continue on their way more easily without them, carrying Court Hardy's memory card.

Obson seemed to read his thoughts. 'The soldiers kill Mr C.,' he said. 'They kill you too when they find you.'

'Will they kill Helen?'

'Mr Kristian,' said Obson. 'You wash now. Give He'len milk. We walk soon.'

Helen screamed with fury as Kit bathed her in the cold water of the stream.

Minutes after setting out again the next morning, they ran into the patrol.

It happened so quickly it was hard to make sense of. Obson was leading them along the stony edge of the stream, looking for the best place to wade across. The soldiers saw them first. They were a hundred yards away on the far bank. They must have been standing back in the cover of the trees; when they began to shout Kit could hear but not see them. Then the grey figures emerged on to the stones, black rifles in their hands, yelling commands.

Kit, who was carrying Helen in the sling, stumbled immediately back into the cover of trees; behind him, Obson was calling to the imps. Kit clambered over logs and around bushes. On his chest, Helen was screaming in alarm, her head bouncing within the sling's constraint.

There was a single rattle of automatic shots. Kit ran until he was exhausted, and rested half-slumped against a tree. Like a beacon, Helen's cries drew the others in – Moon Moth, Eagle, three of the boy imps, and Obson, who sprinted out of the undergrowth carrying Frog on his shoulders.

The sisters were nowhere to be seen.

Obson was gabbling questions at the children, who replied with gasps and sobs. No one knew what had happened to them.

'Raila,' Kit said to himself. 'Tayla, Silk Mouse.'

Obson turned to Kit. 'The soldiers catch them perhaps,' he said. 'I have to go back for them.'

'If you do that they will catch you too.'

Obson screwed up his face in the agony of the dilemma and rubbed his hands on his temples.

Kit imagined stopping here, feeding Helen, waiting as the boots came closer, waving his shirt as a flag of surrender.

'Let me go for them, Obson.'

But the others were already running on, and Eagle had picked up the rucksack. Behind them, Kit could make out the sound of a labouring engine.

Obson and Eagle led the way, but it was obvious to Kit that they had little idea where they were going. They ran up and down the obstacle course of jungle, sometimes along notional tracks, sometimes through thickets of bush that they hacked with their machetes. Twice, Kit made out the engine sound; once he heard shouts. His chest was burning and pain was shooting up his legs. At times, he slipped so far behind that he was unable to see the others. Then a child would appear, offering a hand. Helen never laid off her crying, but he refused to hand her over. She stank again. He sensed physical collapse circling him, like a hunter stalking an animal. Finally he caught up with the group as they crouched panting on the slope.

Helen's screaming echoed around the tall trees, louder than the insect and bird sounds. All their pursuers had to do was to follow it.

'Obson,' he said. 'I need to change Helen's nappy.'

Obson shook his head. 'Further, further. Up here,' he said, pointing.

They scrambled on and up. Ahead of them the trees were thinning into light. At the top of the slope Kit saw brightness and glimpses of the sky. And then he was stepping out of the trees, on to the great platform of limestone with its stone upright and the sweeping views of sky and jungle. Obson and the imps were smiling in relief; Kit was amazed. It was appalling how close the place turned out to have been. For two days, they had been walking in a circle.

Obson and Eagle were overlooking the river gorge, standing by the tree trunk that tethered the bamboo bridge, and shaking it to test its soundness. Helen's cries had dwindled to a parched croak of protest, but now they rose again, a dry, sawing racket that echoed off the limestone surface and made it impossible to think about anything else.

'We're going back over the river?' Kit shouted over the din.

'We can do what else?' said Obson. 'The soldiers come here soon.'

'I will not carry Helen on that bridge.'

'I carry. Do not worry, Mr Kristian.'

'No, Obson.'

Eagle began to speak, and Kit understood that he was offering to go with him and Helen down the cliff path that had brought them here two days before.

'OK,' Obson said. 'But it is long. You must go now.'

Kit shook his head. 'I have to clean her. I have to feed her.'

He opened the pack and set a billy can of water on the stove. Then he unrolled the mat on the flat limestone and laid the thrashing Helen on it. The sequence of simple actions, so routine and familiar, soothed his shaking hands.

'Mr Kristian,' said Obson. 'The child – please, the child can wait.'

Beneath the whine of his own anxiety, Kit felt a throb of anger. Helen had never cried like this before, or been for so long without milk or a clean nappy. He began to fear that her screams would do some damage to her, like a spring mechanism broken by an excess of strain.

'You go ahead, Obson.'

'You know what they will do to you – to all of us. We go together.'

'I have to change her. I have to, Obson.'

Obson muttered incredulously in the Tongue.

Mustard yellow poo had leaked out of the nappy and through the cotton suit. The front of Kit's shirt was saturated by it. Helen's legs thrashed as he undid the poppers, and peeled off the sodden garment and the mash of swollen paper around her hips. He gathered up leaves and did what he could to wipe her off. He splashed her with the water that remained in the bottle, then unfurled and fastened the clean new nappy. Now he had to sterilise the feeding bottle. But his hands and upper body were coated with a glaze of shit.

'Mr Kristian, Mr Kristian. We cannot wait. We go now.'

'I have to feed her.'

He rinsed his hands from the water bottle, and rubbed them against his shorts. They were still filthy. Kit's heart flexed in panic: Helen had to be fed, but he was too dirty to feed her. Moon Moth, as always, was close at hand. Compared to Kit, she was unsoiled. His heart jumped with relief. He called her over, tipped the last of the water over her hands and mimed for her to rub them together.

'Like this, like this. Between your fingers, under the nails.'

He led her back to the billy can, where Obson and the imps stood tensely watching. His hands were steady as he tipped the boiling water into the bottle and over the cap and nipple. Moon Moth helped him to pour the water for the formula backwards and forwards from bottle to billy can to cool it. When this was done, she measured out the powder from the tin, and shook the bottle to mix it. Then she took Helen in her arms and put the bottle to her mouth.

Helen moaned and twisted her head away from the teat.

Kit thought: it's too late. She's too tired to feed.

Obson was pacing back and forth, snorting.

The girl sang to Helen and stroked her head, and Helen took to the teat, first grudgingly, then hungrily.

Soon the bottle was almost empty. Helen's eyes were closed, the motions of her mouth and chin were slackening and slowing. Her limbs and neck slumped against Moon Moth, and she was asleep.

'We go, we go,' hissed Obson.

Kit strapped Helen into the sling and followed Eagle to the edge of the cliff from where the bridge extended across the ravine and the steep downward path began. But now the imps were shouting.

– Soldiers, soldiers.

There were crashing sounds coming from inside the forest and again, at the thought of capture, Kit felt flutterings of relief.

Obson spoke to him in the Tongue.

– Kit, you have to cross the bridge. The soldiers are coming. If you take the path, they will catch you and Helen. They will kill you. Move your feet along the lower bamboo. Hold the upper bamboo. Keep moving. Don't move too slowly. Don't look down. I will go first, I can take your hand. I will carry Helen.

'No,' said Kit. 'I have to carry her.'

– OK. Obson nodded. – We have to go *now*. We are going now.

The bridge was a well-made structure that had fallen into disrepair. The two parallel lengths of bamboo were bound to one another and to trees on either bank, but the vines had sagged and loosened with time. Obson held on to the trunk of the tethering tree and gripped the upper support, then edged his feet uncertainly on to the lower. The whole bridge succumbed to a visible tremor. Obson shuffled along it, and held out his hand to Kit, who sidled into position, and on to the bridge. It wobbled, but less drastically than he had feared. Gusts of breeze tousled the slack vines; the sun had made the bamboo of the handrail warm to the touch. It was frightening, but easier than he had expected. The trick was to keep your weight on your feet and to use your hands for balance, without leaning on to the upper support. Helen was asleep, but the burden of her weight made it all the more difficult. Why had he insisted on carrying her? It was not that he believed that he alone could save her. But if she fell, he wanted to fall with her.

It was sixty feet across to the far bank. Kit looked down, and saw low water frothing noisily over exposed rocks. It was sickening, but he had known that. Everything was a bit less horrible than he had feared. He looked back and saw the group of children. The oldest boy, Eagle, was holding them back; they were waiting for Obson and Kit to reach the far side. It had not occurred to him to let someone else go first.

The barrier of glass was in place again. It separated him from the children, but it also extended beneath him to prevent him from falling. The recognition of this lulled him, and he found his mind wandering in unexpected ways. The drops of sweat on his face made his nose itch; he had to stop himself removing a hand from the bamboo to scratch it. He realised that he hadn't burped Helen after her feed, and worried about the gas trapped in her stomach. The weight on the bridge caused it to sag deeply around the middle. But soon they were ascending its upward arc, and Obson was gripping his hand and pulling him up on to solid ground.

From the other side the imps began to make their way across. Eagle was lining them up and telling them when to go. He could see the boy looking down the line of the bridge, reckoning the tension in the bamboo and the depth of the sag; Kit's pack was still on his back. He sent the imps across in pairs, an older child leading a younger. Soon there were two of them on the bridge, then four, then Obson was lifting the first one off, followed by his partner. The bamboo was flexing, but not uncontrollably.

A group of soldiers appeared on the limestone platform.

Immediately, the remaining children were on the bridge, jamming and pushing up against one another in a frenzy of movement. The pair of imps who were in front had separated, the older one abandoning the younger to hurry to the other side and jump into Obson's arms. His smaller companion, Frog, was clinging to the bridge in terror, eyes clenched shut, blocking the way; behind him were Moon Moth and Eagle. On the stone platform, the soldiers were kneeling with raised rifles. Two of them had begun to edge their way on to the bridge. They moved deftly towards the clog of clambering children. Then, in response to a shouted order, they nimbly turned back.

The soldiers gathered instead at the tree that tethered the bridge. They were so close that Kit could see their faces and the patterning on their grey uniforms. The children on the bridge had started moving again, the oldest boy half pulling, half carrying the small, terrified one. Now the soldiers were arranging themselves on either side of the bamboo poles where they were attached to the tree. Working in opposing teams they began to push and pull, push and pull. The motion, slight at its point of origin, transmitted itself along the poles in a wide, majestic swing. The children on the bridge were swept from side to side in the air above the river. They sank to their knees. They clung on to the bamboo and one another. The swings increased in breadth and speed. They were still holding on. They were crying. Then, in a final flexing, the bridge shrugged them off, and they dropped into the gorge below.

The glass, when Kit needed it most, had fallen away. He rose from his crouch and stepped to the edge of the cliff. He looked down, and saw the unmoving shapes, sprawled across the rocks and the narrow channel of water: the yellow dress of Moon Moth; Eagle, with Kit's pack still strapped to his back; tiny Frog, face up with the clock on his chest.

The soldiers were starting to edge again across the still swinging bridge. Obson was hacking at the tethering vines. The soldiers could see him. Two of them raised their rifles. There was an explosion of shots that bit splinters of wood out of the trees. But the bridge was already slipping and breaking, still rippling from the energy that had been imparted to it, uncoiling and thrashing and throwing the soldiers on to the rocks below.

7

They stumbled through the forest until it was dark. No one spoke of what had happened, or what was to be done. All that mattered was to place distance between themselves and the bridge. Kit worried about Obson's sense of direction, and his habit of leading them in circles. But he found it impossible to address him, or even to look him in the face. A change had taken place in Obson. His limbs moved clumsily; he faltered and tripped. Even his tattoos were more visible, as if there had been an alteration in the transparency of his skin.

Obson blamed him, of course, for the delay in crossing the bridge and for the deaths of the children – if he had let Helen cry, and crossed the river at once, the children would be alive. He recognised this fact, which throbbed on the edges of thought and feeling. But in his heart and panting lungs, it was eclipsed by something else: the loss of the rucksack. Helen needed to be changed again, and soon she would start crying for her evening feed. The camping stove, billy can, bottle, powdered milk, changing mat and nappies were gone. The situation expressed itself in the form of three sentences through which his mind toggled helplessly. Helen needed milk, to live. But there was no milk. How was she to live?

You are mad, Kit said to himself. *I am mad.*

They came through a patch of dense vegetation and stopped in a narrow clearing where rotting trunks had toppled to form a rough U-shape. The three surviving imps kindled a fire and roasted green bananas on it. The oldest boy, Ridwan, placed one of them on a broad leaf, mashed it with his fingers and offered it to Kit.

– For He'len, he said.

'No, no, she's not weaned,' said Kit. 'She can't eat banana.' In the Tongue, he said, – She drinks only milk.

– She has teeth, said the boy. – She can eat banana.

– She cannot, she cannot, said Kit. Then in English: 'She has to be six months old for that. She needs milk.' He tried again in the Tongue – We have no milk. She must have milk.

The imps looked at one another in patient exasperation. Obson lay awkwardly against a fallen trunk, his head facing upwards, his eyes unfocused. The boys whispered among themselves, then Jefy produced the last of the cigarette lighters. All three disappeared into the trees.

Helen's grizzling gave way to rasping wails. Kit removed her filthy cotton suit and held her against him. His stroking fingers encountered roughnesses on her skin, a row of livid insect bites, made raw by scratching. He looked at Helen's nails, which were ragged and uneven. In the Koolroom, he had kept a pair of tiny steel clippers for just this purpose. Fleetingly, he contemplated the idea of using the rusty edge of the machete in their place. Instead, he laid Helen on the earth, took her fingers into his mouth, and nibbled off the ends of the soft nails with his teeth. Her arms jittered and her head moved from side to side.

He was aware of the flickering of the lighter as the imps pottered in the forest. They came back with a coconut and a branch of glossy leaves. Jusley hacked and split the fibrous husk and shell. Ridwan folded one of the leaves into a tight cone deftly pinned with twigs. Into it he dribbled the clear coconut milk. Kit loosened the sling and held the leaf beaker to Helen's mouth. She writhed and cried and puckered up her mouth. Kit angled her head back and tried to pour in the fluid. It dribbled over her neck and ears and hair. She thrashed and screamed. He wasn't sure that she had swallowed any of it. He tried again later, and twice more before the sun rose. But Helen cried all night.

Rain was falling when he woke the following morning. Beyond the cover of cloud the sun had risen, but the forest floor remained in soupy twilight. The rain reached it not in discrete drops, but in rivulets that cascaded down the trunks like gutter water. Murky light glittered on pools at the feet of the trees. Obson was leaning against his log in an attitude of abstraction. The three imps were crouched around a large beetle to which they had tied a thread of wiry grass. The other end of the thread was bound to a stick jammed into the earth, and the beetle toddled round and round it on an ever-shortening tether.

Helen lay on a mat of leaves. Kit had removed the soiled cotton garment and put it to soak in a puddle. She had stopped crying and lay naked on her back, batting her arms listlessly. Her lips were dull and dry, but her eyes darted and focused on Kit's face as he leaned over her. Using a half coconut as a bowl, rinsing his hands against a seeping tree trunk, he mixed a paste of coconut pulp, rainwater and banana, dabbed it on her lips, and attempted to push it into her mouth against the resisting bud of her tongue.

High above, the rain ceased, and sunlight and heat struck the forest again. Soon the trunks were steaming. Kit looked to Helen to see that she had shitted over the leaves, without any of the preliminary straining that usually preceded such moments; already, flies and ants were bearing down on the glistening mess and porting it away.

Kit knelt and sniffed at his daughter's shit, alert to its smell, colour and texture. It was darker, he thought, and thicker than usual, with a dry sulphurousness about it. She smiled up at him, looking more than ever like Lara.

Obson's stupor lasted for most of the day. He lay awake with his head against the log. The bruises on his face had become puffy and the cuts were bright and raw. Sweat from beneath his arms spread across his T-shirt in overlapping rings. The boys foraged among the trees and set bananas and tubers on a fire of twigs. They lodged coconut cups beneath the trunks to catch the rainwater, and Kit brought one of them to Obson. He drank it quickly, and then a second. The water seemed to make him sweat more.

Part of Kit was grateful for the crisis in feeding Helen, because it distracted him from questions that he was afraid to ask. Such as: what were they to do now, and where were they to go? The severing of the bridge could not protect them for long. Why were they slumped here on the forest floor, not far from the place where they had been shot at? Twice that morning, the Siskin Ferox had passed by, unseen above the trees, but felt unmistakably as a throb in the inner ear.

'It is the nomads,' Obson said. They were the first words he had addressed to Kit since the bridge. 'It is the filthy people. They betray us.'

'You think so, Obson?'

'We talk to the nomads. We talk in the nomad village. In the morning the soldiers are there, waiting.'

The insects had subsided into one of their mysterious silences.

Kit said, 'We should leave here.'

Obson's stomach gave out a rumbling gurgle. He grimaced, stood up with difficulty, pushing himself up with his left arm, and shuffled off into the trees. He was frowning when he returned. He slumped back against the log. 'Sometimes we must rest,' he said. He gave a deep sigh, turned on his knees to face the log, and lifted up his T-shirt to expose the right-hand side of his torso. Just above the line of his shorts was a four-inch trench of pus and congealed blood. It was rough with the embedded fragments of leaves that he had pushed into the wound. A dark rash of web-like lines spread outwards from the gash.

'The bullet, it touches the tree and then it touches me,' Obson said. 'Just passing by my skin. My skin comes open. The blood is not so much.'

'Obson, that looks infected,' said Kit, attempting to sound unconcerned, as he absorbed this information. 'It's a flesh wound, but it could be . . . well, we need to – I should wash it.'

He cast around for something clean with which to

dab the path of the ricochet. There was nothing. He took another coconut of water, and rubbed it on to the wound with his fingertips. He could feel the heat radiating from Obson's skin. The edges of the wound were raised and in places it was sealed with a cap of yellow matter soft to the touch. Obson winced, and thrust Kit's hand away.

'It is OK, Mr Kristian. I can do, I can do. Look to He'len.' He raised his left arm to point. Helen had rolled off the leaves and was lodged uncomfortably on her side, with her cheek in the mud.

When Kit looked again, Obson appeared to be asleep. He had not been reproachful after all; the alteration in his manner was caused by something other than anger. Kit felt a pulse of relief and despair.

The following day, Obson seated the children before him and recited to them the songs and legends of the village, of gods and god-like animals, and the numberless unseen denizens of the forest. He was visibly sicker than the day before. The wound on his hip was bloated, and the pain of it made it difficult for him to move. There was an air of delirium about the stories that he told. Some of them were chatty and anecdotal, rambling shaggy dog stories punctuated by jokey rhymes. Obson's sweating face gurned and beamed as he took on the voices of conniving toads and prim pheasants. The three boys chuckled and joined in the refrains, and acted out the tales with jerky dances. But then a change came over Obson, and the imps were solemn and still. His back straightened, and his eyes grew glassy. With an air of trance, he intoned the legends of the deities of the sun and moon, and the avatars of the elements, in a voice high and level, chopping out a rhythm with his hand.

Kit found himself able to understand more of the Tongue than ever. Obson told tales of the monkey bandit, Rotto, and the tricks that he played on Rampian, the pompous crocodile king. He talked of the village deep in the jungle inhabited by badger bears, who walk upright and talk as people do. He told the story of Bayl, the melancholy catfish, who always looks sad despite the efforts of the other creatures to cheer her up. He recited the saga of the war between the rocks and the trees, of how the bark fell in love with the moss, and the moss betrayed him for the stone.

He was chewing on the leaves of a jungle plant that was meant to suppress fever. The green juice dribbled out of the corners of his mouth and into his stubbly beard. Each story was directed to one among the imps, who had to repeat sections of it. 'I teach them the stories to remember,' Obson said, while the boys were out foraging for food. 'They are the treasures of our village that is gone.'

Kit looked at Obson. The tendrils of discolouration beneath his skin had spread as far as his armpit and thigh. Obson was reaching the end, consciously settling his affairs with the world. How to bring him back? He was the only hope in the forest, for Kit, for Helen and the imps. The prospect of his death was like the absence of milk, impossible to ignore or to accept. Panic beckoned to Kit like a ghost between the trees. He twisted his head away.

Obson extended a wet hand to Helen, and stroked her cheek. She was propped on Kit's lap as he sat cross-legged on the ground. Her lips were flaking, and the insect bites had become infected. The skin on her head had tightened or shrunk, exposing the throbbing flat gap in the unclosed plates of the skull.

'Just once I see Dr Mochtar,' Obson said. 'I never forget it.'

It was the afternoon of the next day. There had been no new rain, but cloud was visible through the tops of the trees. The puddles had resolved into mud in which small biting insects were breeding. The imps repelled them with cords of vine tied around their heads, stuck with the twigs of a pungent bush. Within the space between the toppled trees, the ground was littered with coconut shells, discarded fruit and small coils of muck, where the boys had squatted. Obson no longer made the effort to haul himself up and crouch under the trees; he seemed no longer to have the need. He was not eating. Everything he drank was sweated out of him. He lay in a dazed slumber, groaning occasionally, then woke, with rolling eyes and chattering teeth, avid for conversation.

– It was in the trading town, Obson went on in the Tongue, his voice a croak. – Two weeks before the election. We walked, and then we took a boat. Justus came too, and the chief and the chief's son. Many from the village. People came from far away, from all around the country. Black men like us, and the brown people from the coast. Yellow men who own the shops and the warehouses. Everyone wearing green, the colour of Dr Mochtar, his party – green T-shirt, green hat, green paint on faces. Some of the people, all they wear is green leaves.

– The market square was too small so they moved to the football field. It was full of people, standing close to one another. Children on their shoulders, so they can see. There are people sitting in the trees all around the field. They make a stage at one side, with loudspeakers. The week before, the government had their own meeting in the same place. The prime minister, he spoke – the old grey man. All round the football field are metal poles with his picture at the top. Tall, tall poles, and a big photograph – the old man in his grey suit. Between the poles, people were hanging green streamers, and banners and flags and pictures they make of Dr Mochtar. So many flags, so many colours. Mrs Lara, she said to me, 'Obson, this is like a ship. It feels like sailing in a ship at sea.'

'Lara was there?' said Kit. 'Lara went to see Dr Mochtar?'
'She come with us. Nurse Jim too.'
He hurried on in his urgent whisper.
– In the field it is so hot. Everyone is standing close to one another. Everyone is sweating. Dr Mochtar is late. The imam says a prayer, the pastor says a prayer, the sorcerer says a prayer. Even the temple priest of the yellow men makes a prayer. Still Dr Mochtar has not come. So Rollo, Dr Mochtar's old friend – Rollo Konrud, now he is minister of security – he gives a speech. He tells the story of Dr Mochtar's life. You know it? His mother dead when he is a kid, the father a poor man with many children. He goes to the pastor's school and he goes to the imam's school. He wins a scholarship to high school in the trading town, to college in the capital, to university in your country and in Mrs Lara's country, and becomes a doctor, and becomes a professor. He comes home, he writes books, he goes into prison, but they have to let him free. Rollo is telling the story, and then everyone shouts because Dr Mochtar is

coming. He is coming through the crowd from the back. The guards try to push the crowd away, but Dr Mochtar tells them no. He stops, and he talks to the people and shakes their hands. But the crowd is pushing and the guards are pushing back. The whole crowd is moving, and we are being lifted up and pushed. People are screaming. It is hard to breathe. I can see Justus, he has lost his spectacles, and I hear Mrs Lara, she is shouting. Nurse Jim, he is trying to protect her. And then Rollo comes on the loudspeaker again, and he says, 'My friends! This is not how we greet our leader. This is how we greet him.' And he holds up his handkerchief and waves it in the air. And the band on the stage starts to play.

> Land of green, land of freedom
> Light on the green sea, shining
> Light in the green trees, glinting
> Light on the green river where the fish jump
> Mochtar Mohamad, light of our land
> Mochtar Mohamad, light of our hearts.

– Everyone stops pushing, and takes out a handkerchief, or a scarf, or prayer beads, or just holds their hands, and waves, and they make a space for Dr Mochtar and he walks through and climbs up on the stage.

– My sisters and brothers! he calls out. Everyone is cheering, and jumping up and down, and laughing. – It is hot!

– Hot! Hot! call the people in the crowd.

– So hot my spectacles steam up.

Everybody laughs louder, because Dr Mochtar has very thick spectacles.

– My sisters and brothers! Let us all sit down.

Everyone moves up for one another and sits down on the ground. I am sitting next to Justus, and he finds his own spectacles on the grass, just one lens broken.

– My sisters and brothers! It has been too long since I saw you here.

– Too long, too long!

– But I am very happy to see that you are looking well.

Everyone is laughing and cheering and singing. – Light of our land! Light of our hearts!

Dr Mochtar looks up at the high poles and the big pictures of the prime minister, and he waves at them.

– Hello, sir! It is a pleasure to see you here too.

And everyone is laughing again – the way he says it is so funny, because he is being polite and he is being rude. And then a young boy, he is no older than these boys here, he jumps up on the stage, and the guards try to make him go away, but Dr Mochtar stops the guards, and the young boy starts to do acrobatics. He jumps and he flips over in mid-air, backwards and forwards. He is bouncing, he is doing somersaults, he is almost flying. It is incredible, and everyone is cheering and clapping, and the band starts to play along. Then the boy gets too tired, and he stops, and Dr Mochtar shakes his hand and hugs him and sits him beside him on the stage, and stands up in front of the microphone again.

– My sisters and brothers! How good it is to be here with you again, in this beautiful town. And I mean that, my friends, I mean what I say: you have made a beautiful place here. In my grandfather's time, in my father's time, this was a place for the white masters and the mosquitoes.

Look at it now! Your river, your forest. Your mosques, your church, your temple. Your schools – the fine schools where I was educated. Your hospital, your market – your magnificent market! All the produce of our land comes to us through here. I live in the capital, Dr Mochtar said, and in the capital is power. But this place where you live, this is the heart of this country, of this nation!

The cheering goes on a long time, but then people stop cheering and singing and tell one another to shush, because Dr Mochtar is looking serious.

He says – And now you have your road.

People cheer, but not everyone is cheering.

– You like your new road? he asks.

People cheer – Yes! but Dr Mochtar is looking strange, and they are not so sure.

– It is a big road, he says. A big, wide, long road – I drove along it myself today. One day! One day is all it takes now from the capital to here. No more need to wait for the boat, and paddle up for three days, getting off, getting on, the rapids, the crocodiles. Now the people of this town can get on a bus, or on a truck, and the next day they are in the capital. To sell your vegetables, to go to school, to college, to find a job, to follow your dreams. One day is what it takes now. The people of this town deserve that. The people of this town need a road.

And everyone is cheering and whooping and singing, when Dr Mochtar leans into the microphone, and says – Not this road.

He says it quietly and not everyone hears, but soon the cheering goes quiet too.

– Not this road. Because this is not your road.

It's very quiet, and he makes a long pause.

He points up at the big pictures of the prime minister, the grey man, looking down from the metal poles.

– This is his road.

Another pause.

– This is your forest, your river, your town. But this is his road. The engineer who planned it? His cousin. The company that got the contract? It belongs to his uncle. The machines that make the road, those big yellow things that break the earth and make the concrete? His other friends, his Superpower friends.

– Who worked on this road, this big expensive road? He points at people in the crowd. – Did you? Did you? No, not me either. None of us got the chance. They bring in the workers from foreign countries. They say we don't have the skills. Another one of his friends brought in those workers.

– And the money, all the money that it cost. Do you know how much? They try to explain the way that they spent it, but it doesn't add up. I ask them, Rollo asks them, we ask them in parliament – but they cannot make it add up. That money – your money – most of it went into someone's pocket.

He looks up again at the big pictures of the grey man.

– Whose pocket did it go into?

A few people laugh, but most of them are quiet, and Dr Mochtar is talking very quietly.

– Into your pocket?

– No! says the crowd.

– Into my pocket?

– No!

He says, – This is a very big road. It is a fast road. The people of this town, they need a road, they deserve a road.

Now he is talking more loudly.

– But not this road.

Every time he speaks it is louder.

– This isn't a beautiful road.

Now he is shouting.

– This is a dirty road.

– Dirty road, shouts the crowd.

– Dirty money, dirty business, dirty men.

Everyone in the field is shouting.

– We have had enough of this dirtiness.

– Enough!

– Enough of these cronies, and this corruption.

– Enough!

– It's time.

– It's time!

– Time to make change.

– Time to change!

People are standing up.

– It's time to throw them out.

– Throw them out!

Everyone is standing up.

– Do you hear me? Throw! Them! Out!

Obson said, – Everyone in the field was on their feet, shouting Throw! Them! Out! The shouting went on and on. People were shouting at the big pictures of the old grey man. Some of them tried to pull the poles down, but Dr Mochtar told them not to. They didn't need to pull down the pictures. Two weeks later there was the election, and in the election everyone, everyone votes for Dr Mochtar. The next day he was prime minister. I'll never forget it.

That night, the imps dug out a jungle root that tasted of soap suds and caused visions. Kit had heard about this plant from Lara; it was what the village sorcerer took before entering his trance. Obson had told the boys to bring it for him, but after he had nibbled on the dirty tuber and closed his eyes, mumbling, they began sucking on it themselves. Later, Kit could not remember if he had chosen to take it or if the imps had mixed it into the drinking coconuts. The water had tasted soapy, and the soap made him clean inside. He was crouching over Helen, pushing broken banana into her mouth. The sound of the mushy pulp against her lips, Helen's weak slobbering, was jarringly loud. He could smell the sound as well as hear it. Kit recognised that he was hallucinating. He had taken mushrooms once at university, and had felt lonely and trapped. But this was quite different. The soapiness was making bubbles within him, which lifted him up. He was full, but very light. He looked down at Helen, lying on her leaves. There was a slackness in her skin and a boniness about her knees that he had not seen before. Anxiety about this, and other facts, presented themselves to him, as if for inspection. But he was distracted – possessed in fact – by something that he had never recognised before, and had suddenly grasped, a radiant fact that illuminated the night, the jungle and everything in it. Helen was not, in fact, his daughter. She was his mother, and she would always protect him, as a mother must.

'Mum! Mum!' Kit cried out to the jungle, which laughed. Helen was laughing too, even if her laughs were like cries.

The imps were running, rolling somersaults and dancing beneath the trees. Obson wasn't somersaulting, he was lying down, and twitching, but he was like a lamp. Kit followed the children, who had made torches and gave him one. Colours were mighty, of course, although the jungle had not changed. It didn't need hallucination. There was a lot of green and a lot of black, and green and black turned out to be the only colours, because they contained everything else inside them. Even the flames of his torch were composed of green and black. Kit danced danced with the children. The leaves tied around their heads had eyes, but the eyes were laughing. The imps were acting out the stories Obson had told the day before: gaping like catfish, growling like bear. Kit became preoccupied, as no child could, with the story of the moss. He stroked it with his fingertips. The velvet on bark and stone became the surface of Lara's body, long ago, and the bodies of other women, long ago.

They ran ran ran through the forest and danced danced with the water in a sandy stream. Moonlight broke on its surface, breeze ruffled it, and the moonlight, wind and water were all things you could drink. Fish danced and frogs danced danced danced. A badger bear danced. Kit laughed, but the imps screamed and they all ran and the torches died out and they got lost in the dark and the imps were screaming more loudly than ever but he couldn't see them. The screaming stopped, and it began to rain, and the rain came down down heavily. With the moon covered by cloud, the blackness all around was complete: blackness of leaf, blackness of blood, blackness of inside of worm. He crawled and crashed blind through the undergrowth and the rain. The lightning through the tops of the trees illuminated split-second images of jutting branch and bark. He shouted to the imps, but none of them replied.

It was still completely black when he found the place of fallen logs. He was drawn to it by a noise, like the sound of a saw. Obson was still there. He was soaking wet to the touch, and his body felt taut, like an overinflated balloon. The sound was his breathing. Kit slumped beside him, exhausted by the night's exertions, and leaned his face against his friend's.

– Obson, he said, laughing.

Although there was no light, Kit could hear Obson opening his eyes.

– Kit, he said between wheezes.

– It's raining again.

– Kit.

– I took a holiday. I came back now. I'm sorry, Obson, about the children.

Obson said something that Kit couldn't properly hear or understand.

– You are a very good black man, Obson seemed to be saying. – You are a black man. You are one of us.

Kit laughed.

– It is good to talk to you, Kit, Obson said.

– Why?

– When you speak, you remind me of my wife, he said and gave a wheeze that might have been a laugh.

Kit's head, resting against Obson's shoulder, nodded into sleep. The rain off the leaves drilled their faces and hair. Kit's neck slipped and slumped, waking him.

– Kit, said Obson. – In my pocket. Pocket, my shorts.

Kit laughed, and reached with difficulty behind Obson's wet body and pulled out the plastic lighter; as he was withdrawing his hand, it brushed against the tiny shape of the memory card. He placed both of them in his own pocket.

– There was a badger bear, said Obson.

The effort of speaking was making his breathing thicker.

– We danced with it, said Kit. But all he wanted to do now was sleep.

– Kit, said Obson. – Where are the imps? Where is He'len?

The thought jolted him to alertness.

Kit stood up quickly, straining by force of will to see through the darkness. The rain was still falling, but the heart of the storm had passed and the lightning was too far off to impart any illumination. He cast his arms about, groping like a blind man for the spot where he had left Helen. He edged forward, straining to hear her; it filled him with horror that she was not crying. The surface of the ground was liquid. It slid beneath his feet, or else it was his feet that were sliding. He crashed backwards, and fell heavily. The last thing he was aware of was the taste of mud in his mouth.

He woke in full light, lying in mud. He was assailed immediately by panic, by the sense of having broken something that could never be mended. He raised himself to his knees and looked about. Obson lay against his log, eyes closed. There, a few feet away from where Kit had fallen, was Helen. She lay on her side, a small wet shape facing away from him on the earth. She had rolled or crawled from the leaves on which he had left her. She was motionless. Panic was quelled by the thump of suspense. He looked from Helen to Obson, and back to Helen. He rose, took two steps and put his hand to Obson's head and neck. He was cold. He took five steps to where Helen lay, and laid his hands around her head, which was warm. Helen was alive. Her fingers were flexing feebly.

He lifted her up and held her to him. At some point in the night, he noticed, he had lost his shirt. Shivering, he pressed his daughter's skin to his own muddy skin. She stirred against him. Enough of the drug remained in his blood for him to register this on his palate, as well as feel it against his chest: the motion of Helen's legs and arms tasted of grapefruit. He carried her to the foot of a tree, and looked around the place of encampment. The rain had smoothed everything into mud: the traces of the fire, the fruit skins, the piles of muck.

He found one of the half coconuts, and cupped it against the water dripping down the tree, and held it to Helen's mouth.

He looked over her, as her mouth flickered weakly. It was as if he was seeing her for the first time. She was the same Helen, but altered in ways that made her strange. Her eyes, which were closed, seemed to have shrunk into her face. The skin on her head was tight, and the throbbing fontanelle more pronounced than ever. The angles of the small familiar body were altered; it was not emaciation, but bagginess, as if the skin had become untethered around her arms, her legs and her bottom.

The rain eased and the sky above the trees was clearing. Kit looked at Obson. He too was changed. The tension was gone from his body, which was gently slumping off the log on which it leaned. Green leaves loosened by the storm had fluttered to rest on his face and chest. His shorts and T-shirt were sucking up the water on the ground and taking on the colour of mud. His arms were becoming pale and the tattoos were manifesting on his skin like photographs in developing fluid.

Stirred by the sun, the jungle was waking after its night of rain. The insects and monkeys took up their din; the birds put out liquid calls. The forest, which had killed Obson and was killing Helen, was a beautiful place. It was not just that horror and beauty were interlinked, Kit saw: they were inseparable; in fact, they were the same. And the thing that the forest did with the greatest magnificence was to overcome time.

He had lost track of how long it had been since the attack on the village. Two weeks, one week – what did it matter? Decades, generations, millennia meant nothing in this place. The jungle was always new. This was its lesson: to show what life had been before the coming of people and what it would be after they had gone. Adrift between these points, Kit was no more than a particle, a flimsy packet of minerals, oils and moisture destined to be swallowed up and digested by the earth. It had already begun; he had been consumed at the moment he entered the forest.

Obson was ahead of him, but only by a little way.

Flies and ants were already gathering on his body. Death was the term that people used for this, but death in the forest was not a simple thing. Here it was not an ending, but part of a cycle, the process of change that began at birth and continued throughout the course of a life. The idea glowed in the fading embers of his high. It was such a promising way of regarding his situation; it was the means of escape from the trap that he was in. The jungle was a living creature of water and leaf. The plants and forest creatures, Kit and Obson and the imps, even the soldiers, were no more than microbes in its guts. He laboured at these thoughts, for the relief that they contained; he felt a longing to succumb to his green fate. Then Helen stirred in his arms again and began to cry, a cry that was half a cough. He looked from the body of his dead friend to his daughter's face, and panic flooded over him again.

Helen would be dead. He would be dead too, but that was only as it should be. Fathers died in the sight of their daughters and their sons – but not a child, a baby. It was inconceivable, the violation of a profound principle: his beloved daughter, stiff, lying cold in the mud. The wrongness of it was like the coming together of volatile chemicals; it threatened an explosion. Above all his mind recoiled from the idea of Helen going rotten. That was the point about her: she was the opposite of decay. She was change as life, not death: the brilliant tableaux of her physical growth, the surges of her emerging personality. Soon, though, she would begin a progress in the opposite direction, as Obson was now changing: black, grey, blue, green; hot, warm, cold; slack, stiff, slack; damp, wet, lumpy, and finally bones and mud.

Helen: dead. He could not bear it, even the thought of it. His heart raced, and raced faster. He was choking, although no sound came out. He attempted some half-hearted bargaining: my life for hers. But the thought went nowhere: with or without divine intervention, her survival depended on his.

The idea of Lara came to him – not her essence, that he had sensed in the touch of the moss, but her face and voice. He pictured himself lying beside her in bed, relating to her his green epiphany. He imagined her wide-eyed irony and elaborate scorn. Even at her most stoned, she would have been withering about such 'hippy shit'. However intense her moments of despair, Lara stood for life.

'Sure, the door's open,' she said to him. 'The worms are waiting – no one can stop you, if you're gonna walk through it. But are you sure you're a fucking microbe? Kristian Rabone: man or germ? 'Cause you look like a man to me. Shall we check? Come here. Oh yeah, I thought so. Mmm . . . Looks manly to me. No microbes here.'

There was no longer any doubt: surrender was the only survival. Kit had to find the soldiers and hand over Helen and himself. The Bird of Paradise was out there hunting them. How to attract its attention? He examined the lighter that he had taken from Obson's pocket. The thinnest residue of fluid was visible within. But what fuel was there for fire? After the rain, everything beneath the trees glistened with water. To signal with smoke, in any case, he needed a space more open than this.

There was a crackling in the vegetation and Jusley stepped into the clearing. He was the boy with the scars on his mouth, the one who had played the part of the monkey the night before. He looked stunned; his face was scratched, one eye glued shut with blood. He looked around with his good eye, and saw Kit and Helen. He ran over to Obson's corpse, reached out a hand to the cold face and stood silently looking down at it. Kit waited, hesitated, then laid his hand on the boy's shoulder.

– Fire! We must make fire.

The boy's limbs were as loose and floppy as Helen's. Kit tugged him through the trees to the stream where they had danced. It had been such a long journey the night before, but by day he saw that it was no more than a hundred yards. Images came back to him of the splashing and dancing. He half expected to come upon a scene of horror, but whatever had happened to the other two boys, there were no signs of it here.

– Find wood, he said to Jusley. – Wood to burn.

The boy came back with sticks that were dry beneath the bark, and a cotton-like floss for tinder. Shivering with urgency, Kit heaped them on the sand at the stream's edge. The boy was muttering through bloody lips and pointing into the forest behind them.

Kit coaxed a small cone of flame out of the lighter. The floss kindled, and the flame caught the twigs and the larger sticks.

When the fire was established, Kit moved Helen closer to it for warmth. Jusley was mumbling again and pointing into the forest.

– Dirty, dirty.

– Find more wood, said Kit.

The boy came and went, still muttering, as Kit built up

the fire. He worried about adding the damp wood at the right moment, when the blaze was sufficiently large and hot, but before it burned itself out. Hesitantly, he began to pile on wet twigs, then green sticks, sodden leaves and coconut husks. The flames hissed and shrank, but soon smoke was billowing off the crackling mass and gathering above it in a narrow white column.

– More wood, he said. We need more wood!

He moved Helen out of the smoke. He sat with her on his lap and fed her mashed banana, breaking it up with sooty fingers and pushing it into her mouth. He was afraid of the fact that she almost never cried now. Part of his heart, Kit recognised, was attempting to isolate Helen, as he had isolated Court, Obson, the imps, the dead of the village, Lara – perhaps everybody in his life. He must not permit his heart to do that. The fire was the important thing; the fire, and its smoke, could save Helen. But the fire must not be the excuse for forgetting her. He scooped water from the stream with his hands, and held them to her mouth, soothed by the weak movement of her tongue against his skin.

The lighter was spent now. This fire was the last and only chance.

Jusley was bringing less and less fuel, at longer intervals. Kit called out to him, but there was no reply. He propped Helen on his shoulder and went into the trees to hunt out dry wood. He couldn't find enough. The fire was falling in on itself. The green sticks were choking the red embers.

The sun had risen to its highest point. After the dark of the jungle, the glare on the stream and its sandy margin was unbearable. Kit placed Helen in the shade, and lay next to her. His heart was beating in his chest and the blood was throbbing in his ear. He placed his hand on Helen's heart: weakly, it was beating still. Water was dripping off the tree next to him, in its own regular rhythm. He lay on his back, and looked up at the blank blue sky. It came to Kit that the fire was dead, that Helen was dead, and that he was dead too. Here, half beneath the sun and half beneath the green, was the point to which everything had led and where it would now end.

Then the sky began to pulse, that familiar inaudible sound felt in the temples and in the hairs on the arms. The black shape shuddered into view, lazily, as if appraising the landscape below. It ceased its movement above the trees on the far side of the stream, and then lines were tumbling from within it, and dark, nimble figures were moving down them.

The loudspeaker was saying something, but Kit was not listening. He picked Helen up and waded across the thigh-deep stream. The sudden cold of the water sliced open his cocoon of stupefaction. His legs began to cramp; his lungs wheezed. He slumped on to his knees, lifting Helen up in both hands to keep her out of the flow. The clenching pains had spread to his stomach; he groaned. In front of him was a commotion of splashes and shouts. Two men were wading to meet him, one black and one white. They were great powerful creatures with rolling shoulders; their chests bore the flag and the badge of the eagle; their rifles were poised in their arms.

They were shouting at Kit as he knelt in the water, holding Helen aloft.

Helen began feebly croaking, and the sound gave Kit hope.

The black soldier slapped a palm to his face, as if killing a mosquito. He dropped his gun. Then he was waving his hands in the air, and flailing backwards. His comrade jerked his head around in confusion, then cried out. A short spine of wood was sticking out of his eye.

Now more of the spines were raining down on the river out of the forest behind Kit. The first soldier was on his knees in the stream, plucking them out of the fabric of his uniform and the skin of his face. He fumbled in the water, and pulled out his rifle, and fired off deafening rounds into the trees. Then he struggled to his feet and splashed back to the other side.

The soldier with the dart in his eye now had them in his neck and cheek. He was retreating too, and screaming. Kit could see the darts arcing above him in the sunlight, to fall silently into the water or embed themselves in the backs of the retreating soldiers. The first man had disappeared into the trees, but the second had fallen on his face at the water's edge. He grovelled in the wet sand, his limbs twitching.

The Siskin Ferox was drawing near, and its loudspeaker was shouting.

Kit rose to his feet, and ran back with Helen across the river and into the forest. Figures became visible, peering out from behind the trees. The men with the blowpipes crouched, reached into their bamboo quivers and released the thin darts again and again at the dying soldier on the far side. Pale children looked on silently. A man offered water. On his wrist there was a shiny watch. A group of women came to him. They wore dirty T-shirts, except for one whom Kit seemed to recognise. She reached out, and took Helen, and stroked her head, and held the baby to her breast.

He knew from the beginning how it was going to end. It ceased to matter at the moment he handed over Helen. The mother was so young, but she never faltered. At first, Helen was limp and listless, but the girl stroked her hair and cooed songs in her ear. Within a day she was sucking strongly at the breast. Movement and colour returned to her limbs as quickly as they had left. The skin on her scalp lost its tension and the dryness lifted from around her mouth. Except when the girl went to wash, Helen hardly left her breast. Kit was no more than a bystander to his daughter's care. The men laughed when he picked up the baby and cradled her. But when she began to smile again and to reach for his face, Kit knew that she had forgiven him.

The girl led him to a small freshly heaped mound at the edge of the settlement. She made him understand that her own child lay beneath it. Even the death of one so small was a contamination. The camp would be moved because of it. She pointed to the mound, then pointed to Helen, and held her close.

Kit followed little of the conversations around him. One of the men spoke a few words of the Tongue, but he asked Kit nothing about himself or what had brought him there. The nomads did not introduce themselves; he wasn't even sure of their names. At the beginning he had taken them to be the same people whom they had encountered on the far side of the bridge. But the pale faces, the bone necklaces, the muddy clothes and the straight-cut hair were so difficult to distinguish that he was no longer sure.

The boy, Jusley, was with them too, Kit noticed without surprise; within a day, it was as if he had become one of the nomad children. To Kit, they gave a T-shirt and a water gourd. When food was eaten, a portion of it was allotted to him. Helen was the object of affection and curiosity among the men as well as the women, but his own status within the group was unclear to him. He was not invited to hunt with the men or to prepare food with the women. He was not offered tobacco. He washed on his own. One of the women gave him a heap of beads and showed him how to drill holes in them using a fine metal bit, and how to thread them into necklaces. After that she showed no interest in him.

The nomads were neither warm nor hostile, attentive nor indifferent. None of that mattered. Understanding was no longer the important thing. He knew how it would end.

He didn't understand why they had saved him and Helen, or why they had acted so violently. As the soldier lay on the far side of the river, twitching with the dart poison, two of the men had waded over to him and pierced his neck with the spear ends of their blowpipes. They had come back with the chain of metal tags, which they handed to Kit, wet with bubbles of blood. The group had moved quickly through the jungle after that, to a settlement in a dim clearing about an hour away. It seemed impossible that such an act could go unavenged; Kit was tense with apprehension about the return of the Siskin Ferox. But it was two days before the nomads dismantled the huts and moved on. The roof tarpaulins were carried away; everything else was pulled down and scattered on the ground. The women and the oldest man went to the grave of the baby and murmured words there; clutching Helen, the mother wept a little. Then the entire group left the clearing and entered the jungle.

They walked for days and days. It might have been for weeks. They would stop for a night, sometimes two, and make rough shelters out of branches. The men hunted and fished and butchered pig or deer while Kit threaded beads, and then they moved on.

They travelled far. Sometimes the walking was hard, sometimes easier. Kit walked with the women, carrying Helen and other young children, and helping to forage for fruit and tubers. It rained for hours each day. He had no sense of the direction in which they were walking, although they seemed to be tending down, rather than up.

They passed beside a deep gorge traversed by what had been a wide concrete bridge. The deck of the bridge had slumped and tipped to one side; armoured vehicles, wheeled and tracked, could be seen, dashed and buckled in the ravine below.

They came upon more burned villages, with corpses heaped outside them, and the wreck of a small helicopter, its round glass cockpit skewered on the branches of a great tree.

They came to a hilltop with a sweeping view of the landscape below. The green of the jungle ended, and gave way to a vista of stripes: tracks of raw orange earth alternating with patches of toppled and heaped trees. Yellow machines moved along the tracks, tugging and pushing bundles of logs into the river where they floated downstream in slow-moving shoals.

They descended the hill, and skirted the zone of deforestation. Later that day they came to a wide passage cut out of the jungle. Walking along it, they reached the place where workers were laying down a road with gravel, tar and rollers. Their torsos were thin and muscular. Beneath them, the flat new surface of the asphalt smoked and glistened.

The man who spoke the Tongue came to Kit, and pointed. – Yellow men, he whispered.

The labourers on the road knew the nomads and greeted them with handshakes and laughter. The machines were halted and the men led them to an encampment of wooden sheds and prefabricated huts. They took them into one of the sheds. It was furnished with bunks, lockers and stoves. The navvies and the nomads squatted on the floor and emptied their pockets on to the mats, and began to barter animatedly, exchanging blades and fish hooks for fragrant wood, and monkey stones, and the dark dried innards of jungle animals.

Kit lingered on the edge of the group. The one who seemed to be the foreman of the labourers was staring. For the first time, the nomads appeared uncertain about what to do with him. He could see the men muttering confidentially, and knew that he was being discussed. Eventually, one of them beckoned and led him outside and into the fringes of the jungle, where they sat out of sight beneath the trees watching the sun go down over the construction camp.

He didn't like being separated from Helen. At dusk, the man who had come out with him grew restless and went back into the dormitory. Lights came on in the windows of the camp buildings. From inside the dormitory there were sounds of laughter, and of a guitar being played. He lay sleepless and alone on the edge of the jungle, tormented by the biting of insects.

The next morning they walked on, continuing the gradual descent. The lowland jungle was hotter and wetter than the one from which they had emerged, and it was crossed by fast-flowing streams and well-defined tracks. Compared to the upper areas, it was well populated. Several times a day, they came upon people out hunting, foraging or washing in the rivers. There were large and well-organised villages with patches of rice and vegetables. The nomads took long detours to avoid them. When they did encounter others, they were met warily at best. Sometimes the villagers sat with them to barter for their jungle treasures. In other places, they were met with shouts and thrown stones.

Kit hung back at these moments and wrapped a rag around his face and hair. He had a strong sense of having entered hostile territory. Overhead, there was helicopter rattle and jet boom. In one of the villages, a group of the grey-uniformed soldiers, their rifles slung lazily over their shoulders, looked on without curiosity as the nomads were chased away.

Cutting through dense jungle, they came one day upon a fence of metal palisades and razor wire. Between its slats, prefabricated buildings were visible and beyond them the aerials and antennae of an airfield. Kit saw people in uniform walking between the buildings. The nomads seemed amazed by the presence of the camp, which had the look of a place newly staked out. They walked for a long way to get around the fence of steel and back into the security of the forest.

Kit knew that he was becoming ill. He went to sleep feeling dizzy and when he woke the next morning his head was beating with pain. After a few minutes of walking, he sat down and couldn't get up. His legs and arms ached, and he was sweating. The nomads fashioned a stretcher of branches and vines and carried him until evening. The fever lifted, and he sat up and ate, but then it returned. He wasn't fully aware of what was going on. He was conscious at one point of being wiped and cleaned after he had shitted himself. The one who looked after him was the same girl who fed Helen. Helen was strapped to her chest; as she bent over him, Helen's face leaned in close, giving the impression that he was being nursed by his own infant daughter.

He saw that she had a new tooth.

Pah! she said. Daa!

He desperately wanted her touch. But he was stricken by anxiety about infecting her with his own contagion. He tried to communicate this to the girl, but she could understand nothing of his gasps.

The fever eased, but the weakness in his limbs remained. He knew that it would come back again, and worse than before. He got them to understand what he wanted – the bore for drilling the beads. He took the memory card out of his pocket. Tremblingly, he forced a fine hole through it, close to the edge of the plastic, clear of the copper contacts. The girl brought him pieces of bone, stone and wood. He threaded them together with the memory card on a short length of twine and tied it around Helen's neck.

He caught the attention of the man who knew the Tongue. He pointed to the necklace.

– Please, he said. Please. Give this to her mother. Give this to Lara.

The man gave no sign of having understood.

The fever returned. Helen's face returned. Faces in conference hovered over Kit's face. There was much that he did not understand, but he knew that he had become the centre of the nomads' attention. There were arguments, and even shouting. The girl-mother did not like it. She held Helen to Kit's face, and Helen touched his face. The mother was crying.

The following morning, he was lifted on to the stretcher. They were carrying him beneath the trees. Helen was not there anymore. They carried him a long way. Then the trees gave out and they were in the sun. They laid the stretcher down. Turning his head, he could see metal and razor wire. Water was tipped into his mouth, a bough of leaves was angled above him to keep off the sun, and he was alone.

Time passed. He stopped being conscious of things. Then they took up again.

He was being lifted and carried, but not in the way that the nomads had carried him. They had moved silkily and stealthily on bare soles. Now he felt himself to be in the hands of large men on booted feet. It was too bright to see much, but he heard their voices and understood all their words. Then the brightness dimmed and he knew that he was inside.

He was laid down. He unsquinted and found himself looking into the face of a woman with fair hair and green eyes. They were wide with surprise.

'Mr Rabone,' the woman said. 'At last we meet.'

III
BLACK

8

In his fever, Kit dreamed of nights in the Koolroom when Helen thrashed all night, and woke to bitter crying even after being fed. The first signs were the whispering of her blanket, and faint sighs and croaks that took on a snuffling rhythm. Kit lay tensely still, willing the noises to recede. He concentrated on the regularity of his own breathing, as if the simulacrum of sleep in the father's body would magically inspire it in the child. But the splutters of complaint became louder and more regular, until Kit levered himself up, shuffled to the side of the cot and lifted Helen to him. The embrace soothed her at once; her head and body nodded and slumped into his shoulder. Gently, after a few minutes of nuzzling, he began to lay her down, his hand cupping her head. But Helen was in the shallows of sleep; at the instant her body was tipped away from the vertical, she woke with a start, and passion gathered within her, like a wave taking shape on a horizon.

It began with a huge and prolonged inhalation; it unfolded in slow motion. The limp body stiffened and arched, the head tipped back, the face twisted as the lungs filled with air, to be expelled in an outraged scream. No one could run fast enough, no distance was great enough to escape its force, as the wave broke over the shore.

He never became accustomed to the violence of Helen's wailing, and the vastness of the energy she discharged. It could not be mistaken for grief or fear; it was anger. Her whole body was convulsed by it – the bone box of her chest vibrating, arms and legs flailing, torso twisting. Once it had taken hold, no physical touch could still her rage. Held upright in the closest hug, she strained away in disgust. The cries came one after another, a pulsing, rhythmic awww! that billowed like a gale. They filled the Koolroom, battering its metal walls, as Kit and Lara huddled, helpless as sailors under the wash of churning seas.

Waking from these dreams, Kit understood that to save Helen it would be necessary to kill her. He was lying in bed in a dim space that smelled of disinfectant. It had the same air as the Koolroom: chilled, dry and even, regulated by the hum of unseen engines. The bed was high and had raised sides. It took time for Kit to realise that he was attached to it by a delicate metal bracelet on his ankle and a loose chain of links.

To one side were tubes, drips, a glowing lamp; on the other a curtain, through which figures would emerge bearing pills and beakers of fluid. A woman sat beside him silhouetted by the light. She was very still. She was looking down on Kit as he looked up at her. He was returning from the dream of Helen. For the first time since the forest, his head and his limbs were not in pain. Eventually, the woman's head moved slightly, and with it the angle of her chin.

He tried to speak, but managed only a dry rasp. His arms, when he moved them, were pinioned by the tightness of the sheets. From the table by the bed the woman took a bottle with a protruding spout and held it to his mouth.

'Mr Rabone,' she said, after he had sucked. 'I hope that you are feeling better.'

Kit lay still, looking up at her from the pillow.

'You were real sick when you came to us,' she said. 'You were lucky to make it. But we got a good team here. They saved your life, Mr Rabone. They tell me that you are in recovery.'

Kit shifted in the bed and succeeded in loosening his arms. The bracelet tugged on his ankle. He became aware that his loins were wrapped in thick paper.

'Mr Rabone, there's a lot we're going to need to talk to you about. You're going to have to help us with quite a few things. But most of that – well, most of it can wait.'

She passed the plastic bottle again and Kit took it in his hands and held it to his mouth.

'There's one thing we have to ask now,' she said regretfully. 'Mr Rabone, I'm sorry to bring this to you when you are sick. But there is something that we're concerned about.'

Kit knew what she was going to say.

'We're real concerned about your daughter, about Helen.'

He knew how he had to reply.

'Where is she Mr Rabone?'

His eyes filled with tears.

'We need to know where she is, Kristian. So we can help her.'

He let his chest heave and his head shake.

'She's such a tiny little girl. You must be so worried about her.'

It was the old conundrum of surrender. He had to protect Helen. But he could not reach her. Why not tell them, and let them bring her here to join him in the cool?

He flexed his mind to squeeze the thought away. He summoned the image of Helen lying in the mud, where he had abandoned her in the storm. Everything else followed.

'She's gone,' he said. 'Gone, she's gone.'

His voice surprised him with its hoarseness and high pitch. The woman's head remained steady, then turned behind her, towards the corner of the room. There Kit became aware of a second figure standing in the shadows, a tall man in a bright shirt.

'Aw, Kris,' he said. 'I'm so sorry to hear that, man. I'm so sorry for your little girl.'

His name, he told Kit, was De Luca. He came to sit by the bed in the afternoons. The woman did not come back, and no one spoke of her again; he wondered, at times, whether she had been a creation of his fevered mind.

After a few days, when he was strong enough to walk, he was moved to another room with a bunk, table and lavatory pan. The heaviness in his limbs lifted; every day he needed to sleep a little less. He understood that he was inside a military compound, a newly established base of the Superpower. Even within this windowless room, he was conscious of the rumbling of heavy vehicles, the boom and percussion of aircraft and the muffled drumming of rain. But there were no preliminaries; no one offered any introduction or explanation. He had woken, barely capable of speech, and by the time he had regained the capacity to question his hosts, the rules of their relationship had been fixed.

They were marked by an atmosphere of courtesy and compulsion. The chain was removed from his ankle when he left the clinic, but the doors of the new room were locked. On its ceiling was a clouded orb that he took to be the housing of a surveillance camera. But the young soldier who brought him his meals addressed Kit as *sir*, and always asked him if there was anything else he could get him. One day, unprompted, he presented him with a New Testament; on another, two battered paperback thrillers. Later he brought a stack of scratched video discs and an old-fashioned player. Kit had ceased to be a patient; he was not, as far as anyone had told him, a prisoner.

'May I ask you a question?' he said to the soldier, whose name stripe identified him as Cuthbert. 'What am I doing here exactly?'

'Sir,' he replied. 'I believe you're an object of ink wearies.'

Time slid by, unmeasurable, as it had among the nomads. How long had it been since he had been carried in here? He soon lost track of the days, which were marked only by the arrival of the meal trays and the visits of De Luca. He always appeared after lunch, with a bottle of water for Kit and a paper cup of coffee for himself. He wore ironed jeans and polo shirts in orange and yellow. His upper arms and chest were defined and muscular, but his neck was scrawny, like a man whose only form of exercise was raising heavy weights. Like Kit, he was neither young nor middle-aged. He was the only one who did not wear a uniform; and it was obvious that he enjoyed his undrilled status. He was jokey and back-slapping with the young guards, respectful, but undeferential, towards the officers. With Kit, his manner was prone to abrupt shifts. Much of the time he was beaming, expansive, given to broad gesticulations and gushing expressions of empathy. But coiled within the good cheer was a cold intensity. The mouth, which gaped with humour, would snap into a thin-lipped slit. The eyes, which narrowed to crinkles when he laughed, would relax into a dead stare, the irises flat as a lizard's.

'You've had a time of it, Kris,' De Luca said, at their second meeting. 'You've had a hell of a time of it. All of that with your little girl. Man, I can only imagine. So what we're gonna do is just go over some stuff, establish some facts, and then we can take it all from there. That OK?'

He was never asked for a general account of who he was, and how he ended up in the village. De Luca, it became clear, knew all of that and more, and needed only to fill out gaps in a story that had already been carefully logged. He was most concerned with recent events: the attack on the village, Kit and Helen's escape. He wanted to know everything about Court Hardy. It was obvious to Kit that the truth was the simplest thing to remember, that his lies should be clear and few, and that he had to devise them early. He found that they came easily; it was more about placing the emphasis on things that were true and harmless, than asserting things that were not.

'So you've told us about your background, growing up,' said De Luca one afternoon. An unsmiling lieutenant sat beside him, taking notes; coloured files were stacked on the table between them. 'Where did you go to high school?'

'I told you about that too.'
'Tell me again.'
Kit told him.
'And your family, your parents. Tell me again about them. Their origins, going back.'
Kit repeated the story.
'So going forward now to the – events under consideration. You were in the village when the police action began. But rather than presenting yourself to the Transitional Committee, you left the village.'
'As I said, I left before all that. I didn't understand what was happening. But it felt like a dangerous situation. I wanted to – I wanted to protect my daughter.'
'And where was Mr Hardy?'
'He stayed. I told him he should leave, but he wouldn't. He only ever did exactly what he wanted.'
'So you hid out in the jungle with your daughter?'
'We just sat under a tree most of the day. I could hear shooting, some explosions. Then the children appeared. And one of the men from the village.'
'That's Mr . . .' – he consulted a piece of paper – 'Hobson?'
'I think that was his name.'
'What did he tell you?'
'He was jabbering away, but I couldn't understand. They all started running, and I followed. I didn't know what else to do.'
'You followed them a long way.'
'So far. So far. It was like a nightmare. They just kept going, on and on, I didn't know where. But it was just me and my daughter. We couldn't survive on our own.'
'And who was with you exactly?'

'That village man. About nine or ten kids – I don't know. They were running round everywhere, I couldn't count. And then some of them went off, and they weren't there anymore.'

'Did you encounter anyone else at this time?'

'There were those people, the strange, pale people I told you about. We got some food from them. We had so little food.'

'Anyone else?'

'There was no one else I saw. There was that time I told you about, when we crossed a bridge, and I went ahead with some of the kids, and then I heard what sounded like shooting behind. I didn't know what was going on, but the local man who was with us bolted out in a panic. Something bad had happened, I don't know what. And then he became ill, very ill, and we just sat in the jungle for days.'

'The bridge that you crossed – tell me about it.'

'It was terrifying. Just ropes and sticks across this great cliff. They made me go over first. I've never been so scared.'

'When was it that you crossed that bridge?'

'I lost track of the days. Perhaps a week after we left the village. Perhaps more.'

The lieutenant opened a folder and produced photographs that he placed on the table. 'Is this the place we're talking about?'

Kit took time to frown over the photographs. 'Gosh, I don't know. My memory's a bit of a blur.'

The lieutenant said, 'It's very distinctive, in fact. You see this limestone feature? These large trees, overhanging.'

'At the place I'm talking about there was a bridge.'

There was a silence. De Luca crossed his arms and laughed. Kit and the lieutenant looked at him.

'"Gosh, I don't know,"' De Luca said. He was no longer laughing. 'Gosh, oh Golly Gosh, oh Goody Gum Shoes.'

The lieutenant returned the photographs to the folder.

'So after you'd crossed the bridge, you stopped, and Mr Hobson was sick,' said De Luca. 'And then he died.'

'He did. It was awful. He had this deep cut, and it got infected. They were rubbing jungle stuff on it, but it just got worse. And then, then – then my daughter died. I couldn't save her. One of the kids, he just disappeared with the bag I had, with all the infant formula in it. And the forest and the water was so dirty. She had a fever. She was getting weaker and weaker.'

Kit thought of Helen lying in the mud, and brought himself to tears, as he did every few hours.

'And then?'

'And then the pale people came. I was – distraught. I didn't really know what was happening. I followed them. What was I supposed to do? It's a jungle – you have to follow someone. And I walked and walked and walked with them, and then I got a fever, and they brought me here, and here I am.'

The weeping was coming easily today. De Luca pushed a bottle of water towards him.

'That's OK,' he said. 'Take a beat.'

Without any discussion, Kit's detention, the succession of long and detailed debriefings, had become the natural order of things. He felt a desperation to get out of the camp as soon as possible, to find the nomads, to take back

Helen. He panicked about how he would achieve this, and how much more difficult it became with each day that passed. But while he stayed here, his ambition was to be unsuspicious to the point of dullness. He was fashioning a character in which to answer the questions, a dimmer, more naïve and more passive version of himself. Every day, in advance of De Luca's arrival, he put on the character like a coat.

One day he was driven to another building within the camp. After so long inside, the sensation of heat, light and humidity was overwhelming. The jeep passed rows of pre-fabricated buildings and a fenced court in which huge men in khaki vests were playing basketball. De Luca was waiting with the lieutenant and a guard. He was standing by the window of the room, which was screened by a heavy blind. There was a small tripod-mounted camera on the table.

Kit said, 'So you're recording this one?'

'We are,' said the lieutenant. 'For purposes of – administration.'

'That's good. I'm glad that this is all official. Because I'd like to do something official myself, if that's alright. I'd like to telephone my embassy.'

After a pause the lieutenant nodded. 'Well, I'm sure that's a conversation that's going to come, Mr Rabone. That's all going to come in good time, no doubt.'

'I'd like to telephone now, if you don't mind. There are people who must be worrying about me. My family. My partner. Isn't it right that I should contact them? To tell them what's happened.'

'Kris, Kris,' said De Luca, who was leaning against the window with folded arms. 'We're going to do this first.'

'The thing is – can I ask? – what's my status here?'

'Your status,' De Luca said, and smiled.

'What am I doing here?'

'What are you doing here? You're helping us out, Kris. That's what you want, isn't it? To be helpful.'

'Of course. But—'

'There's a few things to clear up. When we're happy, then we can talk about making calls.'

Kit frowned, and was about to speak. De Luca cut him off. He was wearing his lizard face.

'We're not happy yet,' he said. 'Gosh, no. We are a long way from being happy.'

There was a silence. Both men were looking at Kit. The lieutenant took a stapled typescript from the folder on the table, its sentences highlighted in pinks and yellows.

He glanced at De Luca, who gave a nod.

'This has got to be difficult to talk about,' the lieutenant said. 'But I need to know more about the circumstances of your daughter's death, about what happened to her remains.'

'Her remains?'

'Yes. After her passing. What did you do with her?'

'I told you.'

'No, we didn't discuss that as of now.'

'Well, she was buried.'

'Who buried her?'

'I did.'

'How did you do that?'

'I made a hole. Christ, do I have to talk about this?'

'You need to tell us, Kris,' said De Luca, intimate and empathetic once again. 'I know it's tough, my friend, but we can bring her back. We can get people out there, and bring back your little girl so you can lay her to rest properly like she deserves.'

'I made a hole,' Kit said, sobbing. 'Those people helped me.'

The lieutenant looked at the typescript. 'So it was after you encountered the nomadic group that your daughter passed?'

Kit hesitated. 'It was before. I carried her there. She was – she had died, though, before.'

'You carried your daughter's remains, after she had passed?' They were both looking at him.

'Yes.'

'And where was it?' said the lieutenant. 'The place of burial.'

He had been thinking about it, wondering whether to offer it or not. But there was no other way now; it might even help. The lieutenant produced maps and aerial photographs. There were more photographs taken on the ground. With sketches and diagrams, Kit told them about the grave mound that the nomads had made in the forest, and how to find it.

The task of identifying the place absorbed De Luca and the lieutenant. Kit detected an air of suppressed relief about them. As they were about to leave, De Luca, almost as an afterthought, said, 'When you laid your daughter's remains in the earth, Kris, how was she – arrayed? I mean, what was she wearing? If anything.'

'I can't remember.'

'Was she in a garment, a diaper? Was she wrapped in something, or laid directly in the earth?'

'It was just her, just her in the ground.' He sobbed deeply. 'Or perhaps they wrapped her in a mat. I was distraught. I was beside myself. I can't remember.'

There were no questions the following day. To his surprise, Kit found the interruption to routine off-putting, almost upsetting. On the second day, later than usual, he was led out of his room by two guards not, as he assumed, to the interview room, but for a walk around the camp.

'Officer De Luca's suggestion,' said Cuthbert. 'He figures you need some exercise.'

The sun was low in the sky, and the air was cool from the afternoon rain. The two soldiers flanked Kit as they walked between identical buildings of prefabricated design. Officers came and went carrying files and briefcases; Kit's escorts saluted as they passed. Through the gaps between the buildings, the scale of the camp revealed itself, vastly larger than he had imagined. Intermittently the glittering exterior fence could be glimpsed and beyond it the darkness of forest. They walked through a succession of discrete zones: a great open space containing hundreds of stationary yellow bulldozers; acres of tents that accommodated the lower ranks; a suburb of pre-fab cubes in which the officers slept. Beyond them, low, warehouse-like buildings were visible, and the dark shapes of military vehicles. Kit's escorts turned in the opposite direction and entered the camp's zone of recreation, a cluster of sheds and hangars with signs above their doors. It was loud with the chatter of men and women in green; the air smelled of their sweat.

'Here's where it's at,' said Specialist McGrew. 'Here's what we call the downtown.'

The two soldiers pointed out the zone's features: bowl hall, game hall, chow hall, driving hall, aqua hall, movie theatre, fitness centre, Pizza Park, Burger Beach and BX. They led him to the last of these, an arched warehouse of corrugated metal. Inside, strip lights illuminated shelves stacked with brightly coloured packets. Broad aisles ran between them, along which soldiers slowly walked, pushing deep metal trolleys.

'They sell everything here,' said McGrew. 'Everything you get back home.'

'There's something you want to purchase here, sir, we can purchase it for you,' Cuthbert said. 'Officer De Luca provided for that. Said you should choose something for yourself.'

'Anything?'

'Anything that's reasonable.'

They strolled down boulevards of training shoes and tennis rackets, decks stacked with cookies and painkillers, fizzy drinks and shampoos, flown across oceans. On one shelf there were boxes of big baby dolls, with dummies in their mouths and gaping blue eyes. On another was the same brand of nappies that Helen used to wear.

'Are there babies here?' he asked Cuthbert, who looked at McGrew.

McGrew frowned, and shook his head. 'I never seen no babies myself.'

Beyond the infant and sanitary products, the aisle opened on to narrower shelves carrying stationery and books. Against the far wall was a rack of magazines and newspapers. Kit made out on one front page a photograph of a crowd of people holding placards. He was walking towards it when Cuthbert applied a diverting hand to his shoulder.

'You can't enter that sector of the BX, sir.'

They ambled on past racks of driving gloves, underwear, game consoles, jelly beans. Stupefied by abundance, Kit could identify nothing that he needed or wanted. At the urging of Cuthbert and McGrew, he came away with a pair of mirrored sunglasses, a packet of beef jerky and a family-sized jar of house-brined half-sour dill pickles. As they were leaving, he saw by the door a rack of clothes, including the brightly coloured polo shirts that De Luca wore.

'That's what I want,' he said. 'I'll have a yellow one and an orange one.'

But the money for the shopping expedition had all been spent. Cuthbert, who had been speaking on his walkie-talkie, said that it was time to leave.

He expected to be returned to his room. Instead, the soldiers led him through the zone of recreation and along a wide road divided by checkpoints. The sun was setting and the lights of the base were coming on. They climbed a shallow rise, and looked down from it on to the illumination of an airfield.

'Figured you might want to see this,' said McGrew. 'What this place is all about.'

They reached the fence that divided the airfield from the rest of the camp and peered through the mesh at the scene within. At the near side was a concentration of tent-like awnings, dishes and aerials. The runway, fashioned out of interlocking plates, extended like a dully gleaming carpet; beyond it were a row of hangars and the huddled shapes of jets. The earth all around was raw and red. Kit marvelled at the volume of forest that had been removed to make space for all of this. On the apron, soldiers were manoeuvring pallets off a forklift and into the back of a stubby transport plane. It raised its rear hatch, started up its rotors, trundled on to the runway and took off with a bass roar.

It was nearly dark by now and Kit began to wonder why they were still here. The mood of respectful joviality that had animated Cuthbert and McGrew in the downtown had gone; they had become silent and watchful. With a thump of apprehension, a thought occurred to Kit – that he had been brought to this distant corner of the camp to be discreetly killed. It seemed unlikely, but no more unlikely than anything else.

The thought was interrupted by the sound of an approaching helicopter. Its lights were visible high against the evening sky. Soon it was looming above the apron in front of the fence in a din of rotors, throwing up a litter of dust and leaf fragments that whipped through the wire mesh and enveloped Kit and the two soldiers. Before the blades had ceased their rotation, a group of figures ran up to the helicopter and stood beside it. Kit immediately recognised De Luca in his bright shirt. The hatch opened and a soldier emerged from it holding an object that he transferred carefully to De Luca's arms: a coffin, small, but unmistakable, made of some polished material, no bigger than the boxed game consoles in the supermarket. De Luca was speaking to the soldier, who was shaking his helmeted head. De Luca was asking him questions; the soldier shook his head again. De Luca turned and walked back briskly in the direction of the tents.

De Luca was carrying the coffin. He was looking up towards the fence as he walked. His eyes were on Kit; the two escorting soldiers were staring at him too. Kit understood suddenly what was at stake. He had to think, or rather to feel, quickly. He forced himself to imagine that it was Helen inside the coffin. His hands gripped the fence. He let his legs relax, and slumped down and against it. He bowed his head and wept.

When he stood up, Cuthbert and McGrew were watching him respectfully. A jeep was waiting to drive them back.

Late that night he was shaken awake and taken to De Luca and the lieutenant. They were scowling and edgy.

'Can I call—'

'You cannot,' De Luca snapped. 'Sit down, there's things you're going to tell us.'

The lieutenant asked the questions. De Luca paced up and down the small room.

'In the period between leaving the village and her passing, what was your daughter's state of health?'

'Her state of health? She was dying, of fever and dehydration. Her state of health was that she died.'

'But not at the beginning.'

'At the very beginning, no. I had the formula. I could boil the water. She wasn't used to the formula, but she drank it. She—'

'So she was drinking normally.'

'The routine was broken, but she was feeding regularly. She—'

'Did she spit up?'

'You mean was she sick?'

'Did she spit up? Did she puke?'

'She posseted a bit after feeding. Yes.'

'She did what?'

'Yes, she spat up a bit of milk after a bottle.'

'She vomited.'

'No, not like that. It's just normal. When her tummy's full, a bit of it squirts back up.'

De Luca sat down.

The lieutenant went on, 'Was there anything unusual, in what she spat up?'

'Just formula.'

'Only that?'

'Yes.'

De Luca stood up again.

'What about her excrement?' asked the lieutenant.

'Her excrement?'

'Her poop.'

'What about it? Christ.'

'Was there anything unusual?'

'Yes, there was. She was dying. It was very, very—'

'No, at the beginning. Before she got sick.'

Kit put his face in his hands. 'Why are you asking me this? What does it matter, now?'

'Bear with me, sir. Be patient with me. Was there anything unu—'

'What was in her diaper, Kris?' De Luca demanded.

'Shit. Baby shit. Her nappy was full of shit. And then she was shitting water, then blood. Then nothing.'

'Where's the data device, Kris?'

Kit smoothed his face into blankness. 'What?'

'Where's the data device?'

'I really don't – what kind of data device?'

'Where's the data device?'

'What do you mean?'

'You know what I fucking mean, Kris.'

'I really don't. I—'

'Where is it, Mr Rabone?' said the lieutenant.

'I genuinely don't know what you're talking about. What sort of—'

'You are a goddamn fucking liar,' said De Luca.

'I'm telling you, I don't—'

'You must think we are really fucking stupid.'

'Not at all, I just don't know—'

'Do I look like some stupid fuck? Does he look like one?'

'If I knew what on earth you were—'

'Where is the goddamn fucking data device?'

The shouting continued. The lieutenant sat silently throughout, with an expression of hurt dignity. De Luca stamped up and down, pausing to crouch directly behind Kit's chair and to bellow into his ear.

'Don't fucking look at me,' he hissed when Kit turned his head. His face was pink and blood vessels were standing out in his bloated upper arms.

De Luca stamped out of the room, and the lieutenant followed him. Kit realised that the other Kit, the character whose part he was playing in these conversations, would have been appalled by this blast of aggression. But he was not surprised at all.

'It checked out,' De Luca said the following morning. 'I mean we found your daughter. But now you need to understand some facts about your situation. It's real important you're aware of all this.'

After the outburst the night before, Kit had been returned to his room in the dark. Overnight, he tried to make sense of the situation. Court was dead; Obson was dead. No one else knew what had happened to the memory card. How did De Luca know that it existed?

He tried to think about Helen, then he tried not to think about her. He told himself: they are trying to frighten you, not to hurt you. As long as they don't hurt you, there is nothing to be afraid of.

This morning, in the same interview room, De Luca was putting on a display of calm. 'You're a smart guy, Kris,' he said. 'You've got an education. But there's things here you're missing, real obvious things. So I'm going to enumerate those for you. OK?'

'OK. I—'

'Number one, no one knows where the fuck you are. No one gives a fuck either – no one who matters anyway, no one who can help you. You're just some aimless jerk who walked off the map with his girlfriend and got caught up in some shit way bigger than he bargained for. Now you've disappeared, probably dead, and no one cares because you're nobody. That's number one. That's just in case you got any ideas about holding out until the King or the prime minister or the United Nations turn up here to rescue you. "Call my embassy"? Call my asshole. You called your embassy, you'd be humming to the hold music a long time. They have bigger things to worry about right now.

'Number two is, you are in some deep shit. You have

no one to protect you, no one who cares about you, and you are deep in deep shit. We know all about you, Kristian. We have looked inside your home. We have looked inside your blood. We know all about you, and you are a fucking junky. Your bloodwork – your blood's full of junk, man. Rare junk. Where did you find that shit? Stuff our lab guys never seen before. Took them a long time to ID it, and they were amazed. You take too much of that jungle juice, you never come back. Guy in the lab was telling me about it – some people they just float off inside of their heads and stay there. We got this, of course—'

He threw on to the table a transparent plastic bag. Kit could see at once that it contained the small pouch in which Lara kept her marijuana.

'—but that's the fucking least of it.' He started throwing down photographs on to the table, rapidly, like a dealer with a pack of cards. They were colour prints of an interior, crowded with people. Kit picked them up; it took time to make sense of the visual information. Then he understood: it was the Koolroom. The figures inside it were the grey-uniformed soldiers of the Neighbour. They were holding objects up to the camera: bulging plastic packets containing dried leaves, white powder, small metal pipes. In one picture, a soldier was pointing at Kit and Lara's bed. On the quilt were glass tubes of varying shape and size.

'Looks like quite a little meth lab you had going back there,' said De Luca, without looking at Kit.

The soldiers in the photographs all wore the same expression, that of a child attempting to mimic shocked, adult disapproval. They were so comically solemn that Kit laughed.

'You think we had a drugs lab in our bedroom?' Kit put the photographs down. 'These are ridiculous.'

For a moment De Luca looked embarrassed. Then he was shouting again.

'You think that's funny? You know what the penalties are in this country for what you've done? For illegal drug use and manufacture? For drug dealing? They hang you for that here. No nice injection – by the fucking neck. You get that? Not so funny, in fact.'

Kit thought: if I'm a drug lord, then so is Lara. He's made no mention of her. They don't have her. They don't know where she is.

'But that,' said De Luca, 'that is not the worst.' He placed another transparent bag on the table. Inside it were the dog tags from the soldier whom the nomads had killed by the river. Traces of dried blood were still visible on their embossed surfaces.

'Young man was twenty-four years old. Mom and dad back home, three sisters. Fine soldier. Throat cut open.'

'He was killed by the poison.'

'So you know all about it? Well, we knew that you know. Else how did these get into the pocket of your pants when we found you?'

Kit had forgotten about the dog tags. They connected him irrefutably to the killing of the soldier; and now he had acknowledged it. He realised with a pang that he had crossed a threshold from which there was no return.

'What was he doing there anyway?' Kit said.

De Luca smiled humourlessly, and ignored him. 'You are not only a drug user and a drug addict and a drug dealer, in a jurisdiction in which those matters are taken extremely seriously. You are also an unlawful combatant. You are a murderer. You are a terrorist. You are so deep in shit. Do you see how deep in shit you are?

'Now, things can be better for you, or they can be worse. I think that you want them to be better. And I can make them better. So tell me where the data device is.'

Kit said nothing.

'She shat it out. You must have seen it. A poppa as devoted as you.'

Kit looked away from him, his face crumpling. Whatever he admitted to, Kit reminded himself, he had to cry about Helen.

De Luca was straining to be calm again. 'Did you drop it somewhere? Or leave it somewhere? Because you tell us where, and we can find it. You don't have to worry about that. We got the equipment to find anything like that. Even in a jungle.'

'For the last time, I don't know what you are talking about,' said Kit. 'You can shout at me, you can swear at me. But I don't know what you're talking about.'

'Oh, I can do worse than that.' De Luca smiled. 'There's options we have. If you remain uncooperative. For one, there's those guys in the photographs, the guys in grey. The "Transitional Committee".' He chuckled. 'Good soldiers, in some ways. Well equipped, by us. But fucking psychos, man. Your friend, the journalist, Mr Courtly-fucking-Doo-dah. You know what they did to him?'

'I heard that he was mutilated.'

'So off the record, Kristian, because they're allies and friendlies and all that, here's the deal with them. The missionaries got to them a while back, and it's all hymns and churchy shit most of the time. But they're only a generation or two from being cannibal fucking headhunters. You do not want to find yourself in a position of vulnerability when they are in charge. You don't want to piss them off. You want to end up like your friend, with your own junk stuffed in your mouth? Because we got a little detachment of them here at the back of the camp. You didn't see them on your walk, but they're here. "Ally Liaison", they're called. And I know they'd love to liaise with you. Maybe they'd have more luck in . . . debriefing you on the information we seek. Their methods are going to be very different from mine. But maybe that's what you need.'

He sat back, as if thinking hard about what to say next.

'There's another option. Likely a more realistic one. Certainly the one that my colleagues, my superiors out there' – he jerked his head in the direction of the door – 'are favoring. And that's sending you away. To Bartok's place. It's a terrible place, Kris. Long way from here. Another world. No friendly butler like Cuthbert here, bringing you your reading matter. No dill pickles. You'll be begging to be brought back here. You'll be crying my name in your sleep.'

'I don't know your real name.'

'Kris, Kris,' he said, like a man done in by weariness. 'We fucking know, man. We fucking know you're lying.'

He stood up, with the air of having reached a decision. 'Let's take a drive,' he said. 'There's someone you should meet.'

They drove a long way. To Kit, blinded by the hood, it felt as if they were traversing the entire camp, passing through zones of distinctive sound. Outside the vehicle, voices rose and receded; aircraft noise drew closer or became distant. The place where they stopped was quiet. Jungle insects could be faintly heard, which made Kit think that they were near the outer perimeter. He had assumed, with dread, that he was being taken to the place of the grey soldiers. But when the hood was removed, he found himself in front of what looked more like a school than a place of mutilation.

A collection of pre-fabs stood behind a low wooden fence; in front of them was a small playground with a basketball hoop, a weathered ping-pong table and a climbing frame. Through the windows he could see tables and a whiteboard bearing the names and images of animals: eagle, bison, wolf. De Luca led the way up a shallow ramp and down a corridor to the back of the building. Beyond a locked door was a dimly lit office with shelves of files and children's books. A young woman looked up without interest as they entered and turned back to her laptop.

On one side of the room was a long high window that looked into the classroom next door. It took Kit a moment to register that it was a sheet of one-way glass. On the far side was a small group of children. Two of them were reading with a female teacher. One, a girl in a wheelchair, was looking at a television screen, which displayed a cartoon of smiling children in tiaras and long dresses. But all of Kit's attention was on the youngest child who sat on the floor on the far side of the room.

She was a baby of about six months. Her face was turned away from the one-way glass and a bonnet covered her hair. She was reaching out to coloured blocks on the mat with the wobbly poise of one for whom sitting up is new and strange. Kit's heart throbbed and his face became hot. He pressed his face against the window; the glass resounded dully with the impact of his forehead. De Luca and Cuthbert jumped at the sound and pulled him back by the shoulders.

'Easy, man – woah.'

The children on the other side turned in the direction of the sound, and then returned to what they were doing. The face of the baby on the mat was clearly visible now. It was not Helen.

De Luca was looking at him thoughtfully.

'My daughter – my own girl,' Kit said. 'That's how old she would be now.'

De Luca nodded coldly.

'Just stand back and take a look,' he said. 'See anyone you recognize?'

The children were dark skinned, but, in their clean bright clothes, it was difficult to place them. Were they captives, like him? Or the children of residents of the base? De Luca had brought him here for a reason – but what? He looked at the girl in the wheelchair. Her face was tilted towards the screen, but he could see that, apart from the injuries to her legs, her nose was twisted and broken. She wore a denim skirt, sweatshirt and clean new trainers; her hair was bound in a sparkly ribbon. Then she looked up for a moment towards the invisible window, and Kit saw that it was Moon Moth.

They cuffed Kit and sat him behind a table. He was protesting about this when Moon Moth entered the office, pushed by the teacher.

'Say hello to the gentleman,' said the teacher.

'Hi,' said Moon Moth. 'I'm Kelly.'

Unmistakably it was her, but here, at close quarters, she was changed. It was not only her injuries. Her limbs, even in the wheelchair, were sleeker and plumper; her face, despite being crushed, was fuller; her rich, dark skin had a gloss and a sheen. She gave no sign of recognising Kit.

'Kelly's been doing real well since she got here, isn't that right?' said De Luca.

'Real well,' said the teacher. 'Haven't you, honey?'

'Real well,' said Moon Moth.

'And her English is coming on just something wonderful,' said the teacher. 'Isn't it, Kelly – your English?'

'I like English,' said Moon Moth. The accents of the girl and the woman were the same.

De Luca began to address Kit in an undertone, as if confidentially. But he was standing next to Moon Moth, and everything he said was audible to her.

'So Kelly was in a bad way when she came to us. A real bad way. A fall like that, and all that time she was untreated – you can imagine, right? It was touch and go she'd make it or not. I say it myself, our guys did an amazing job fixing her up. She's not just alive, which is a miracle itself – she's doing great. She's had the spinal work done here, she's getting great physio, and super-specialist stuff to come once she ships back home. Spinal surgery, cosmetic, corrective – the whole suite.'

'Ships back home?'

'It's all in hand. There's lots of folks'll be happy to welcome a kid like this into their family. And there's a whole lot she's going to be able to do. That kind of disability, it's no obstacle now – school, college, employment. She's a bright kid. She's gonna be OK.' He raised his voice and spoke to the girl with exaggerated cheer. 'You're gonna be OK, right Kelly?' He raised the palm of his hand and she slapped hers against it with a clap.

'Gonna be OK!' Her voice had taken on the intonations of the princesses in the cartoon.

The lizard look chilled De Luca's face, and his voice became a whisper.

'We had a lot of conversations, Kelly and I. Lot of debriefs. She's told me all about what happened. Out there with you and your daughter in the jungle. Climbing up in the tree. The data device in the diaper. You and Mr Hobson talking it all over. How your friend Mr Hardy must have had her swallow it, so he could pick it up later. 'Cept he never made it – got detained by some dudes with machetes. We've been over it all. Great amount of detail.'

Kit said, 'You made her one of you.'

De Luca smiled as if Kit had paid him a compliment. 'Everyone becomes one of us eventually,' he said. 'You're one of us too, man. We're on the same side.' He sighed. 'This is it. You can see it – you can see where we're at. We know. We know you're lying. So just tell us – where is the data device?'

Kit found that, in his tension and amazement he had stood up, with his fists clenched in the cuffs. He was conscious of facing a decision with little time in which to make it.

De Luca was right that he was nobody. If he guided them to the memory card, or if he convinced them that he knew nothing of it, then his life no longer had value. He was the only witness to events that had to be concealed; and he was long assumed by the rest of the world to have perished invisibly in the forest, a fate that could easily and undetectably be brought about. He was worth keeping alive only for what he probably knew, but had not yet given up. Moon Moth had created doubt about Kit, and doubt was his salvation.

She was being wheeled out of the room. She had not once met his eye. As she was passing through the door, Kit said, – Thank you, imps. Now we go to eat.

She looked up quickly at him and smiled.

The door closed, leaving Kit alone with De Luca and Cuthbert. They took off his cuffs, lowered a blind over the window of one-way glass, and turned up the lights.

De Luca pulled up a chair and sat opposite Kit.

'So that's it, my friend,' he said resignedly. 'It's your choice. Your choice, my friend.'

Kit reached into his pocket and took out the new silver sunglasses. The illumination dimmed as he placed them over his eyes.

'Fuck off, De Luca,' he said.

The change came violently; the journey was underway before he understood what was happening. He was sitting at the table. The other chair lay on the floor, where De Luca had kicked it before stamping out. Kit rested his elbows on the table, as the noise of shouting continued beyond the slammed door. Standing guard in the corner, Specialist Cuthbert met his eye.

'Don't look at me,' he said in a whine. But it was he who

looked away. Kit smiled, conscious of how calm he felt, and how strong.

Then the door burst open and men in uniform were in the room, and all around him. Arms seized his upper body and black fabric was pulled roughly over his head. His hands were cuffed behind his back and he was propelled into a vehicle. It drove with lurching stops and starts, then he was hustled out and the hood was pulled off his face. A torch was shone into his eyes, a hand took his pulse, eyes looked into his mouth and scrutinised his tongue. The bag was pushed back over his head, followed by unfamiliar and disturbing sensations that he identified as metal cutters slicing through his shirt, trousers and underpants. He stood naked and hooded in the air. He had an image of how he must have looked – a skinny, headless body swaying among the strong, uniformed, armed men around him.

A crinkly pad of heavy paper was wrapped around his loins. Cold, latex-covered fingers brushed against his cock; he felt it shrinking away to nothing, retracting into the cavity of his trunk. Then some kind of body suit was being zipped and buttoned on to him, and the cuffs were on his wrists.

He was lifted and shoved into another jeep. The absence of human voices was making him afraid. He began to say *Hup* and *Oop* in response to the movements being forced upon him, in the hope of encouraging a response. But no one so much as grunted. He was shoved out again into air choppy with engine noise. Thick mittens were pushed on to his hands. He was led up a ramp, and strapped into a narrow seat. Now he was conscious of heavy doors crunching shut to seal off the outer world and the faltering sensation of lifting off from the earth.

He was in a place new to him, but familiar. This was not one of the smaller choppers with their juddering din. He could see and touch nothing, but that did not matter because sound was all there was, or rather its opposite. It was as if sound had been overthrown and usurped by something else, a silence that was a positive thing in itself, thick and suffocating and irresistible. He was a passenger in the Bird of Paradise.

9

He woke to find himself looking into the face of the woman with green eyes.

He didn't know whether he had lost consciousness, or simply fallen asleep. He remembered the journey of soundless noise, his senses suppressed by hood and gloves. It had been impossible to reckon time, speed, direction, even gravity. It was like floating in fluid; even the pressure of the handcuffs was at a remove from him. At times, pinpricks of light penetrated the weave of the hood. He was able to smell the sweat inside it, and his own sour breath. Every few hours, they had landed, for refuelling he assumed, and he had been frogmarched out, unhooded in a darkened room, then hooded and manhandled back again. After flying for so long, he could be anywhere in the world. But of the end of the journey he remembered nothing; no thread of memory connected the interior of the aircraft to the bed where he now lay. The air was heavy and humid and stirred lightly as if moved by an electric fan. His body was held down, but the restraints were concealed by a sheet pulled up to his chin; moving his head he could see the walls of a dimly lit room on either side.

The face of the woman came into vision, and

immediately withdrew. He had time to take in the eyes, sharp chin, and an open-necked blouse.

'Hello, Mr Rabone,' she said. Her voice came from somewhere behind him.

'I know you,' said Kit.

There was a pause. 'Not really,' replied the voice. Then, 'Are you thirsty?'

Kit licked his lips. 'No, not this time.' He wasn't hungry either, although he could not remember eating or drinking; and there was no pressure on his bladder or in his guts.

'Let's begin then,' said the woman.

'Where am I?' he asked.

'A long way off.'

'What is this place?'

'You have . . . graduated, you might say. It's going to be different here.'

'How is it going to be different?'

'There have been changes, to agency. There's a different set of protocols now, a new chain.'

There was silence and then the sound of papers being shuffled.

'I can't move,' said Kit. 'May I sit up?'

'For now, stay as you are.'

The leg of a chair scraped against the floor. He wondered if the woman was alone. He strained to detect the sounds of breathing, to know whether there were others in the room. The woman said, 'You have travelled a long way, Mr Rabone. And now here you are, with me. We have important matters to discuss, real important. I need to impress that on you, Mr Rabone. This is a serious situation. You got caught in the middle of something very big, something much larger than you were able to see. So to begin with here we're just going to return to the basics. Some of this you know, some you will have missed.'

'Oh, I'm aware how serious this all is,' said Kit. 'Your - colleague, the last guy, he made that very clear.'

'Hear me out, Mr Rabone. There's aspects of this you may not have grasped.'

'OK, but can I—'

'It's better that I talk and you listen.'

She spoke firmly, but without impatience. Looking up at the whitewashed ceiling, Kit pictured her resting her elbows on a table and touching her fingertips together to form a steeple beneath that distinctive chin.

'There has been a change of government in the Country,' she said. 'As you know, following the disputed elections last year, a group of corrupt and incompetent politicians took over for several months.'

'You mean Dr Mochtar? He didn't take over, he won.'

'The results were disputed, and the dispute was unresolved. And what followed was a disastrous period. Everyone could see that. The economy tanked, there was unrest. Widespread lawlessness and criminality. Well-intentioned nations - including mine, including your own - reached out to offer help and guidance. To no avail - they weren't listening. There was a lot of anxiety, globally, and within the region. In response to border incursions and rampant criminality, including cross-border drug trafficking, the neighboring government found itself with no choice but to launch a limited police action in the western province. The governing faction completely overreacted to this. They rejected all efforts at diplomacy—'

'Diplomacy?'

'I guess you missed all this, Mr Rabone. You were in an isolated community, with defective radio equipment. There was outreach, a lot of it high level. The Mochtar regime overreacted disastrously. They made a difficult situation worse.'

She went on. 'In the capital, my nation's embassy was attacked. A military detachment was inserted to defend it. Later, in response to rising disorder, this force was augmented. The scope of its mission was expanded to offer security to democratic forces in the country, at their request. With the engagement of key international partners, my own country's military intervened to restore order and to support the formation of a transitional administration headed *ad interim* by the previous premier. Since then we have provided further advice and training to government forces as they deal with disorder and criminality coordinated by the Mochtar elements.'

Kit's judgement, he sensed, was unreliable. He felt unnaturally refreshed and alert; he suspected that he had been drugged. About one thing, though, there was no doubt: the woman had a remarkably beautiful voice. She spoke quietly and steadily, without any obvious regional accent. It was the voice of an actor: smooth, flexible and unselfconscious, expressive in a way that imparted depth and subtlety to the hackneyed script that she read. After the silence of the Siskin Ferox, it hardly mattered what the words were; all human speech was delightful.

A dog barked somewhere.

'What this all means – what you have to understand, Mr Rabone – is that there is a war going on here. Over there.

This is a war situation, and my government, and folks like us, are facing some exceptionally malign actors. Resourceful, sophisticated, cunning, determined individuals. We know these people are networked – they've got connections with established international terror organizations. And we're using all the resources at our disposal, everything we can lay hands on, to stop them making things even worse, and to protect our friends – people like you, and your family – while the interim administration makes plans for a popular consultation. It's a mess, Mr Rabone, everyone agrees that – a terrible mess. What we've got to do is to give our friends some space and some time to clear it all up. And that's where you come in, Mr Rabone.'

A chair moved, and footsteps sounded on the hard floor, the woman's voice moving closer to Kit, then further away.

'You're an intelligent man. That's why I'm going over all this, because I know you've got the capacity to see where we're coming from here. This data device – well, we think that it might contain information, intelligence if you will, that could be of value in our endeavor. Do you understand me, Mr Rabone? To you, it might look like nothing – even to me, I might not see it. But to our people it could be real useful. That's why we've got to find it, Mr Rabone. You've suffered a terrible loss, and you've been through an ordeal. We sympathize, we really do. But this is not about just one person – there's too much in play here. You got to tell us what happened to the data device, where it is now.'

'As I said, I just don't know—'

'I know what you said Mr Rabone. And I don't believe it. No one does. I'm not expecting your response right now. Like I told you, we're doing things differently. But what hasn't changed is that you're in control of what happens here. There is just one question and it is very simple: where is the data device? You can tell us whenever you like. You can make the choice at any time – any time – to end all of this.'

There was another pause.

'Where is the data device, Mr Rabone?'

Kit sighed. He rolled his eyes, then realised that no one could see them rolling. He said nothing.

'I'm going to ask you one more time: where is the data device?'

A prolonged silence. It was broken by the sound of more chairs scraping – three chairs, four chairs or more. So they had been here all along. A qualm of trepidation jabbed Kit's guts. He realised that he was not wearing a nappy anymore.

'Carry on, gentlemen,' the woman said.

There were people all around him, and the bag was on his head again. He was being unstrapped, and hauled up and handcuffed, all in darkness.

'We're going to talk again real soon,' the woman said. 'But that's me done for now.'

Voices were shouting at him and he was being pulled back and shoved forward. His ankles were loosely chained and, with his head covered, it was impossible to keep balance. He staggered and fell, to be caught and propelled into a new stumble by one set of arms and then another. Hands on his shoulders pulled him up, the hood was removed and a tall skinny soldier pressed a stethoscope against his chest and shone a light in his eyes. He saw that he had been dressed in a bright yellow shirt and trousers. The young medic nodded, a blindfold was wrapped tightly around his eyes, and he was forced down into a squat. He toppled on to his knees and a boot in his back sent him sprawling on to his chest. His chin jarred against a cold floor.

'Squat!' shouted a voice, and hands pulled him up off the ground. 'Squat up!' He kept falling forward and kept being kicked. When he managed to remain upright, the pain in his legs became unbearable. Soon he was groaning with the effort. Then he was being pulled up, marched forward, and pushed into some kind of seat. To his relief, the manacles around his legs were being removed, but then they were pulling off his trousers and his shirt, and he was jerked to his feet again, blind and naked. His cuffed hands moved instinctively to shield his groin, and he jumped as a voice shouted into his ear, so close that he could feel the exhalation of hot breath: 'Where is the data device?'

And then from equally close on the other side: 'Where is the data device?'

The second voice belonged to a woman.

Before he had time to answer, a clanging din exploded all around him. It was the sound of heavy metallic objects – chairs, Kit assumed – being hurled against the walls and concrete floor.

'Where is the data device?'

'Where is the data device?'

There were five or six different voices in the room.

'Where is the goddamn data device?'

'I don't know. I don't know.'

He sensed the vibration of the chairs' legs in the air. They were bouncing off the walls; he bent double clutching his balls in anticipation of the impact as one of them ricocheted into his naked body. Amid the shouting, somebody laughed.

'He shit scared.'

There was breath in his ears again.

'Where is the data device?'

'I don't know.'

'Where is it you piece of shit?'

'I don't know.'

'You're a lying piece of shit.'

'Can I have some water?'

'Shut the fuck up.'

The clangour and shouting went on and on. Kit cowered and trembled in private darkness. But the metal chairs did not strike him; the angry bellowing began to sound forced and unconvincing. Abruptly, calm fell on the room, as if a silent order had been given. Kit heard booted feet walking away. The clothes and the manacles were restored, and he was led slowly and carefully through several sets of doors. The blindfold was removed in a small windowless cell containing a mattress, a bucket and a bottle of water.

Kit fell on to the mattress, trembling and sobbing. His heart slowed its beating. He drank thirstily from the bottle. Soon his stomach was gripped by a violent pang. He pulled down his trousers and squatted over the bucket with shaking legs.

The door opened. It was a female soldier; she gave a small nod of acknowledgement when she saw what Kit was doing. 'Excuse me,' she said, and pulled the door to. 'Give him a moment.'

She came in when he was done, accompanied by the young medic with his stethoscope. He shone a torch in

Kit's eyes, took readings of pulse and temperature, and recorded them on a clipboard. The woman had the accent of somewhere far south. It was the same voice that had been spitting in Kit's ear moments before.

'So your partner, Mr Rabone,' said the woman with green eyes. 'Ms Hueffer-Lee – she comes from a place not far from my home. Next state anyway. Similar town, similar kind of people. Hers is a military family, right?'

It was the following morning. Kit was sitting upright in a low-backed chair, with his ankles chained to its legs and his wrists cuffed in his lap. The hood had been removed, but the woman was behind him, still beyond the scope of vision.

'I knew a lot of families like that, growing up,' she said. 'Sweet folks. Sincere, genuine folks, but they – they kind of live in their own world. The horizons are wide out there, and people don't look beyond them. It can be frustrating, for someone ambitious, someone with a wanderlust. You know what I'm talking about. I'm guessing that was your partner's situation.'

After the medical examination the night before, Kit had been given a plate of rice and tinned fish. The cell lights had dimmed. He had slumped into a dense sleep. Breakfast was a fried egg and a square of bread. Then he was hooded and returned to what seemed to be the same room as the day before.

'You know, I get that there are things to dislike about my nation,' the woman said. 'I see that, I really do. I'm talking to you as an educated person, Mr Rabone, and as a skeptical person. I'm not some bright-eyed true believer. I'm not looking to the shining city on a hill. There's a *naïveté* that a lot of people have, and it does – it does shade into complacency, into arrogance sometimes. The culture – there's a shallowness, a violence, sometimes ugliness. There's things to be ashamed of in our history, at times, and plenty of folks are ignorant of that. You know what bothers me the most, I think? The obesity. I notice it whenever I go back. I mean the size of these people. I don't know what you do, when people make bad choices like that.

'So all of that is there, Mr Rabone. And lamentable, in its way. But beyond that, when you do read the history, when you really know it, all of that is insignificant. I mean it's meaningless, next to what my country has achieved, what it has given. I mean the greatness, the sheer good' – her voice rose in pitch, and almost broke into a laugh – 'that my country has done in the world, since its foundation. I'm talking about the contribution that we have made – to the peace of the world, to the wealth of the world, the freedom of the world. A gift to humanity, unique in history. Is that in doubt? Do I have to give examples of how we have helped? Helped your own country, for one, at crucial junctures?'

Kit's mind was still reeling from the previous day's violence. He had expected flattery, menaces, appeals to duty and common sense, but not this impassioned soliloquising. The woman spoke with frustrated intensity. It was as if she was working from notes that failed to match the heat of her convictions and from which she lifted off in flights of rhetorical excitement.

She began to furnish examples of national virtue, reaching back into the past. The historical account led into an analysis of present international conditions. She spoke of *we*, not *I* or *they*. Phrases lodged in Kıt's mind: Unprecedented power and unprecedented vulnerability. The world order we have birthed. Full-spectrum dominance. 'Nothing has ever existed like this,' she said, 'in the history of power.' Kit's grasp of such matters was weak, but even to him the shallowness of her understanding, the second-hand character of her judgements, were obvious.

Soon he gave up following the threads of contention, and surrendered to the sensation of the woman's voice.

'So when people around the world complain about the superficiality and the materialism,' she was saying, 'yes, I can see that. But they know, those people, they know in their hearts that we are a power for good in the world. They know that when we intervene, there may be snarl-ups on the way and, just now and then, some bad people doing bad stuff. But they also know that we have democracy, we have laws, we have transparency, and that above all we have ideals – ideals that carry us – and for all of those reasons, you are better off dealing with us than with anyone else.'

Kit imagined her face. He pictured its fervour and animation, the emphatic chopping of that sharp chin. 'The world on fire demands a first responder,' the woman said. 'It has fallen to us to be that country. It's not romantic. It's not arrogant. It's just a reality, that we've been needed to lead in so many situations. And if you're living in a poor village in some disadvantaged country someplace, and trouble comes, and the soldiers are pointing guns and asking questions, then you better hope that they are our soldiers, because behind them are all of those institutions and those ideals, and they constrain and impose responsibility, and you got a better hope of justice and fairness and freedom from out of our guns than out of anyone else's.'

The words, which had been tumbling out, stopped. He heard the sound of sipping from a cup.

'But I'd like to hear, Mr Rabone,' she said, after a pause, 'I'd like to hear what you think about these matters.'

Kit's bounds were loose; after a night on the lumpy mattress, it was a pleasure to be sitting up. He wanted her to continue talking, and to bask in the flow of firm, passionate words. What was to be gained from entering into debate?

'You're very persuasive,' he said.

'And are you persuaded?'

'I don't see what it has to do with me.'

'Mr Rabone, I think that it has everything to do with your situation. That's why it's me talking to you now. I happen to think that you are a good and responsible person, Mr Rabone. I think that we share the same values, the same goals, broadly speaking. We believe in the same virtues. I think there's something blocking you from recognizing that – stubbornness, rebelliousness, resistance to conformity. And those can be virtues too. You have a questioning mind. So my job is to show you the answer to your questions, in a way that allows us to cooperate.'

There was a silence, marked by tiny sounds that might have been the scratching of pen on paper. Kit became aware of the presence of the unseen others, the soldiers with hood and chains. He had the strong sense that they were close at hand, sitting alongside the woman, bored probably, each resisting the urge to scratch, to yawn, to shuffle feet, to pollute the atmosphere of tense tranquillity.

The silence extended itself. He had expected her to badger and hector him with repeated questions. But it was over suddenly. There was the scrape of a chair. 'He's all yours,' the woman said, and the other chairs scraped, and Kit was bundled into darkness again.

He was manacled and blindfolded, jerked up and frog-marched at a faster pace than his legs could match. He gave up trying to walk and let his feet drag and bounce against the ground.

Jagged, panicked thoughts overcame him. He was no one, here. He had nothing. They could do whatever they wanted to him, the worst, most horrible thing, and nothing could prevent it. He would never again see anyone he knew or loved. No one would know what had happened to him. Most terrifying of all, Helen was over there in the jungle, thousands of miles away, unprotected, quite beyond his power to intervene.

How was any of it possible? None of it had come about by choice. Who had the right to demand that he be a hero? But if he told them what they wanted to know, they would kill him and kill Helen. This was the choice: betrayal and death; or silence, torment and a postponed death. Anguish flared within him; his mind searched out for someone to blame or beseech. There had been a terrible wrong step – what was it? The soldiers flanking him must have subtly adjusted their pace and posture, because he sensed what was coming next a moment before it happened: a sudden explosion of pain, jagged and blunt at the same time, in his right shin. He cried out, and staggered forward, gripped around the shoulders by the guiding hands. There was some kind of sharp, low obstacle; his escorts had marched him into it. Everything in him strained to sink to the ground and to rub, rub his bruised bone. But he was cuffed and held fast, writhing as he stood. Unsoothed, the pain ricocheted around his nerves. He groaned and swore. Such a simple, banal torment – a banged shin, a stubbed toe, a smashed nose – and yet, in the moment, completely unbearable. If he had known what was to come, really known it, and if they had put the question the moment before, he would have done anything to avert that pain. He would have told them at once where the memory card was. It was hopeless to pretend otherwise.

He was marched on and then yanked to a halt. In an instant, he was drenched in cold water. His sodden shirt clung to him as he spluttered and gasped. Close at hand, someone suppressed laughter. Then he was being shoved and propelled from one pair of burly palms to another. It was as if they were standing in a ring and tossing him like a ball. When he lost his balance and fell, they jerked him up and threw him between them again.

'Where's the goddamn device, you piece of shit?'

'Piece of shit, where's the data device?'

But now the pain in his leg had passed its point of crisis; the shock of cold water had chased it away. He was frightened, but being frightened was different from being in pain. Kit thought: these are the worst moments of my life. It is unbearable. And yet I am bearing it. The last thought generated a numbing surge of excitement. Fear and exultation flowed into one another; it was impossible to distinguish one from the other. He gave a breathless laugh, although to anyone else it would have sounded like a croak. As if his thoughts were being read, a blow connected with his solar plexus, throwing him on to the floor again, where he moaned and cowered.

He was jerked once again to his feet. The skinny medic pulled up the blindfold and looked at his eyes. A bottle of water was tipped into his mouth, and he glugged and gagged. The medic nodded. The blindfold was replaced by a hood. He was led a long way and thrown on to the floor of a new room, which hummed with powerful air conditioners. It was piercingly cold. Soon he was shivering and whimpering in his wet clothes.

They left him there for hours. It was the worst so far. As bad as the aching cold was the boredom. He called out for a drink, and for somewhere to piss, but no one came. He sucked water out of the yellow shirt. He relaxed his bladder, and the fast-fading warmth was a small relief. The effort of constant shivering exhausted him. He fell half-asleep, and then they came in and pulled him up, and put dry clothes on him, and took him back to his original cell.

He was woken again in what felt like the middle of the night. Four or five soldiers were in the small room and he was hooded again. They pulled down the loose trousers. He heard the click of a lighter and screamed in panic as he felt a heat around his scrotum. Delicately and painstakingly, adjusting his penis and pushing aside his balls to avoid burning him, an unseen hand singed off his pubic hair.

As much as the heat, cold or blows, the hood became a thing of terror. It made violence redundant: deprived of vision, his hearing muffled, he anticipated pain and shock at every turn. He saw that it was important to hide this;

when the hood was being tugged over his head the following morning, he strained not to flinch, or to gape with relief when it was removed. He was seated at a table. There was a plastic bottle of water and a cup. With cuffed hands, he poured it out and drank. He became aware of his own stink, a mixture of sweat, piss and scorched hair. He sensed the woman's presence. Upright and unbound, he could have turned around to look for her, but something constrained him, connected to shame at his filthy state. He glugged down the water and gave a heaving sob.

'I guess you've had a rough night, Mr Rabone,' said the woman's voice. 'I understand that they increased muscularity.' She sighed, as if in resignation and concern. 'That must have been tough. Have a drink. Take your time.'

Kit drank and sobbed again. A coldly detached part of his mind reproached him for showing weakness – but what difference did it make? Strength or vulnerability, cowardice or courage – here they were the same. It was so obvious, so lamely and dully predictable, that he was going to tell them what they wanted to know, that the question was no longer interesting. The mystery was what prevented him from doing so right away.

His shackled hands reached under the table. He rested his right palm on his leg and with his index finger began to trace letters and words on his thigh. *Helen. Lara. Moon Moth.*

'My name is Alice, Mr Rabone,' said the voice. 'Can I call you Kristian?'

Kit's heart gave a small jolt. He smiled at the cleverness of it. To be forced to attach a name to the voice robbed him of strength and imposed subtle obligations. He knew that he could never gain the advantage in any spoken exchange. Even the meaningless, preliminary exchanges yielded something that he did not want to give up. And yet it was impossible not to speak.

'You can call me whatever you like,' he said. 'Can't you, Alice?'

There was a softer quality to her voice today. Dirty or not, he turned his head to take in the world behind him. This was a different room, strip-lit and windowless. There was a partition of mirrored glass a few feet behind his chair that stopped short of the ceiling. In the gap above it, he could see the darkness of the space beyond.

He nodded into the mirror, then turned his head to the front again. A camera peered down at him from the facing wall.

'Increased muscularity,' said Kit.

From behind the screen, Alice gave a regretful chuckle. 'That's a euphemism, I guess.' She sighed again. 'It doesn't have to be this tough, you know, Kristian. You understand what we need. Just tell us where it is – your best reckoning of where it is – then we can get you a shower, fix the paperwork, put you in touch with your folks, and we can all get on with our lives.'

Kit poured himself more water. 'Why should I believe you?' he asked.

'Because you know who we are, Kristian. You know what we stand for. You know our values.'

'You are criminals,' he said, thrilled to be uttering the words.

'Legally, jurisdictionally, that is not accurate.'

'You are liars,' he said, drinking the water. His heart was

racing; his fear was numbed. 'I was there, remember. I saw what you did. I saw your invasion, your illegal invasion of another country.'

'Kristian, there was no intervention. There was no presence in the western region. It did not happen.'

'I saw it.'

'You must be mistaken.'

'I saw the soldiers. Court filmed it.'

'And where is that footage now?'

His thoughts had become darting and daring. He looked appreciatively at the bottle of water that he had just finished. There had been nothing strange about its taste, but he was beginning to feel wide awake now – punchy, argumentative, almost cheerful. The urge to retort had become irresistible. He was flexing the muscles in his face and rotating his lower jaw against the upper.

'You say that you're proud of your country,' he said. 'But there's more to it than pride, isn't there? Your pride in your country requires that everyone else should be slightly ashamed of theirs.'

'Not at all. My nation has the highest—'

'You talk about your nation and how much you love it, and its goodness and its greatness. You say, "As a nation, we do this, we believe that." But what do you know of your nation? The village where I was living, the place where I took my child – I knew the face of everyone in that village, and everyone knew my face. And even in that place, that tiny place – no one spoke like you do. No one, not even the chief, ever said, "The people of this village believe . . ." Because it would be an absurdity. Even among a couple of hundred people, there is no statement you can make that applies to all of them. In a country – sorry, a *nation* – it's fucking ridiculous.'

She said, 'But Kristian, that's simply not true. Our nation is diverse, but it is united. That is its beauty and its strength. We, all of us, are individuals, but we acknowledge an allegiance to something greater than ourselves, something that unites us with other people who we recognize as . . . our folks. That identity completes us, it fills out the gaps and the holes and the shortcomings and the confusion that we all experience from time to time. None of us are alone in this world – you neither.' There was a pause; from behind the screen, Kit sensed whispered consultations.

'Take – just as an example – take sports,' she went on. 'You know what I'm talking about. Imagine a soccer stadium, and a big match, with seventy thousand people, eighty thousand. All united, all cheering for the same thing. You must know that feeling.'

He thought about the last time he had been to a football match. It felt like yesterday, and also years ago. He remembered the excitement of his friends, the pleasure that he had taken in their high spirits. The stadium had been immense; it reared above the city like a cathedral. Even before the kick-off, a tumult of sound came from within, a single voice that rose and fell. But after they had entered, squeezed side by side in the stands, the noise broke down into particles. It became ragged and complex: shrill cries, oaths, laughs, whistles, barking shouts, like the calls of creatures in a forest. Kit tried to imagine a collective, an organism, and himself as a part of it. But all he could see were people, like him, in small groups. There were three laughing women dressed for the office, and a dour father with a young daughter and son. There were two tough-looking men who kissed one another whenever their side scored a goal, and a middle-aged woman on her own who followed the action through a pair of binoculars. It was to their faces, voices, clothes that Kit was drawn, rather than to the crowd as a whole. There was no crowd as a whole. And far from emoting in a common cause, there were two sides, each willing the defeat of the other.

Kit said to Alice, 'Diverse – yes, I'd say you're diverse. There's – what? – 300 million of you. "You" – you see you've got me doing it too. You're not a *You* or a *We*. You're not even an *it*. You give me your speech about foundation, and history, and values. It's all in the head. This idea that you have some magical connection to people you've never met, will never meet, people in completely different circumstances from yours, in places that you don't know and will never see – just because you have the same passport. And the idea that you would die, and kill, for those people, and that this is not even a choice, but a duty. Who do those ideas serve, in the end? You personally? Ordinary people collectively? Or someone else?'

He paused. His mouth was dry again. He wanted more of the bottled water, but the bottle was empty. He said, 'It's a total fucking con. It's like ghosts, it's like God. If you don't believe in them – poof! – they don't exist. And then they can't touch you. Isn't it really so very obvious what it's all about? Who gains from all this. You're being used, you're being imposed upon, you're being ridden, for money and for power.'

A luxurious numbness was spreading throughout his limbs. He had never felt so powerfully the conviction of being in the right. He looked up at the camera on the wall and smiled. There was a long silence. Eventually, Alice's voice returned, strenuously calm.

'Let's go at this another way,' she said. 'Where is home for you, would you say? Simple question. Where do you come from?'

'You've got all that in your file.'

'I got the facts. But the facts only take you so far. I want to know how you feel. Who are you, Mr Rabone?'

'Who I am is my business.'

'The spelling of your name – Kristian. What kind of a name is that?'

'I'm bored by that question.'

'You have that very interesting . . . complexion. Where does that come from in your family, going back?'

'My skin is none of your concern.'

'Don't you have feelings of duty, of patriotism, Kristian?' Alice said, sounding genuinely confused. 'Don't you love your country? Aren't you proud to be who you are? Don't you have a country?'

'I have a country. There are places there I love. There are people I love. But where does it come from, this idea that I must love the whole thing? What is the whole thing? And to be *proud* of something like that, an accident of birth. You might as well be proud of being left-handed, or having brown hair.' He stopped. I have a country, Kit thought to himself. Lara is my country. Helen is my country.

He said, 'My country is none of your business.'

'You say that a lot of things are none of my business. The point is I'm making them my business. You're in detention. I'm torturing you. So everything is my business.'

There was a heavy pause. Kit savoured the delicious languor in his legs.

'I thought that you didn't control it,' he said.

'Well, I'm consulted. Bipartisan decision making, you might call it.'

She said, 'You know how this is going to go, don't you, Kristian? You get it, right? It's going to get worse every time. There's no way that you can hold out. It's not about politics or psychology. It's just biology. Everyone gives up, Kristian. The only reason that you haven't already is that we're trying real hard not to do you any lasting physical harm. Imagine how much worse it can get.'

'If you all love your country so much,' he said, 'why isn't it enough for you? Why are you over there at all? Why does loving your country require you to invade someone else's?'

'Perhaps that's the difference between you and me,' she said. 'I never need to go home. I carry home inside me. See it? It's right here.'

Kit turned his head to look, but the mirrored barrier gave back only the table and bottle, and his own black, frowning eyes.

10

At night, waking on his pallet in the dark cell, he kept dread at bay by imagining Helen. He tried to recreate her in his mind: delicacy of fingernail and eyelid, softness of skin and hair, the weight of her in his arms and against his shoulder. She must have grown and changed by now in ways that he could only guess, for he had lost track of time and couldn't say whether it was weeks or months since he had become a captive. Stricken by the dark, attuning himself to consciousness, he concluded that she was alive. He would know if she was not. There would be signs, palpable to sense: a shift of temperature or pressure, an alteration in the quality of air, a change in the texture of the darkness.

After his last session with Alice, he had been thrown into a new cell with a dim bulb and no windows. It was foul with dirt and insects. He was left there for days. Mosquitoes stung his face and arms. The bucket was not emptied, and overflowed. The soldiers screamed at him, and made him mop up his filth with a small piece of rag.

At his next meeting with Alice, he launched into a rant about his rights. He demanded access to a consular officer and a lawyer. He shouted that he should be charged or released. They took him out and left him alone in his cell for three days. The solitude made him panic. He understood that he had reached the limit of his mental strength. He decided that when the next meal was brought he would tell them that he wanted to speak to Alice. He would give her what she wanted. He would ask something in return. Perhaps they would not kill Helen. Perhaps they would be kind to her. As these thoughts were rotating in his mind, they came in and hooded him before he had the chance to speak. He was placed in a padded room, with speakers in the ceiling. Unbearably loud and harsh music was played, for hours and hours. Soldiers, wearing ear defenders, came in and slapped his face. The noise made him nauseous. The shock of it relit his anger, and chased away any urge to talk. After what felt like an entire day, he fell into a tranced stupor. They came in, yanked him up and slapped him awake.

The more they hurt Kit, the more casual the soldiers became in their treatment of him. They would forget to put on the hood, even when they moved him from room to room. In his presence, they spoke in barking parade-ground voices. As soon as he was out of sight, they reverted to the weary, whining tone of those forced to spend too much time in one another's company. He overheard their baiting of the race of people that they referred to as the 'chonks', the cohort of migrant cooks and cleaners who came and went at all hours, spraying for insects and removing Kit's bucket. They sneered about their superiors. When he heard them muttering about 'that fancy-pants Agency bitch', he felt an obscurely located sense of hurt.

They had moved him to a block constructed in the form of a conventional lock-up. A row of barred cells faced one another across a dingy corridor. The jailhouse was newly built; the black bars still gave off the smell of paint. There was a small high window that let in a slat of sunlight. The other half-dozen cells were empty, or at least silent. When they were not hurting him, the soldiers lingered in some kind of office at the end of the block. Kit could not see it, but clues reached him through its open door about the life they lived there: the smell of cheeseburgers; the chirping of video games; muffled chatter, laughter and swearing.

The corridor of empty cells amplified small sounds. Sometimes he would hear the click of arriving footsteps, which he took to be those of superior officers. The soldiers would clatter to attention and the barking tone returned to their voices. They would huddle together for hours; sometimes Kit could make out raised voices through the closed door of the office. The subject of these meetings seemed to be Kit himself. They were often followed by new torments.

They forced him to stand in his cell for hours on end. Once he stood all night; the guards rotated in shifts to prevent him from sitting or falling asleep. When he was reeling with dizziness and pain, they looped a rope through a ring in the ceiling, tied it to his hands and pulled him to his feet.

'Please let me down,' he said.

'Where is the data device?'

'Please let me down.'

'Where is the goddamn data device?'

The conversations with Alice were a giddy pleasure, for the absence of pain, for the water that was supposed to make him talkative, and for the talking itself. Kit knew that this was part of the scheme, that they were rationing these encounters in order to break him, and that it was important to disguise gratitude and relief. Sometimes this was impossible. Several times, after being led in and chained to the table, he spent the first minutes crying beneath the strip light. As soon as he was capable, he summoned up sarcasm and indignation; his hand moved to his thigh, where he traced out words with his fingertip. The important thing was for Alice to talk, and to continue talking for as long as possible. She liked to talk; often Kit detected boredom and even neediness on the far side of the mirror. Either way, Alice was full of speeches, awaiting their occasion; his task was to prompt them.

'I could give you a whole story about me, Kristian,' she said one day. 'Shall we try? So, I'm a teacher, happily teaching senior high-school literature. My husband is a software engineer, we got two kids, the girl is disabled. Or maybe I'm a lawyer, not a teacher. Or I work in finance, or I'm a doctor – and it's a wife, not a husband, no kids, but it's the same story. There I am, in my life, when – bang. World events, those moments all of us remember. Maybe they hurt me directly, or people I love, maybe not. Maybe it comes to me all at once, maybe it builds up over years. Either way, I get to understand that it's my duty to do something, to make a personal contribution to the fight that's being fought. So I apply, and I join, and I reskill, and I get one post and then another, and then I get sent out here. I leave my family behind – and here I am.

'The details don't matter, Kristian. There are so many stories, so many of us like that. We're normal folks. We're not monsters. Things had been different, you could have met me someplace, or someone like me. And we would have got on fine, Kristian. Found we had things in common. Shared beliefs and assumptions – I'm pretty sure we've got those. I'm not what you might think. I'm not a person of faith – doesn't trouble me if others are, but I'm not. I got my politics, Kristian, like we all do, but they're not what you might be assuming. I don't go for the "isms". I'm not one for joining a cause. I'm just a patriot, like everyone. At a certain moment I recognized that our way of life is precious to me, and that it is under threat, and that it's the duty of all of us who feel that way to step up and protect it, or at least do what we can.'

As she spoke, Kit thought about the layout of the room in which he sat, and his position in it: the mirrored partition behind him, the camera facing him from the wall in front. Alice, he assumed, was looking at the back of his head through the one-way glass, and his face through the camera.

She said, 'No one wants any of this, this program that we have embarked on with you. No one is excited by it, by the muscular measures. It's horrible that we have to do this. But it's a horrible situation that we find ourselves in as a nation these recent years. There are people out there who hate us. They hate us more than they love life.'

His bruised wrists throbbed and glowed; he drank the water and waited for it to take effect. He said, 'Why is it, d'you think, that they hate you?'

'They hate us for what we are.'

With his finger he traced on his leg the letters of the word *hate*.

'For what you are – not for what you do. Well, that lets you off every time.'

'They hate our values. They want to destroy our way of life. That's not some secret that we've worked out. It's not an interpretation. It's what they say openly and explicitly. And it's what they have done, time after time. How much evidence do you need? What do you need to persuade you to act? A mushroom cloud? Our people dead – many, many of them dead? That's not going to happen anymore.'

'You think that Dr Mochtar, or people he knows, have got a nuclear bomb over there, in the jungle?'

'It's possible, Kristian, and the possibility is too terrible. With a threat like that, of that magnitude, you have an obligation, you have a goddamn duty, to overestimate.'

'With all your snooping and eavesdropping, that's the best you can do? You don't actually have an enemy in this war, do you? Not a physical enemy. All you've got are fears.'

'Well-grounded fears are a worthy enemy, Kristian. And take it from me, the more you know, the less confident you feel. There's always something more, beyond what we know. There's always something more to fear.'

Kit thought: it's not just fear. It's a kind of mania. That's the most forgiving way to understand it. Alice had said it herself: *Bang!* – like a great blow to the skull, a traumatic head injury. And then the reeling and the lurching, the striking out, crashing into things, into friends as well as enemies.

He said, 'It's never ending.'

'It used to be these things did have an ending,' said

Alice. 'The great moment was when the troops came back home, right? Bands, cheering, tickertape, and life back to normal. But there is no normal now, and home has changed.'

Kit frowned encouragingly, for he could tell that she would soon be in full spate.

She said, 'It's not a place with a fence around it anymore. It's a system, this global system. It's like the blood, like the lymph, with all this money and ideas and power flowing through it, in and out and back around, making us healthy and fit and strong. But there's other things that can flow through too. The viruses, the bacteria, the bad cells. And if they start breeding in one part of the system then before you know it they're passing through those same veins, and they're spreading from place to place, and soon enough they're with us, inside us, making us sick back home where we thought we were so safe behind our oceans, and those walls we put up don't mean anything now, because it's coming under the ground and in the soil and through the air and the ether, and we can't block them or shut them down, any more than you can switch off your blood. So our job is to stop it breeding – find the places where the cells first turn bad, and kill them off before they do. Sterilize those places. Because it can happen anytime. You do your best to make the system healthy, but you're watching, watching all the time. And there's no homecoming parade from that.'

'That's what I am, then,' Kit said. 'Cancer. And you're chemotherapy.'

On his thigh he was tracing the word *girl*.

There was another silence. She said, 'There's other

people, Mr Rabone, want a go at you. I'm a guest here – you get that. I have an influence, but only as long as there's a chance of you cooperating. We can't just go on like this, round and round, and nothing changing. There are other levels, other leaderships. There are other organizations that have a different personality from mine.'

One night in his cell Kit woke in alarm from a dream of Helen. A sound had broken through sleep, and moments later he heard it again – a flat crump, as of a distant explosion, followed quickly by another. Soon there was a commotion of booted feet arriving in the jail block, and urgent voices from the office. A pair of boots came down the corridor and he blinked as a torch beam was shone through the bars of his cell and on to his face.

The following day more boots came and went and there were long meetings behind the office's closed door. Kit was left in his cell all day and night. He was woken by an unfamiliar trundling in the corridor outside the cell. His guts turned over when he saw what it was. A group of soldiers was looking at him through the bars. Between them they were pushing a hospital stretcher mounted on a low trolley.

The medic took his pulse and looked into his eyes and mouth. He was hooded, strapped down, and rolled into the back of a vehicle. The vehicle started up, drove, stopped and he was rolled out. There was warm air on the skin of his hands. He was wheeled inside. He felt the cold of a stethoscope against his chest, and clips and bands were attached to his fingers and wrists. Hands braced his arm; a needle pricked him, and he could not prevent himself from whimpering. The hood was removed, and he was looking up at faces in a brightly lit room.

The straps were loosened and the back of the stretcher was angled upwards to elevate his head. Two of the faces were familiar: the middle-aged sergeant and the female soldier with the southern accent. Sitting with them was a doctor with a thin face. The needle had come without warning. It aroused in him an animal dread, the panic of a beast in the slaughterhouse. He waited for unconsciousness to seize him, or for something worse – a choking in his lungs, the sensation of unstoppable burning. He tried to speak, but horror was interrupted by an explosion of ease that made him gasp.

'You feeling OK, Mr Rabone?' said the doctor.

Kit could not stop himself smiling.

'Feels good, right, Kristian?' said the sergeant, who was smiling himself.

Kit laughed.

The others looked at one another, and laughed themselves.

He was saturated in unbearably sweet and benign feelings. It was as if the air he breathed was composed of effervescent honey. He knew what they were doing to him, and why, but understanding was so much less important than how he felt. It wasn't happiness or elation so much as a profound recognition of the rightness of all things, radiated over him by the universe itself.

'Oh, oh,' he said.

'How ya doing?'

'It's like – champagne.'

'Champagne is good, right?'

'Champagne is fucking delicious.'

The others laughed.

'Cheers, Kris!' said the woman. It was the first time he had looked closely at her face. She was young, and had wide wet lips.

Kit said, 'I thought you were killing me.'

They laughed again, and the sound of the voices, at their different volumes and pitches, was outrageously complex and interesting.

'Kris, we're not killing you.'

'I thought that's what it was.'

'But it feels good, right?'

'I felt very sad, about that. Sad and afraid. I felt sad a lot recently.'

'No need to feel sad now, eh, pal?'

'I feel great now. This is great.'

'That's terrific. Terrific.'

There was a pause. The sergeant and the specialist were looking at the thin doctor. He glanced at his watch, and nodded.

'So, Kristian, it's good to talk,' said the sergeant, suddenly brisk and awkward. 'Good to talk like this. And I'm guessing there's something else you want to talk to us about, huh?'

Kit laughed warmly. He wanted to soothe and calm the sergeant's nervousness, to reassure him that everything was going to be fine.

'You know what I'm talking about, right, Kristian?' he said, as they all joined in the laughter. 'I think you know what I'm talking about.'

Kit was laughing and spluttering so much that he could hardly get the words out. 'I know, I know.' Then he said, 'I like you, sergeant. I like you, specialist. Didn't know I did, but I do.'

'Kristian, Kristian, I love you too, man. We all do. There's a lot of affection, really is. But you know, by now, after all this time, we just got to know . . . Where's the data device, Kristian?'

Kit laughed.

'You want to, Kristian. You want to say it. Where's the device?'

He did want to say it. He wanted to say the word. So much, because he loved the sergeant.

'Won't you just tell us where we can find it?' This was the woman spanking now. Not spanking! She was speaking, not spanking, but the confusion convulsed Kit in a new spasm of hilarity. 'It's not so hard,' she said, confused by his giggling. 'It's easy. "The data device is . . ."' She paused, then tried again, '"The data device is . . ."'

'The data device is . . .' He was laughing again.

'That's it, Kris. "The data device is . . ." Where?'

'With the. No—No—'

'Oh yes, Kris, yes. You can do it.'

'No mad,' said Kit. That was true, too true, and although the world – in fact the universe – was in exquisite harmony, there was something wrong about saying that true thing. He had to remake it, not as something false, but different.

'Not mad,' he said theatrically. 'Not mad.'

'We're not mad with you, Kris. We just want to know—'

'He means crazy,' said the doctor.

'What?'

'He means crazy mad, not angry mad. Not mad mad. He means he's not crazy.'

'You're not crazy, Kristian, or mad,' said the sergeant. 'What you're experiencing now is a very normal reaction to the little shot the doc gave you. And you've got something to tell us. There's something you want to tell us. You're going to tell us.'

He was perfectly right. He had to tell them. He experienced it as a necessity, almost a physical compulsion, as natural as releasing the muscles above the bucket. But even as he yielded to the irresistible he was able to do so in his own way, to give the muscle a jerk as he let go.

'Where is the data device, Kristian? You know where it is, and you're going to tell us. Kristian, where is it?'

'No. Nome. Not. Not mad.'

'You're not mad, my friend. We know you're not mad.'

'No mad.'

'We got that, Kris. You're not mad. It's just the champagne, right?'

'Not mads.'

'No one thinks that. You're the sanest one here, right Doc?'

The faces looking down at him were nodding earnestly.

'Just tell us where it is, Kristian?'

'No, not mad.'

'Please, Kris. Let's spare ourselves all this, this whole—'

'No mads.'

'WHERE IS IT, YOU FUCK? WHERE IS THE GODDAMN DATA DEVICE?'

The spittle sprayed Kit's face. His expression became solemn.

'Not mad.' He smiled, then burst into laughter again.

*

Sometimes he fell asleep at once, toppled by exhaustion and by whatever it was they put in his food; sometimes, he lay awake for hours, shaping thoughts of Helen and Lara, and listening to the insects clicking against the window. There were more dull explosions. Many of them were barely audible, but once they sounded close at hand: three percussive crunches, answered by the noise of barking dogs and vehicle engines. Lamps came on outside, casting an illumination through Kit's small window. The soldiers in the jail block clattered into wakefulness and torchlight was played on to his face again.

The next day he heard the arriving footsteps of a group of visitors. The tone of the barked greetings suggested that these were senior people; a muffled conversation could be heard in the office. Then there was another set of arriving footsteps and a voice that he immediately recognised, speaking in unfamiliar, strident tones. 'You will unlock this door,' it said. 'I will be admitted to this meeting.'

It was Alice.

The door opened and clicked shut behind her. Beyond it, voices were raised, including hers. Her proximity to his cell was disturbing to Kit, as if a boundary had been violated.

After the visitors had gone, the soldiers placed in front of his cell a cage of thin steel bars four feet square. They rattled it as they walked past.

'You wanna go in there? You want the dog cage, piece of shit? Tell us where the fuck it is.'

The following day they locked him inside it. He could not stand up, or stretch out his legs, which began to ache and cramp unbearably. When he managed to sleep, soldiers would come into his cell and rattle and kick the cage, shaking him awake.

They placed a new object in front of the cell – a black box, like a cuboid coffin, even smaller than the cage. Daubed on it were the words 'General Bartok's Butthole'. They put him inside it and closed the lid. Air came in from somewhere, but it was stifling and dark. Soon he was shouting to be let out. The lid of the box opened.

'Data device.'
'Can I have some water?'
'Data device.'
'I need to—'
'Data device.'
'Please, can I—'
'Data device.'
'Please, please, I don't know—'
The lid closed.

It would be Alice he would tell when the moment came. He longed to see her, but they had stopped taking him to the room with the mirror. It became harder to reckon the passing of time. Night and day were difficult to distinguish. They locked him in the room and filled it with deafening sound. It was the noise of a baby crying, the recorded cries of a real infant, played back through the enormous speakers. The sound, so familiar to Kit, and so longed for, was unbearable at this volume. He lay on the ground, cringing in the battering waves of noise. The light went out. He called out Alice's name. The crying of the baby went on and on, louder and louder, as he clung to the floor. They left him there all night.

They left paper and a pencil in his cell. He knew that it was another ploy, but it brought him relief. He wrote, 'This is the time for a god or a devil.' The soldiers took it away, and he heard them in their office, reading the words to one another in mocking imitations of his accent. He wrote, 'Helen is alive with the nomads the memory card is on her necklace.' He laughed, and chewed the piece of paper up, and swallowed it.

'Dearest Lara,' he wrote:

Who are you where are you what have we done. Did we did we take the wrong step. I can't know any more. They put things in my food that make it hard to get to the point. Do you understand. But I'm not sorry are you. We found one another and we made Helen. We loved her. We knew we had to get away without getting away we couldn't have found one another wouldn't have had Helen who made us get away. Helen was the escape. We couldn't not have escaped. Does any of this make sense. We saved her as well as killed her. We saved ourselves. They are always going to catch up but you have to run you have to make them chase. We will always fail. They will always win in their minds. I love you I. You always told me to come back to be present and I have and I am I came out of the cave Lara. I pushed up the glass. Are you proud of me. The stuff they make me drink makes it

       hard to write. I worry that it made a ghost of me am
       I a ghost. Was he right that I slipped away drifted off.
       I saw you in dream the other night you were all in
       white robes with a worm or a snake coiling round you.
       I want to come back I will come back I am back.

He told them that he and Lara had manufactured and distributed crystal methamphetamine. They shook their heads. He confessed to the murder of the soldiers on the bridge and at the river, but it wasn't enough. He told them that the memory card had dropped from his pocket after he had eaten the jungle root, as Obson was dying. They sat him at a large table, and spent hours going over diagrams and photographs. The soldiers were suspicious, but he could tell that they liked his story; surly caution gave way to a grim sense of purpose. New faces sat in on the interrogation, men and women with technical know-how and questions about soil type and vegetation. Then on the second afternoon of the debriefing, Alice walked in, nodded in greeting, and sat down at the head of the table.

    Kit was transfixed by her proximity. He had spent hours in her company, but had caught only glimpses of her, so fleeting they might have been dreams. Suddenly here she was, a few feet away, available to unlimited scrutiny. It was like finding himself in the presence of a badger bear; it was like travelling back into the past. She did not look him in the eye; she addressed him with cool formality. But it was delicious to submit once again to the soothing, ardent rhythms of her speech.

    It was her voice, he realised, that had deceived him about her age. From the beginning, he had registered the sharp chin and unlikely green eyes. But now he saw that the skin of her neck and hands was lined and mottled. Her cheeks crinkled around her eyes when she smiled. She was old enough to be his mother.

The soldiers didn't know how to treat him after that. They had only two modes of address, contempt or respect, and Kit qualified for neither. The torments were suspended; but torture had filled the days, and without it they were restless. The medic produced a chess set. For reasons that he couldn't identify, Kit claimed not to play and allowed himself to be taught. One after another the soldiers sat down at the board and chuckled as Kit let them win.

The artillery explosions were becoming more frequent. They came during the day as well as at night. Sirens wailed in warning; at first they were met with a commotion of boots and revving vehicles. Soon the warnings had become routine, and the soldiers reacted to them with boredom. But there was a new tension among them, which filled the void created by Kit's confession. They swore foully at the menial 'chonks'. Shouting, verging on the berserk, could be heard through the door of the jailhouse office.

He was fed three times a day, not in his cell but in the mess hall, after the soldiers had eaten and gone. The cooks and servers watched him as he ate, smoking and bantering with one another in their own language. His patterns of sleep and digestion returned to normal. The soldiers lent him books. He experienced once again the pleasure of being at liberty in his own head. He thought about the search that was now underway in the faraway patch of forest. They could not know that he had lied to them. If they found nothing, they had no way to be sure that it was never there. Eventually they would conclude that it was lost forever. Then he would be of no use to them.

Being hurt, Kit reflected, was unbearable, but easy. You experienced fear and pain. You begged, screamed, pissed and shitted yourself. The torture stopped. Then it began again. Physical cruelty was obvious. It was either present or absent. It was when the bruises were fading into his skin that he became conscious of what lay behind the fists and boots. In his imagination, it took the form of a vast apparatus, humming with electricity and pulsing with lights. It was an unimaginably sophisticated machine, the product of generations of expertise in compulsion and manipulation, using finely wrought tools of psychology and pharmacology, underwritten by violence. The chemicals in his food, the behaviour of his interrogators, the temperature and quality of the light in the rooms in which they held him: all of them, he had no doubt, had been considered, calculated and dosed. It was a game that he was incapable of understanding, let alone winning; he was like a child playing chess against the world's most powerful computer. But throughout it, at his core, he felt himself possessed of something unconquerable, a nugget of certainty, hard, light and indestructible, an alloy compounded of the secrets he held, and a conviction difficult to put into words.

It was connected to the grandest abstractions: good, evil, right, wrong, justice, oppression. He pictured it to himself as a ball of shining, metallic green, embedded deep inside him, spinning at incalculable speed. No one could ever grasp it. Even if Kit's insides were cut open, the ball would spin off and outwards into the world, beyond the fingers of his killers, unstoppably brilliant and dynamic.

'You were right to tell us,' Alice said. 'You did the right thing, Kit. And at the right moment. Things were getting – well, if it had gone on much longer, I don't know what would have happened.'

He was in the usual room, but it was not the same. The mirror partition remained, but Alice was in front of it, at Kit's table. He was unshackled. On the table were plastic cups of coffee.

It was hard to sit with her like this. Her hand was so close he could have taken it in his own. After so long as a creature of his imagination, the reality of her presence was too much.

He said, 'They'll never find it out there.'

'You don't know the equipment they've got. You would be amazed. Believe me, we won't fail to find it.'

He could have reached out and touched her cheek.

He said, 'What happens to me now?'

'Well, when it all checks out, we move on to the next stage. You move on, anyway.'

'What do you mean?'

'I won't be here,' she said. 'I'm shipping out.' Quickly she went on, 'So there's a few things I need to check with you, for the file, in the hope that very soon we will be closing it.'

'Where am I?'

'That's not the important thing right now.'

'Who is General Bartok?'

'You don't need to know any of that.'

'Why did you hide your face? Why are you showing it to me now?'

'That was just the protocol. Now we're in a different place, right?'

Kit said, 'Don't go.'

There was an explosion outside and close at hand, and a shiver shook the mirrored screen.

Alice glanced into her quivering reflection and sighed. 'I do like you, Kit,' she said. 'I respect you. You've made me think some. You're a good man.'

He was assailed by details of her appearance: the clips that held her hair in place, a scar on her hand.

'Please don't go,' he said. 'They'll kill me.'

'Kit, you got to tell me this, for the file—'

'Please, you know it's true.'

'Right now, let's focus on these things I got to ask.'

'You're the only one who can help me.'

'What is CSF?'

'What?'

'What is CSF?'

'Where did you hear that?'

'It came up.'

'She called it that.'

'She called what that?'

'Your country, her country.'

'This is who?'

'Lara.'

'And what is that?'

'CSF.'

'But what does that stand for?'

'Confederated States of Fuckface.' There was a pause as Alice noted it down.

'Kit,' she said. 'I won't let them kill you.'

Alice said goodbye to Kit. They took him to the mess hall to eat. The escorting soldier left him there, and seemed to forget about him. The cooks and kitchen servers were chattering to one another in the highest of spirits. It was late by the time he was returned to his cell. When the soldier removed the hood, he was already in darkness. Even before the departing footsteps had echoed away into nothing, he had become conscious of something else in the silence, a human presence, invisible, but unmistakable.

'Hello,' said Kit to the dark.

'Hello,' a voice replied immediately. 'You must be Mr Rabone.' It came from the cell opposite. A man's voice: warm, richly accented, ironic.

'I am,' said Kit.

'You will be surprised to find me here,' the voice said. 'Allow me to introduce myself.'

'That's all right,' Kit said. 'I know who you are.'

11

There was another round of explosions, close enough to impart a buzz of pressure to the air even within the walls of the cell block.

The voice gave a chuckle and a sigh. 'There are more and more of them, are there not? It won't be long now.' Then it said, 'I know you too. I heard about you.'

As Kit contemplated the darkness, he saw that it was not absolute. A trace of exterior light, from clouded stars or the arc lamps that lit up the perimeter, set the small high window at the back of his cell dimly aglow. It was the faintest kind of radiance, little more than a variation in the texture of black. But by it, Kit made out the bars of his own cell and the one opposite, and a shuffling of shadow in the space beyond.

'I heard about your little girl,' said Dr Mochtar. 'Our hosts here told me. I am sorry.'

'Thank you,' said Kit. He had trained himself to choke and weep whenever Helen was mentioned but here, with a thump of exhilaration, he realised that it was unnecessary. 'Thank you. But you see she's—'

The voice interrupted him. 'Let us not talk of it,' it said, almost sternly; Kit saw or imagined a hand raised in the darkness. 'Let us talk of cheerful matters.'

Nothing cheerful came to Kit's mind. The silence filled with the sound of insects in the trees outside. A large number of questions occurred to him. It was difficult to know which one to put first.

'What are you doing here?' he asked.

'I was . . . snatched, I suppose you would say. I was betrayed. We tried to take precautions, but they have such resources.' Kit detected a thickness in his speech, as though from a swollen mouth. 'I thought they would kill me quickly, but that wouldn't have been enough. They wanted me to make certain . . . declarations. Recordings. They wanted me to call everything off. I declined.'

'Did they hurt you?'

'They did hurt me. In various ways. Did they hurt you?'

'Yes, they did. In various ways.'

'And now they have done with me, and tonight they have put me in here with you. They are sentimental people at heart, are they not? That old-fashioned idea that, although they are justified in doing what they intend to do, it is not right for me to be alone the night before.'

Kit became aware of an individual insect, which had fetched up in a loud trilling close to the cell window.

'Tomorrow?' he said

'At dawn, I'm informed – another cliché. It could be one more of their games but I choose to believe it this time. It will not be carried out by our hosts here, of course, but what they call the "interim administration". There has already been a "tribunal". I am convicted and I am sentenced. I am to be "custodially transferred" and then—'

From the darkness came a click, or a swallowing noise.

'For what?'

He chuckled. 'Treason. Murder. Terrorism. Collusion with foreign powers. Embezzlement. Corruption. And unlicensed possession of a satellite telephone. On the last charge I am guilty, by the way. I knew there was some document that was needed. My secretary had inquired – there was always so much else to get done. Ah – and drug trafficking.'

'I confessed to that myself,' said Kit.

'I confessed when I was bleeding and in pain. But not to the camera that they set up after they had made me look respectable.' He chuckled again. 'That made them angry, of course, but I think that confessions make them angry anyway.' He paused. 'When you hurt people, you give up the pretence of believing that you are in the right. All that you assert is your own power. They know this, at their core. They believe that they want you to talk, but when you do they are humiliated.'

There was another series of flat explosions.

The darkness rippled around him, as Dr Mochtar laughed again. 'Closer! They are getting closer.' Then he sighed.

'I cannot sleep,' he said. 'Will you stay awake with me tonight?'

Time passed, but it was impossible to reckon it. The square of the window was Kit's only clock, but its dimness was unaltered. The voice in the opposite cell became silent. He heard rustling, as of a body extending itself along a pallet, and gabbled articulations that might have been prayers.

Tears came to Kit's eyes. So much about the moment

was overwhelming. Partly it was the experience, all but forgotten, of exchanging speech with a human being who had no power over him – and with this man, of all people. In the village, no one had been spoken of with greater excitement or love. He had the status of a figure from folklore: to meet him here in the dark was like encountering one of the demi-gods from Obson's stories. His face, the face from the posters, was invisible, but Kit knew his voice from the speeches that the villagers used to listen to again and again on the chief's cassette player. The prospect of what was to come was horrifying, but it was kept at bay by the absence of obvious panic in Dr Mochtar himself. How, Kit asked himself, was he to behave in such a situation? To talk into the darkness, to solace and divert? To remain tactfully silent? For the first time since his separation from Helen, he experienced a sense of responsibility for another creature. To his surprise, in the presence of a man condemned to die, his strongest feeling was embarrassment.

'Do you want to talk?' he said into the dark.

The rustling renewed itself. There was a snuffling exhalation that might have been sobbing, but which turned into a chuckle.

'I do, in fact,' said the voice. 'There is nothing left for me but talking.'

The silence extended. Kit's discomfort increased. He had to say something.

He said, – I learned to speak the Tongue.

The language clothed him like a carnival costume. He said, – I speak it poorly.

To his relief, Dr Mochtar laughed in delight. 'You speak it beautifully. You speak it like my mother.'

– I studied, but I was a poor student.

'She came from one of the villages close to yours.' He sighed. 'The land is beautiful there – the forest, the creatures of the forest. I used to love travelling through it, when we were campaigning. The boats, the walking. We used to walk for days. I didn't go to every village, but I must have gone to most.'

– The people of my village loved you, Kit said.

'They are a precious people, given to love.'

– Especially my friend. My good friend, who died. He loved you very much. You are a hero.

'And that is true. By common consent. And you know that is one of the saddest things? The need that people have for heroes.'

The voice in the facing cell talked, and kept talking, in its supple and ironic English. Kit listened, and prompted it with words of his own in the Tongue. The simplicity of the expressions available to him tamed the situation; the clumsiness of his speech washed away sophistication and left what remained pure and true. Sometimes Dr Mochtar fell silent; sometimes he soliloquised without pause. He laughed and sighed; he veered between rambling anecdotes and theoretical abstraction. The obvious way to understand this, Kit supposed, was as an expression of suppressed terror. But there was a self-consciousness about him, an air of mockery and defiance, not directed at Kit personally, but almost as if he was speaking in front of an audience.

'Mr Rabone,' said Dr Mochtar. 'May I call you Christian?'

– Yes.

'There is something I remember, Christian.'
He began to sing, in a clear, surprisingly high voice.

> Who would true valour see
> let him come hither
> one here will constant be
> come wind, come weather

Dr Mochtar said, 'I went to good schools, you see. I went to the church school, as well as the mosque school. I went to every school I could.'

He talked about his childhood. Kit encouraged him with questions and murmurs of understanding. He knew much of the story from Obson, who owned a battered book, printed on pulpy paper, that recounted it in reverent terms. Mochtar was the youngest of six; his mother had died when he was small. His father was a remote, silent man who caught river fish, and drank. The children were brought up by the oldest daughter, Bessa. When Mochtar was still a boy, she was wooed by a young man.

'She, he, both of them – they were only a few years older than me,' he said. 'They were kids themselves. But she had looked after me from when I was tiny. She was more like a mother than a sister – she was the only mother I had. And I felt as if he was stealing her from me. I hated him.' He laughed. The young man was Rollo Konrud, who would become his brother-in-law and his greatest friend and ally.

He worked hard in his schools. The pastor and the imam took personal interest in his education. After his father slumped into drunkenness, the family was supported by

Rollo, who married Bessa and became a teacher. Mochtar won a foreign scholarship, one of a handful given out across the whole country. He said goodbye to his family and flew to Rainland. 'It took two days,' he said. 'I was crying all the way.' The city in autumn was cold and grey; he knew no one there, and had no money. In his second year, he began to make friends; in his third, he won prizes. He loved dealing with patients; the patients responded to his humour and his warmth. He qualified top in his year.

Wherever he turned, there were opportunities: famous hospitals, research institutes, private practice. To everyone's surprise, he gave up medicine completely for a new scholarship and a new university in the Superpower.

'I wanted to see that country,' he said. 'And I wanted to use my mind in a different way. I understood the body, I understood it enough to treat it. But I wanted to study the world. I wanted to understand how power works.'

He won more degrees, honours, prizes. Within a few years he had a place on the faculty; there he met his wife. Kit knew the story from Obson – the older politics professor who had been his teacher. It was a time of tumult in the Superpower. 'These gulfs, these big crevasses, were opening up in the ground,' said Dr Mochtar. 'They opened so quickly – you had to react immediately, and jump, and then there was no going back. You were stuck on one side or the other.' As a brilliant young Muslim, his opinions were in demand. He gave speeches and made television appearances. He said angry things that were misunderstood and impossible to take back; he fell out with many of his new friends.

'I wanted to be original in my thinking,' he said. 'It's not that I didn't find people out there to admire. But it is not my habit to admire people. It was the quest I was on, to find my own way. People do not like that.'

His wife had a baby. The child was, in Obson's words, a 'defective'. The marriage did not last.

He returned home, alone. 'Those who remembered me were glad to see me,' he said. 'Some of them were impressed that I had come back. But many of them assumed that I had done so because I had failed.' He was reunited with Rollo, who had become a famous activist in social causes. Mochtar joined him. He lived in the capital, working among the poor.

Steadily, the humanitarian work became political. The grey man had come to power, by crooked means. The social work developed into a movement against him. There were marches and boycotts, raids and arrests. The struggle went on for years, running down dead ends, exhausting itself, picking itself up again. Finally, overconfident and under pressure, the grey man permitted an election, believing that he could not lose.

'That was when the hero was born,' said Dr Mochtar. 'We talked about it for a long time – Rollo had many ideas. We were agreed in theory: the hero should be the movement itself, the principles behind it. But you have to show a face – you have to give people something they can feel. We spent years organising, building capacity, making networks. Nothing moved. Then one night Rollo and I tossed a coin. One of us would be the face. And I won, or lost.'

It began with a speech in the football stadium in the capital, and then another, and then a speech every week, in markets, churches, schools and mosques all over the country. Mochtar and Rollo rode trucks, took boats and walked. The crowds became large, then huge, and then immense. 'Ten months later I won a national election,' he said. 'The grey man was out. And I found my own face turning grey.'

'Up there where you lived,' Dr Mochtar said, 'that was some of the hardest campaigning. Not the people – they were always kind. I mean getting across the idea to them, to the older ones at least in that region. Until my mother's time, those people had no idea of nation. You can imagine how it was: a village or two within walking distance, a jumble of languages, similar, but all different. The border with the Neighbour is so close there, but it means nothing. When you asked a man who his people were, he would tell you his village or the name of his father. It was only when they put in a teacher, that was when it began. My mother remembered it. The green flag on the wall of the classroom. The big map. Singing the song every morning, and all of it in the Tongue. They didn't know it, those teachers had no idea, but they were missionaries.'

He said, 'You, however, are not a missionary. What are you, then? What brought you here?'

The square of the window continued to register its minimal illumination. Kit considered this question. Even in his own language, no explanation that he could give was clear or adequate. With an inward shrug, he gave up fumbling for clarity and precision, and fell in with the few words that were available to him in the Tongue.

– I came for the sake of my woman, he said. – I came

to join a village. I came to live with other people, and to be alone.

'It is a strange impulse that makes someone choose to go far away from their home, and to stay there,' Dr Mochtar said. 'I went away to learn, to get an education, to qualify. Then I came back. But you, you had all those things, those opportunities I wanted – they were given to you there, in your home.'

– I wanted to escape from country.

'From your country?'

– From country. He struggled to locate the right words. – From the idea of country.

'But why escape that? It is a beautiful idea.'

– It is a trap.

'You are thinking of the people who keep us here – of our hosts. You are thinking about them and what they call their pride, and what they do to us here. And you are right: there is a straight line between that kind of patriotism and torture. But the idea of a country – a country in itself is not a bad thing. It can be a magnificent thing. Power concentrated out of the will of the people, employed for the common good. But there has to be humility.'

Dr Mochtar said, 'Do you know the words of our constitution? Rollo wrote them. I was the orator, perhaps, but he was the poet. Everyone knows those words, even when they do not understand them – even the imps in the villages remember them.'

Kit knew the famous words. Dr Mochtar began to recite them in a soft, even tone, distinct from the droll inflections of his English.

– No child of this land, born and breathing beneath

its canopy of green, shall exalt any other above the rest because of his race or the colour of his skin. Man, woman; black, dark, brown, yellow, fair; hunter, fisher, farmer, poor man, beggar; teacher, student, man-without-letters – all are equal and partake of the same spirit of life. The differences between them – in body, gold and accomplishment – are as many as there are men and women. But they are one in their essential nature, and their capacity to serve the cause of justice.

Dr Mochtar said, 'Such words – everyone responds to them. The feeling of being joined to other people. To your family, your class, your school. You must know that feeling, from your own life. What about in sport, what about—'

– Football, said Kit.

Dr Mochtar laughed.

– I don't care about football, said Kit.

'You are lucky that you do not have to care. Football is what people care about when they care about nothing else.'

Kit said, – I was with my daughter and her mother. We lived together. I fed my daughter, and I washed her. I carried her through the forest. Does that make us a team?

Through the darkness, Kit sensed that Dr Mochtar was either nodding, or shaking his head, but could not tell which.

– I am not typical. I know that.

'But you are, you are! Even in rejecting it, you are a true-born man of your country. I cannot think of one more typical – that is your pride. You carry it with you. It is tattooed on your bones.'

*

'Rollo was a great footballer,' said Dr Mochtar. 'He played football the way he wrote – such natural rhythm and fluency. If you don't care for the game, it won't mean much to you, but it's true. He was a great tall, gangling man. Those times when we had to wear suits and ties, for the ambassadors and the foreign delegations – in the photographs he always looks so uncomfortable. But in his shorts and his football boots – he wore these long shorts, very old-fashioned – he took on this elegance. I was stronger, smaller, more aggressive. But he was so much . . . sweeter on the pitch. We used to play every week, even after the election, for a while at least, until – well, until there was no time.'

Kit remembered Rollo's face, which used to appear at the bottom of the election posters: a crooked, clownish smile; a thin, elongated, comical face. When Obson had talked of Rollo, it was only ever in passing, as a secondary player in the political drama. But powerful currents of reminiscence were driving Dr Mochtar. To listen was the important thing.

'Too sweet, perhaps,' he said. 'Too soft and subtle. So, I remember when we were quite young. I was just a kid, and he was trying to win my sister. She told him to take me out, and make friends with her kid brother, because I was so angry. He should have just played football with me, but he wanted to take me fishing on the river. He thought that was an exciting adventure. He was trying so hard. But that was no treat for me – that was what I had been doing with my father all my life. We went out anyway. I was small, but I was a good fisherman. I knew exactly how to handle the boat, and where to take it. I remember my sister waving us off – she looked so worried. I took the boat to the best pool, and we baited the lines, and soon we were pulling out big fat fish. And I was yanking them off the line, and banging their heads, and dropping them bloody into the bucket. Rollo was carefully removing the hook, holding them gently as they thrashed, and exclaiming as he looked at them, at the fins and the scales, how delicate they were, the green of them in the sunlight, and then he was gently lowering them back into the water and letting them go.'

Dr Mochtar said, 'When it came to the technicalities, Rollo was the expert: economics, development theory. He just didn't have the nose for the deal. He couldn't identify compromise, in the way you have to. But sometimes I think it should have been him. And when we tossed the coin, I knew that he wanted to be the hero.'

'They gave me these,' said Dr Mochtar. 'And this.' There was a flinty click and the low flame of a lighter flared in the darkness. By its illumination, Kit registered a hand, an arm, and a cheek rough with beard. The other hand held a packet of cigarettes. Then the flame disappeared.

'The consolation of the condemned man – such cliché. I don't smoke and I don't intend to start now. Here.' There was a clattering sound as he tossed the objects between the cells. The packet bounced off the bars, but after a few moments of groping Kit laid his fingers on the lighter and held it in his fist. The flame shed a dim glow around his hand, but its brightness cast the cell opposite into darker and more impenetrable shadow.

'Who was it who hurt you?' said Dr Mochtar.
– The soldiers. What about you?

'All of them, at different times. The soldiers didn't mean it. I mean their hearts were not in it. The woman meant it.'

– The young woman?

'The older.'

– Alice?

Dr Mochtar exhaled humorously. 'Don't put too much faith in the names they give you. Or the personalities they project. Or even the colour of their hair and eyes.' He laughed, then spoke in a serious, confiding tone. 'It was the older woman. The spy. She took me to her – kitchen. And then there was the general.'

– The general?

'You haven't met the general yet? That's just a formality really. It's the last thing. But before that there was a lot of talking. It's touching, in a way, the effort they expend to prove themselves right. For someone like the grey man and his thugs, it was enough to have you in their power, completely. If they could hurt you, and you couldn't hurt them back, they had won. But these people need more. They have a truth, and a need to reveal it. They need you to see the world as they do. They talk about fundamentalism – they're very anxious about that. And yet they assume, without even recognising the assumption, that their own system, their own way, is true, now and forever, and that one day soon it will be the faith of the whole world.' He clapped his hands together suddenly in the dark, and made a *brrrr* sound, as if shivering. 'Democracy!' he said. 'Such a glamorous word.'

Kit was thinking about Alice and her appearance.

'Democracy's not perfect,' he said in English. 'But it's better than any other way.'

'It's a vehicle,' said Dr Mochtar. 'Not the destination.'

Kit was trying to remember her hair. He had not paid it close attention, but perhaps it was dyed. Was the green of her eyes imparted by lenses?

'It's everything, isn't it?' he said. 'What other destination is there?'

'A decent life.' The voice was strained with irony. 'Dignity. The components of self-respect.'

'But that is what you offered,' Kit said. 'And you won.'

'We certainly won. We beat the grey man. But not through democracy alone.'

'What else then?'

'We used every means.'

'What means did you use?'

'We *mobilised*.'

'You mean – do you mean that you cheated?'

'Cheated!' said Dr Mochtar. 'We brought about the just result. The grey man, he had everything. Money, so much money, control of the election commission and the counting machines, control of the security forces and the courts.'

'But you had everyone on your side. Everyone wanted you to win.'

'My friend – if only that was enough. It was not. It wasn't enough that people supported us, that everyone wanted him out and us in – we had to make a victory.'

'So you did cheat.'

'We *won*. Do you understand how difficult it was? And an election – that is only the start of it.'

The feeling of unease that had been growing in Kit coagulated into a physical queasiness. 'What does that mean?' he said.

'Do you know how difficult it is to run a country like

this? Not even to run it well. Just to keep it going without extremes of plunder and incompetence? To run a modestly corrupt government – it is very hard. Because everything is pulling you, pulling you towards the old ways.'

He paused. There were sounds of drinking, and of a cup being placed back on the cell's concrete floor. He went on.

'Even the good people, the best people – they are all suffering in their own lives. Everyone has a sick grandmother, or a nephew who needs an education, or a baby with a cough that won't go away. The big men, the rotten ones, the bastards – they want everything, and it's easy to say no to them. But everyone else just wants a little bit, a small piece for themselves, to pass on to the people they love. And when you are face to face with someone like that, it is a cruelty not to help them, to refuse to share what can be shared.'

'You're talking about paying bribes,' said Kit. 'You make it sound like social security.'

'We don't even have that. Because of this system that we inherited. It wasn't us who made it, you know. It was white people – the people who raised you. They arrived and forced their rules upon us, and when the whole idea of ruling people thousands of miles away became too ridiculous even to bother justifying, they upped and left and handed over to people like the grey man, who was just like them, but greedier and more stupid.'

The explosions continued; most of them were muffled and distant, so frequent as to have become part of the background. Much louder was the large insect rasping just outside the window.

'You know him, that creature?' said Dr Mochtar. 'I don't know the English word. You must have seen them – an extraordinary-looking thing, like a cross between a mantis and a wasp. There are many stories about him. It is good luck to have him in your house. But he is so loud that nobody can sleep.'

There were questions to which Kit needed answers; this, he saw, might be his only opportunity to ask them.

'What are the explosions?' he asked.

'Some kind of field artillery, I believe. There were heavier things too, but they seem to have stopped for now.'

'Who is firing them?'

'I believe that it is our people. And our friends.'

'Your people? What are they doing over here?'

'They are trying to liberate our country.' He gave his snuffling chuckle again. 'A lot has been happening while you've been confined by our hosts.'

'But how did they get here?' he asked, before reflecting that he did not know where here was.

There was a puzzled pause. 'In the usual ways. As for our friends, they made an amphibious landing and a series of airborne assaults.'

'Your friends?'

'Who else would help us?'

'Who are your friends?'

'The only people who have the capacity. The only ones prepared to take on our invaders.'

Kit understood with a sudden chill of surprise.

'The chonks!'

'Good grief, man. You can't call them that.'

'That is them, that is their army, firing artillery?'

'Some of it is, as they say, "outgoing" – but yes.'

'A foreign army. How?'

'I invited them.'

'When?'

'Very shortly before I was betrayed.'

Kit stood up and paced between the walls of the cell.

'It was a difficult decision. There was opposition. In the end I had no choice.'

Kit had the lighter in his hand and was flicking it on and off. The exhausted blue flame was close to dying. 'But you know what it will mean?' he asked.

'It means that we have a chance.'

'Even if you win, even if they win – afterwards, they won't just leave. They will expect to have influence. They will change your country. They will change everything.'

'We will change our own country. And, as you must have noticed, there have been some changes anyway. Imposed upon us, through violence, without our consent.'

'There is a difference. The Superpower—'

'Must we still call them that?'

'Call them what you like. I don't defend them. At least, I don't defend everything – it would be ridiculous. But there are freedoms.'

'You sound just like Rollo – you would have got on well.'

'It is not perfect, but it is better. It is much better.'

'I will say to you what I said to him. We had a choice – a narrow choice, but a choice nonetheless. By the end, it was the choice of whether to accept defeat, or to accept help in fighting back. And it is not only that. In the long run, it is the choice of how to live. Our hosts here believe that their way is the only way. To put it at its mildest: more and more people in the world are questioning that.'

Kit was shaking his head.

'You think this is it?' said Dr Mochtar. 'That these existing arrangements are humanity's final, perfect form?'

'It's not – it's not so bad.'

'It is not so bad for you.'

'You have to give people the right to choose. That government that is helping you – they take away that right.'

'Rights are not enough in itself. They're nothing on their own. You have to have the education to understand them. You have to have the money to take advantage of them.'

'But your – "friends". It's a dictatorship. Everyone, in their guts, everyone wants freedom.'

'And everyone who's honest knows in their guts that's a delusion. Those who are free, who have the wherewithal to be free, naturally give the impression that it is easy. That anyone can do it, if they try hard enough – if they "compete". But in the real world – it's so obvious, isn't it? What do I need to explain to you, of all people? You are the one who flew across the world to a jungle because you wanted to be left alone. The people in your village, the people who gave you a home, they do not have such choices. They are stuck. Born stuck, grow up stuck, die stuck. And not despite the way the world is, but because of it.'

'You were not stuck. You were given all that opportunity.'

'I was one of three very lucky ones – three a year, in the whole country. It "trickles" down? Who really believes that now?'

Dr Mochtar said, 'Even for people in the rich places – the people on top, the winners – I wonder: is it really the life you want, that life of competition? At the church school they taught us about the gladiators. Think of that – little black kids in a schoolhouse in the jungle, learning about the Romans. Some of those gladiators got a sword, some got a net and a trident, and some just got a little dagger. Is that what you wanted for your child – to throw her into the arena, like the gladiators? Maybe your kid's a lucky one and gets a shield and one of the big axes, and she fights and wins, and walks out a champion. But even if she does, what about the ones who don't, the ones who get the little knife? Is that what you hope for your daughter, that she leaves bodies behind her, bleeding on the sand?'

'You don't give people opportunity by forcing yourself on them from above.'

'That's exactly what our friends have done. A billion people have become affluent and educated. Nothing like it has ever been achieved in history.'

'But at such a cost – the oppression and the violence.'

'Mr Rabone, Christian – do I need to point out the irony in what you have just said, and where you are saying it?' He stood up and gripped the bars of his cell. He shook them so that they groaned and clanged. 'You can't look at your own face, but look at mine. Look at the state of it. See what they have done to you.'

It was still too dim to make out the bruises and scars. But the outlines of Dr Mochtar's face were becoming visible as the first traces of light entered through the small window high in Kit's cell.

'I have a daughter too,' Dr Mochtar said.

'I heard that,' said Kit.

'She is with my wife, over there. My ex-wife. I used to speak to them, whenever I could.'

Kit was trying to make sense of what he had been told, turning over in his mind the new information.

'With my daughter,' he said, 'you have to be in her presence to communicate with her. She does not really understand a voice. Only touch. So, if I am honest, there has been no communication.'

'That must be very hard.'

'It was hardest when she was born. It was obvious at once that something was wrong. I didn't handle it well. Why not? That kind of thing is always a possibility. I am a doctor – I understand the nature of that condition. We made a fuss at the time, got lawyers on to the hospital, but even then I knew it was no one's fault. We learned quickly what the situation was, what the limitations would be. I never forget that sense of helplessness. It was like walls closing around you. You could batter at them, but it made no difference. All you can do is accept, and in time it becomes possible to do that. I love her, of course, and love makes the difference. I realised something early on, about the pain that I was feeling. It wasn't that she will never read a book, or get a joke, or be a mother. The hardest thing is knowing that throughout her life she will be vulnerable. Life is hard enough, when you are tough and cunning. But she has no defences at all.'

He laughed. 'Rollo had so many kids. I lost count of them. Big, strapping, healthy boys and girls.'

He was silent, then he said, 'The hospital where my wife gave birth was by the sea. I spent days there in the room with my wife and daughter. During the tests and the surgeries, I used to go out for long walks on the beach. It was the first time I'd seen anything like that – cold ocean smashing down, great white waves, wind making your eyes water. It was a long beach, and all the way down there were plastic bottles, and lumps of polystyrene, and planks of broken wood. There was this kind of foam that I had never seen before, this froth of fine grey-brown bubbles that had been pushed up and dropped by the sea. The waves were big, but the froth was so fine and delicate that it lingered after the waves had pulled back, like piles of feathers. The wind worried away at it, and broke off bits of it, and then flung them off. The bubbles are trembling on the beach, between the sea and the wind, and being blown away and soon they're gone. I never felt sadder than when I watched that foam, lifting off and blowing away.'

'The things they say about you are true,' Kit said.
'Many people say many things about me.'
'Collusion with foreign powers. Treason. Corruption.'
'I preferred it when you spoke like a woman.'
Kit hesitated. – What happened to Rollo?
'He died.'
– Did you kill him?
'The thing I will miss the most,' he said, 'the best thing of all was the election campaign. The rallies, the songs. The day of victory. What a moment! People all over the world saw that, and they cheered. And yet after all that, what actually changes for the better? Perhaps nothing. Perhaps something changes, and then four years later it changes back. It's a carnival. It's a circus that distracts everyone from what is under their noses – things that should never be allowed. Disease, parasites. Children hungry, growing up stunted.

You know that out in that jungle, those highlands where you lived, there are people who don't even have villages?'

– I know.

'They don't plant. They don't build. They have no access to medicine. They just shuffle through the forest, sleeping on logs, eating grubs. They live like animals.'

– I met them.

'That was one of my biggest arguments with Rollo. We almost came to blows. Some anthropologists, some activists – people from your country – they got to him. Persuaded him that those people had to be preserved, protected, like some endangered rhino. But there had been a contract agreed with my friends, for the highlands. An enormous contract: timber, roads, even hydro. I had been negotiating for months. It would have changed everything for those people. There would have been so many jobs, there would have been new schools – the investors would have built them. Rollo was against it all the way – the debt, the environmental damage. He argued. I told him that I had made my decision. He always denied it, but went behind my back. He went to the partners, to the financers – he must have done – and he undermined me. He made them doubt. There was so much money involved. They began to worry about our commitment. And the whole thing fell through.'

He banged the bars, which clanged dully. 'I weep to think of it even now. Hundreds of millions, billions in the end – for decades to come. But they walked away. They went to the Neighbour and made their investment there. All that lost for one man's stubbornness and pride.'

– I met those people. I met the nomads.

'Then you know what I am talking about.'

– You talk about freedom. Well, those people are free.

'Now you are sounding like Rollo again. They are prisoners. Of ignorance, illiteracy, of the simplest diseases. They refuse vaccination. Do you know what their life expectancy is?'

Kit shouted, – They saved my daughter.

'Stop, stop.'

– I will have my say. You have had yours.

He spoke in English again, and it was like landing punches. 'The nomads saved her life. They saved mine. And they have Helen, and they have the memory card, and that is what will save all of us. Those people are free.'

Dr Mochtar looked up and Kit could see his smile. He could see the thick spectacles, and the swelling of his face, the knees pulled up, his bandaged hands around them. He looked up at the square window high in his own cell. As they had talked, it had become fully light.

– Dawn, he said.

'It is past dawn,' said Dr Mochtar.

– But I thought that at dawn—

'It seems that I am saved.'

Kit could make out the pallet on which Dr Mochtar sat. On the floor beside it, there was a tray with a cup and an empty dish. On the pallet, Kit could see wires that trailed through the bars of the cell, a glint of metal, a bulb of black foam.

– What is that? Kit said.

'Speak English, man, for God's sake,' he said. 'Use your words.'

He didn't know the word anyway. 'It's a microphone.'

'It is.'

'Is that – is that recording?'

'I am sorry,' Dr Mochtar said.

'You betrayed me.'

'You have saved me.'

There were sounds at the end of the corridor: the voices and boots of approaching soldiers.

'They've been listening to the whole thing?'

'I am sorry.'

'They never were going to kill you.'

'They were. I believed they would. But I negotiated.'

'So you are safe now.'

'It depended – on your information. I am sorry.'

'You betrayed me.'

'I tried to stop you. I tried to stop myself. But they hurt me too much. And I don't want to die. Not here, not this morning. You understand – another day of life.' He squeezed his hand over the end of the microphone beside him. He whispered, 'And, listen – there! It may not matter.'

As he spoke, explosions could be heard, distant and close at hand.

'You see! You see! It's close. They are coming.'

He began to sing:

> Hobgoblin nor foul fiend
> can daunt his spirit
> he knows he at the end
> shall life inherit.

The soldiers were in the cell, pulling Kit to his feet.

'As for Rollo,' said Dr Mochtar. 'The situation had become impossible.'

Kit's wrists were being cuffed behind his back.

'The nation was at war, and he was blocking everything. Like driving at speed on a wet road, and the passenger is grabbing at the wheel.'

The hood was being tugged over his head.

'And I was right, as it turned out – he betrayed me. They picked me up before he had even died.' He laughed. 'He thought that he had fired first, but I had already pulled my own trigger.'

12

The soldiers led Kit outside, removed the hood, and ran with him at a jog-trot as the sun rose. It was the first time that he had seen anything beyond the cluster of buildings in which he had been confined; outside, the camp was twitchy with movement and disorder. Voices were echoing from unseen loudspeakers, imparting calm but urgent instructions. Khaki vehicles were racing along the roads between the pre-fab cubes. Soldiers were converging from all directions on the mustering stations, fastening shirts and webbing as they walked.

'What's with the chow situation, corporal?' Kit overheard an officer saying as he ran past.

'Chow hall closed up, sir. The chonks all gone.'

'All of them?'

'Every man jack, sir. Cooks, KP, cleaners, drivers, maintenance. They all upped and went.'

Artillery was being launched from across the camp. The batteries were obscured by the low clutter of the buildings, but the rockets themselves rushed into the air on parabolas of grey vapour before disappearing beyond the horizon. For a while the whoosh of the outgoing shells overwhelmed the sounds of those coming in. But then, without any premonitory whine or fizz, an explosion lit up the ground a hundred yards away, transmitting a flash of white light and a punch of heat and pressure. The soldiers flattened themselves on the ground and against the floor of their vehicles. The sergeant leaped nimbly on to Kit, pressing protectively on his back.

As the air regained its equilibrium, everyone jumped up again, whistling and whooping and shaking their heads.

Kit had expected kicks and abuse, but his escorts were more anxious than angry. They uncuffed his hands to make it easier to run, and strapped a loose-fitting helmet under his chin. Wherever they were leading him, it was far from the jail block that was their home. They were confused and uneasy in the new territory. There were frowning consultations and hissed muttering into the walkie-talkies.

Beyond the aluminium roofs, the sun was rising above the horizon of the camp. Kit and the soldiers ran towards it between shadows and golden stripes of light. Every few minutes the sergeant halted to take stock of time and position, while his men sipped water from oval flasks. They paid Kit no personal attention; his status had shifted from that of despised captive to a consignment to be delivered on time and intact. Above the noise of vehicles, the explosions were increasing in frequency and volume. Columns of smoke rose from a dozen places. A flight of black helicopters struggled into the sky from a distant spot and darted out over the trees.

The desertion of the migrant workers had left the camp in a state of extreme disorder. Trucks carrying fuel, water and rubbish had been abandoned at angles across the roads on slashed and deflated tires. Heaps of dumped refuse bags had burst under the wheels and tracks, discharging squirts of plastic and kitchen slime. Among the soldiers, the absence of the camp's domestics was a cause of greater indignation than the rockets that were falling upon it. Every conversation that Kit overheard reflected on the treachery and cunning of the 'chonks'.

'Little fuckers just scat, sweet as fucking rats.'

'They was sabs all along, man, just watching all the time. They were waiting for this, waiting for the word.'

The flow of traffic on the road thickened and became dense. The green vehicles slowed to a stop before an unseen obstruction. An awful smell filled the air, intimate and overpowering; the soldiers grimaced and pressed hands and neckerchiefs to their faces. The sergeant went ahead to investigate. He returned with a face knotted in disgust.

'Back up, and reroute. Fucking chonks took the sewerage vehicles and bent them cross the road and emptied the tanks. There's a sea of shit up ahead, hundred yards of it.'

They trekked back out of the zone of stench, and traced a new course around and in between buildings. Kit could see from the sun that they were moving towards the east.

They came to a mess hall at the far edge of the camp. The outermost fence was visible beyond it, a cliff face of electrified razor wire. A red civilian car was pulled up in front, incongruously sporty, with a rolled-back, open top; a single sentry stood in front of it cradling his rifle.

'Is this building secure?' the sergeant asked.

The sentry nodded. 'Fire crew, EOD been and gone. She's waiting for you.'

The kitchen of the mess hall was a scene of extravagant

disorder. Cabinets and freezers gaped open and everything edible had been heaped on the floor: legs of meat, discs of pink mince, quarts of milk, crunching hills of dried noodles. One wall dribbled with the residue of hundreds of eggs that had been hurled against it. The gas stoves had been left with the flames turned up beneath pots of oil. Several had caught fire, blackening the ceiling and filling the air with bitter smoke. One saucepan contained a freshly boiled stew of human shit. Foam and powder from fire extinguishers added to the disorder of smell and texture. On the wall facing the eggs, a line of huge ideograms had been sprayed in red paint, and beside them the cartoon of a snarling, smiling, victorious face.

The soldiers picked their way through the hall, stepping disgustedly around the worst of the floor drool. Kit walked beside them.

'Jesus fucking Christ.'

'They animals.'

'Damn waste of good chow.'

A loud explosion rattled the windows of the mess hall; everyone ducked.

Kit became aware of someone else moving through the smoking kitchen, a slight, intent figure in civilian colours, stepping between the upturned drawers and cupboards of utensils and placing objects into a rucksack.

'Ma'am,' the sergeant called out. 'The detainee is with us, as instructed. Apologize for the delay, ma'am. It's hell out there.'

Alice turned towards them. She wore a baseball cap, and her hair was tied up under it. She had on dark sunglasses, although the light inside the mess hall was dim.

'Take the detainee to the CO's mess. Through that door, out back.'

She returned to her examination of the contents of the kitchen.

The soldiers put the cuffs and hood back on Kit. Then they took them off again, because it was too difficult to lead him through the litter of hazards.

The officers' kitchen was smaller than the main hall and, apart from more graffiti and a token turd in one corner, it was unvandalised. The soldiers looked about uncertainly, then cuffed Kit to a chair. At the far end of the room were sinks and stoves. In the middle there was a table, with rings burned on to its surface by hot vessels. The sergeant went out. The soldiers who remained stood about, ill at ease. The sergeant put his head around the door, nodded, and all of them left the room.

Kit was alone again. The explosions continued, remote and muted in this marginal zone of the camp. He could hear the irregular drip of spilled liquids, and the faint singing of the insects beyond the fence. The cuffs dug into his wrists. He became conscious again of his life as a line, wavering at times, but strong and unbroken, and of this moment as its destination. Here he was: here, and nowhere else. The present bore down on him with insupportable weight; he made a conscious effort to think about the past.

He remembered a moment when Helen was still tiny, when he had warmed water on the fire, and given her a bath. She grizzled and complained as he sponged and soaped her on the plastic mat. Until then her cries had always been soothed at the moment of being lowered into the warm water: a grimacing spasm at the transition, then a glazed peace came over her. Kit took it to be a remembrance of the earliest part of her existence, those months of semi-being in the fluid of Lara's insides. That evening, though, the cessation of wailing was momentary; the water brought no relief. She had ceased to be a thing of water and become a creature of the air.

Alice was in the room. Kit was afraid of her. She was standing over the chair to which he was bound. Beside her stood the sentry from outside. She was smiling down at Kit. It was the same smile as the red face sprayed on to the wall by the departing servants. The dark glasses concealed her eyes, but Kit looked at the hair tucked into the baseball cap and, sure enough, dark roots were emerging from the scalp.

'You lied to me, Kristian,' said Alice.

'You think – you think that I owed you something?'

'I trusted you. I went out on a limb for you. I risked my reputation.'

'Your reputation?'

'I explained your situation very clearly to you, and the reasons why it was in your best interests to tell the truth.'

'Well, you know the truth now.'

'You fucked me over.'

'You're not being very clear-sighted about the nature of our relationship.'

Alice had on her back the rucksack. She slid her shoulders free of its straps and placed it on the table. She turned to the sentry.

'An instructor of mine used to say that everything you

need to persuade someone to cooperate can be found in an ordinary kitchen.'

Something was changing in Alice's way of speaking. Her accent had become drawling: her intonation was bright and sarcastic.

'Gonna have ourselves a little cookout,' she said. 'We're not outside it's true, but we're gonna do our best to enjoy ourselves – right, specialist?'

'Right, ma'am.'

'Cookout, specialist!'

'Cookout, ma'am.'

Alice unzipped the pack and rummaged around, producing cellophane-wrapped packets that she waved in front of Kit's face.

'I found these, still good and fresh. You like sausage? I *love* sausage! How about you, specialist?'

'Love sausage too, ma'am.'

'And the specialist knows sausage, right, specialist? Grew up on a hog farm. Am I right, specialist?'

The young man smiled shyly and flushed, as if flattered that this detail had been remembered.

'I sure did, ma'am.'

'Gas is cut off to this facility, but I got this.'

From the pack, she produced a camping stove which she placed on the floor between the table and Kit's chair. Then she took out an iron frying pan, a metal spatula, still in its cellophane packet, and a rectangular block of butter. She ignited the flame on the stove, placed the pan on it, and dropped in gobs of butter.

'Rightly we should season this skillet first,' said Alice. 'But that's not going to matter for our purposes.'

She pierced the skins of the sausages with a fork, then lined them up in the pan where they sizzled and spat.

She tended carefully to the sausages, poking and turning them over. The smell of fried meat filled the air. The savour and richness of it were overwhelming. When the sausages were cooked, she divided them between two tin plates which she set on the table with knives and forks.

'Specialist, have you eaten? Please, join me. Let us partake of this outstanding produce of our country.'

Alice paused respectfully, fork raised, as the soldier clasped his hands together and mumbled words of a grace. Then they fell to their meal. Their metal knives scraped against the plates. Kit's mouth filled with drool.

Alice looked over at him and nodded at the pan.

'I left one in there. That's for you if you tell us where that data device is.'

Kit, who had resolved to offer no reaction, gave an involuntary snigger.

'Oh, you're amused,' Alice said. 'I see you're amused. Specialist, he's laughing and saying to himself, *They think they can buy me with sausage!* But we know we can't do that, don't we, specialist?'

'We know it, ma'am.'

Alice put down her knife and fork and crouched by the camping stove. She dropped the remaining block of butter into the pan. She turned the flame up high. Then she went to the pack and took out a flask and two cups.

'Coffee for you and I, specialist.'

'Thank you, ma'am.'

'Last one overcooking anyway.'

They drank the coffee and finished the sausages. The

butter in the pan slumped and melted, and began to boil in small frothing bubbles.

Alice said something, but the words were indistinct because her mouth was full of meat.

'Did you hear me?'

'No,' said Kit.

'Where's the data device?'

'You know that. You were listening.'

'Where's the data device?'

'It's with my daughter.'

As if by prearrangement, the woman and the man put down their knives and forks and stood up abruptly. The young soldier stood behind Kit, reached around to grab the front of his shirt and yanked it with a single strong movement, tearing off the buttons and exposing his naked chest. He jerked the shirt awkwardly down so that Kit's shoulders and the tops of his arms were bared. Alice was standing over the spitting, smoking pan. She jabbed her fork to spear the last sausage and brandished it in front of her as she stalked towards Kit.

'Where's the fucking data device?'

The sausage was black, carbonised, and boiling butter was falling from it on to the floor. Alice held it under Kit's nose.

'Where's the fucking data device?'

Drops of liquid butter were spilling on to Kit's chest, burning him. Alice pushed the fiery sausage against his cheeks and eyes. The meat smell was in his nose. He writhed and twisted, but the young soldier was holding the chair from behind and keeping it upright.

'It's with my daughter, with the nomads!'

Alice took a deep breath and her words came out in a single exhalation. 'This is your last chance. Where's the fucking data device? I swear to God I'm gonna hurt you so bad.'

'I told you! It's on a necklace, around her neck.'

Alice exhaled loudly as if with relief. She picked the pan off the flame and advanced towards Kit holding it before him.

'I'm gonna burn your fucking skin off.'

'I swear that's where it is.'

'Gonna fucking fry you.'

She was dipping the spatula in the pan and using it as a paddle to splash molten liquid on to Kit's chest and shoulders and face.

Kit could hear himself screaming. His skin was registering multiple points of unbearable pain. He knew what was coming next. He had, he noticed, pissed himself. And yet the screaming, and the piss, and the pain itself, were also detached from him. They were his, and yet in possessing them, he placed them at a remove from himself. It was like grief and guilt: to be tortured and to resist was the image of grief.

He became conscious of the crying of the insects beyond the perimeter fence.

'Out of the chair!' Alice yelled at the soldier, panting, once the butter was all used up.

'Get him out of the chair, get his shirt off. His pants. I want his back, his butt. Sit on his back.'

She placed the empty pan back on the flame. The residue of the butter smoked and charred; the metal vessel became a disc of radiating heat. It took a long time; when it was ready, the piss in Kit's trousers was cold. Alice's breathing had calmed and quietened. When the metal was an angry blue, she lifted it off the heat and carried the pan to the prone body on the floor.

What was he? He knew that it was a foolish question, but it was one that had to be asked. Since the night of dancing in the jungle, Kit had often felt imperfectly tethered to himself. Now, as lightly as a balloon, his consciousness began to expand and lift up, above the floor, above the frying pan, above the mess hall. Poised over the camp, it took in the activity in the flimsy buildings below: the grinding of shredders, and the smoke of burning documents. Beyond the perimeter, artillery and rocket launchers were emplaced in the jungle, and columns of armour were converging on the camp from all sides. From a higher point, he could see warships docking at ports and fighter jets on airfields; from higher still, skirmishes at sea and in the air. The world, Kit understood, was under a dark shadow. Its foundations were being broken up and refashioned, violently and forever. All of this was fantasy, of course, but it was also true. Kit had one duty: to find his family. From his position of god-like elevation, he scanned the world for Helen and for Lara, then paused. There were so many people: how could it be right to take responsibility for only two of them?

Seeing everything, it now became possible to look into the grave. He hovered over those of his parents, beneath their heavy crosses, far away. He sought out those of Court and the boys who had fallen from the bridge, shallow heaps of earth and bones in the forest. Butterflies gathered there, which gave him comfort; but so did worms. Finally, he settled on the grave dug by the nomads. The investigative team had dug, scooped and sifted, but not every trace had been removed. Filament of decayed hair, skin reduced to powder, smear of spit, lymph, blood. The searchers thought that they had taken it all away; but everything essential remained, at the spot, and within memory. He lingered here for an unknowable time, in the green eternally alive forest, envious of the dark ground.

Later, he understood that the rocket had landed in the kitchen. It felt at the time as if he was inside the explosion. Violence of concentrated light, and a blast of sound and heat that propelled the room's metal contents in all directions. Kit, pressed against the floor, was already in a position of cover. Alice and the soldier, astride and above him, had no protection.

The crunch of subsiding rubble continued for a long time. Above him, shelves, metal counters, and the stuff of the walls and ceiling pressed down. Kit found himself sealed in a space created by the still bodies of Alice and the soldier, and the legs of the table that had been thrown on top of them. The weight of the torturers was firm, but soft; he was able to shift beneath it to find a more comfortable position. He lay like that for a long time. He could not bend arms or legs, but he could breathe and call out. Even the smoke did not reach him, although it was stiflingly hot and completely dark. Eventually, it became so quiet that he could faintly hear the insects in the forest. Fluid was dripping on to his face. By turning his head, he could lap it up where it pooled on the floor.

*

De Luca had come to him, after the return of the helicopter and the removal from it of the small coffin.

'I got some bad news, my friend,' he said. 'We just got these back from the lab.'

He pushed a thin folder of documents and charts across the table. Kit leafed through them, and pushed them back.

'So these, my friend, are—'

'I know what they are.'

'These are the results of—'

'I can see that.'

'She's not your kid, Kristian.'

Kit smiled.

'That doctor she was working with. Or was he a nurse? They were – you knew that? The whole time.'

De Luca shook his head in an imitation of despair at human iniquity. Then he smiled.

'You wanna see the pictures?' he asked.

He showed him a picture. Kit looked at it for a long time.

'You can fake tests. You can fake pictures,' Kit said. 'You'll fake anything.'

'Pretty good fake, huh? If it is a fake.'

Eventually, he became aware of muffled sirens and the clanking of machines. There were huge vibrations as the broken fragments above were removed piece by piece, but his mouth was too dry to call out. He supped up more of the floor's ooze, which was cold now and thick. Excited shouts responded to his croaking. The jagged surfaces that held him down wobbled and shifted as boots tramped upon them. He croaked more, and louder. Slowly and noisily, the broken building was being removed one layer at a time.

Glimmers of light appeared. At this point, when salvation became imaginable, physical pain returned to Kit, and he groaned and writhed against his constraints. As the shards of rubble above him were pulled away, the air became clearer and less choking. A tube appeared, worming its way into Kit's cocoon, with a blinking camera eye. It withdrew and was replaced by a different tube that dispensed drips of water.

Kit sucked thirstily. Finally, the table confining him was removed. It was night time, but light flooded over him from electric lamps. The faces of soldiers became visible. They were pulling out the parts of Alice and the specialist. Then their hands were grasping and lifting Kit, with words of reassurance and encouragement.

'What's your name, buddy? What's your name?'

'You're doing good, Kid.'

'Kid, you are one lucky individual.'

'Kid, the deceased here, the people we found with you, who are they? Are there others in this structure?'

Kit told them. He found that he could move his arms and his legs. He could even stand. Beneath the halogen, his torn trousers and bare skin were dyed a glittering black. They wiped clean a patch on his arm and injected him with a needle that quelled pain with an icy lurch. He was helped into the open back of a jeep. The explosion that destroyed the mess hall had also split open a section of the perimeter fence. Buildings across the camp were blacked out, but the horizon was rosy with the glow of fires. They drove him to a medical station where he joined a line of injured soldiers on benches. Those who were not engrossed in pain turned their heads and stared at him. An orderly came with a towel and basin of water, and rubbed at the stuff covering his face and hands. As he did so, Kit slumped over gently and fell unconscious.

He dreamed many dreams. They were either impossible to remember or impossible to express in language. The one that he woke from was about numbers. Kit, Helen, Lara and Alice were not people, but numbers of different kinds. It was a comedy, not a tragedy. The meaning of it, Kit recognised, was to do with the truth. Not that 2+2=5, but that two different things can be true at the same time.

It was day, although he could not be sure which day, when soldiers drove him across the camp for the last time.

The siege had entered a new stage. The smoke from individual explosions was merging into a haze that lingered over the ground. The camp's roads were punctuated by checkpoints and nests of guards hunched behind sandbags. Soldiers on foot sprinted between them, squat in helmets and body armour. Apart from the explosions, the sound of jet aircraft could be heard high overhead.

The jeep in which Kit sat, unbound and unhooded, drove at reckless speed. It pulled up at a large two-storey structure with signs bearing divisional crests. Concrete barriers were being positioned in front of it with a crane; at the side of the building, soldiers were tossing armfuls of documents and oblong computer drives on to a bonfire.

Officers with tensed jaws came and went through the double doors. Kit was led inside, to the back and into a room containing a low table, sofa and a beige carpet. The walls were hung with framed photographs of a uniformed man with short grey hair, grinning and shaking hands with people whose faces Kit knew: a famous politician, a film star, a golf champion.

The door at the far end of the room bore the words:

> Major General Eno Bartok
> Commanding Officer
> Camp Water Hyacinth

The soldier who had escorted Kit loitered uncertainly in the anteroom. He picked up a magazine from the table, then put it down. There were more explosions outside. In the corner, there was a television mounted on a stand. The soldier pressed the remote control and an image filled the screen. There was no sound; quivering horizontal lines distorted the picture. But Kit could make out a correspondent standing before lines of troops on foot and in personnel carriers, smiling and raising their arms as if in victory. Flags were being waved. The screen was dense with lines of excited text.

A young officer stuck his head round the door of the office.

'Mr Rabone. Please come in.'

The inner room was large, and in a state of advanced disorder. Chairs and tables were littered with eviscerated computer equipment. Depressions in the carpet indicated where cupboards and filing cabinets had been removed. There were more celebrity photographs on the walls, and a large wooden desk with a leather top and a carved nameplate bearing the general's name.

The young officer sat behind the desk, and pointed to the chair facing it.

'Please sit, Mr Rabone. Can I get you a cup of water?'

Next to the water cooler was another silent television, flickering uncertainly. Kit looked around. There was no one else in the room. The bandages on his chest and back rubbed against his shirt, but the numbness of injections lingered in his limbs, and he felt no discomfort.

The young man returned to the desk, and consulted a file of papers.

'Mr Rabone, I am Captain Barney, I serve under General Bartok. The general regrets not being able to meet with you himself. But he has deputed me to speak with you.'

'Where is General Bartok?'

They were the first words Kit had uttered for a long time. It was an effort to do so, as if the drugs suppressed the capacity to speak as well as to experience pain.

'He is occupied elsewhere. There's a lot going on – you understand.'

Captain Barney, who appeared almost nervous, gave a squirming half smile of apology.

'The general has authorized me – he has mandated me – to tell you, on our behalf, that we regret the recent treatment to which you were subject.'

He clasped his hands together on the desk and looked into the corner of the room.

'It was unauthorized by any command chain.'

He glanced down at the desk, as if consulting notes.

'It was excessive. It was unacceptable.'

He looked Kit in the eye, frowning with sincerity.

'Those are not our values, Mr Rabone. That is not who we are.'

Kit waited for more, but the captain suddenly relaxed,

as if a demanding duty had been successfully discharged. He took a sip from his beaker of water and turned to the television. The screen was displaying a map, with sections divided into red and blue, and arrows indicating progress and retreat.

The door behind Kit clicked open. Captain Barney stood up and snapped to attention with an expression of surprise. Kit turned and found himself facing the man in the photographs, accompanied by a young soldier and an older officer with a bald head.

In person, the general was shorter than he appeared alongside the celebrities. His hair was more bristly, spiking from the top of his skull. The atmosphere in the room altered in his presence, as if by a change in air pressure.

'Captain.'

'Sir. Is there—?'

'Just one thing we neglected earlier. The colonel will brief you.'

Kit was the only one not standing up. General Bartok flashed white teeth as he turned to him and looked him over.

'This is him, then,' he said. 'The famous Mr Rabone.'

He held out a hand, which Kit was too surprised not to take. The general's grip was conventionally crushing and prolonged. The bald colonel was standing by the desk, engaged in an intense mumbling dialogue with Captain Barney. They shuffled through papers on the desk and extracted one, which was held up before the general at eye level. He quickly nodded, then turned to Kit.

'The captain's been over this already, maybe – but she

was wrong to do that, Mr Rabone. Morally – put all that to one side. Just in practical terms. It doesn't work. You could have said anything to make the pain stop. It's better just to wear them down. Desperation – that's more powerful than pain.'

'That's true,' said Kit.

'I took my eye off. Good deal going on, but I should have supervised more closely. You have my genuine apology for that.'

Kit didn't know what to say.

'We should go, sir,' said the colonel.

They turned to the door, then the general paused, looked over at Barney, and turned to Kit again.

'Captain told you our proposal?'

'Not yet, sir,' said Barney. 'We were just getting on to that when—'

'Well, let me take a moment to brief you myself.'

The bald colonel looked anxious.

'To cut to it,' said the general, 'you've got a choice, and the choice is yours.'

He pulled over a chair and sat in it, facing Kit. He nodded his head slowly, as if carefully putting together words and thoughts.

'Maybe put it like this,' he said. 'As a military we are good – we are very good – at treating burns. Even in deployed units like these. We've got burns specialists as good as any in the world. Excellent care. So if that's what you choose, you can stay here with us, and take a bed in the treatment facility. You can see, however, that we are . . . preoccupied by combat operations here. In circumstances like this, it's probable that yours would not be a priority case. And the attitude of the medical personnel to someone with your status, rather than one of our own – you can see that might be complicated. We're looking at evac for certain elements, in any case—'

The colonel leaned in and whispered into the general's ear. He listened and nodded.

'So then there's your other choice. That shot they gave you – that's good stuff, right? No pain now, and none for a good few hours. Your injuries have been dressed, so provided you maintain hygiene in the tropical environment you got a good start. If you wish, Mr Rabone, you may choose to leave. I mean walk away from here, straight out the door.'

'You're going to let me go?'

The general smiled with his very white teeth.

'Why would you let me go?'

'It's a fair question, a fair question. Remember, Mr Rabone, that you're a little out of touch here. It's a long time since you watched TV, am I right? Out there in the big world things change – sometimes they change suddenly. Maybe you've become the beneficiary of those events. Or maybe not. You would be walking into No Man's Land. The space between two contending armies – it is a dangerous place to be. The decision is yours. No one here is putting you under any pressure.'

'But where am I?'

The colonel leaned in close again.

'That's classified, I'm afraid,' said the general.

'Why won't you say it?'

'Well, maybe you know where you are. Maybe you're right where you started. Maybe we hooded you, and spun you round, and flew you up and around, and brought you right back to where you started out. Maybe. Maybe not. But maybe you'll find out if you just walk out of here.'

'This is a trap. There's no way you'd let me go.'

'Well, maybe.' The general gave a wry smile. 'Maybe you're going to step out and I'm gonna tell Corporal Gruber here' – he looked up at the young soldier – 'to put a bullet in the back of your brain.'

The colonel and captain smiled admiringly, as if at a sophisticated joke.

'Or maybe something else,' the general went on. 'Maybe we need people like you, people who oppose us, in their hearts.'

He turned and addressed the colonel, rather than Kit, as if taking up a conversation that had been broken off.

'Maybe that was the problem when we thought we won the last time round,' he said. 'Got to have people to argue with, to keep the argument going. Even when you've won it. Otherwise, when you've won, you lose. Because you go soft – intellectually.'

'Lot of truth in that, sir,' said the colonel, nodding.

They all looked at Kit.

'Why should I trust you?' he asked. 'Why would anyone ever trust people like you?'

Now the general was looking away from Kit, his attention distracted by the television. The screen was stricken with wobbling lines. But the sequence of images was clear enough.

They were filmed in and around the village. There were shots of the forest, and Justus, the schoolmaster, walking through it. Then there was the bloodstained uniform, held up to the camera by the mountain people, with the name McPugh on its breast and the flag on its sleeve. There was the Siskin Ferox hovering over the village at night. The quality of the picture was so poor that the captions were difficult to read, but through the quivering of the screen Kit made out the words *SECRET INVASION*. People he knew were visible in the film, among them Obson, looking scared and fierce. And now it was cutting to a still image of Court Hardy, a formal photographic portrait, in which he looked young and very pompous.

There was an explosion outside that shook the room, and the television image became grainier still. Was the woman talking on screen now Lara? He couldn't be sure. If it was, she looked older. But that was certainly a still photograph of him and Helen, standing and smiling in front of their house.

'What's happening?' he asked.

'I don't know,' said the general, as more explosions sounded from close by. 'Maybe it's all over.'

He stepped up to the television and switched it off.

'We got to go, sir,' said the colonel.

'It's a jungle, anyway,' said the general.

'Right now, sir.'

'As for trusting us,' said the general. 'There's no special reason, I guess. But what else are you gonna do?'

He smiled at the colonel. 'Trust, not trust, la-di-dah.'

He nodded quickly to himself, as if he had just remembered something important; walked to the desk, opened a drawer, and removed from it a compact object which he handed to Kit. It was a small ceramic urn, decorated with an inlaid cross.

'I'm real sorry for your loss.' The general nodded conclusively, strode to the door and held it open, turning again to face Kit.

'Wanna try?'

Outside, General Bartok strapped on his helmet and climbed into his jeep.

'Corporal Gruber will escort you to the perimeter. Can't spare you a vehicle, not at this juncture.'

Gruber stood by, looking tough and resentful. Captain Barney handed Kit a backpack containing a water bottle, syringes, and a first-aid kit, along with the urn. He presented a pen and a densely printed document of numbered paragraphs; Kit signed, without reading it. The captain climbed in beside the general, who leaned over and muttered to him. He stepped out of the jeep and held out a black pistol. Kit weighed it in his hands, surprised by its lightness and by the delicacy of the moulded grip. Then he handed it back.

The general's jeep departed at speed. Kit and the soldier stepped on to the road in front of the headquarters. With rolling shoulders, rifle in arms, Gruber set off along it.

There were few people now on the routes through the camp; their place had been taken by machines, visible and invisible, that thwacked and boomed, or loomed out of the haze. Artillery shells launching and exploding; jets overhead. Squat double-rotored helicopters could be seen in the distance landing and taking off. The zone through which they walked had been abandoned; the sandbagged emplacements were unmanned. Three tanks overtook them noisily, the tarmac crackling beneath their tracks;

an open-backed lorry covered by a camouflage tarpaulin motored past in the opposite direction.

They came to a crossroads. A hangar-like building next to it had been hit. There was smoke, but no sign of life. In one direction, the road ascended to a shallow rise; it was beyond there that the helicopters were rising and descending. Gruber and Kit turned in the opposite direction.

They found themselves in the square of recreation. It had been devastated by rockets and fire; the plastic Burger Beach sign drooled, half-melted, over the broken takeaway window; the soft metal walls of the BX were split and bent outwards like the skin of a giant soft-drink can. The square was deserted except for the driving hall where soldiers were loading golf clubs into the back of a pickup. Gruber nodded at them, and the soldiers nodded back expressionlessly.

They walked past the residential cubes where the officers slept, and past the encampment of tents. Both were blasted and deserted. Soldierly possessions – T-shirts, charging cables, a sagging basketball – were scattered across the road.

They walked a long way. They paused frequently to drink water. Kit began to falter. Gruber helped him with one of the painkilling syringes, which made him surge with energy and optimism.

Kit would find Helen. She would be healthy. She was with Lara in the city. They were waiting for him. Dr Mochtar would be there too. Kit would seek him out. He would forgive him for what he had done. They would wait for the war to end. Then they would return to the village. Kit, Lara and Helen would help to rebuild it. They would rebuild their own house. They would ship in a new Koolroom. They would place fresh skulls in the eaves.

Kit and the soldier walked and walked so far that the act of walking, the rhythm of one step after the next and the memories and dreams that it unlocked, came to be the natural state of things. But then the atmosphere began to alter. They were close to the perimeter; through the smoke and between the buildings, the fence could be glimpsed. A battle was going on there, not the plodding exchange of artillery, but a fast bitter fight at close quarters with pattering automatic rifles and a small helicopter dipping angrily in and out of sight.

Gruber led Kit forwards, scuttling from the cover of one abandoned building to the next.

They reached a point where the fence could be clearly seen, a hundred yards away. They were crouched beside the last human structure before the jungle. The sound of shooting became louder, and the shouts of men. Gruber was pointing towards the fence, and talking about perimeter breaches and voltage failure. It was difficult to follow everything he said, but it was clear to Kit that from here he would be alone.

It began to rain. It was as if a window had been raised, a pane of glass removed. The light had always penetrated, but now the air flowed freely. It warmed the inside of Kit's nose.

He stepped out and walked fast and upright into the open without looking back. The fence extended in both directions and looking along it he could make out wide holes. Through them, people were coming in from the outside, slight figures with rifles, silhouetted against the smoke and then obscured by it.

The rain fell hard. The closest hole was a few yards away. Kit stepped over a marshy creek, spiky with raindrops, and walked close up against the wire in the direction of the firing. He could see the forest on the far side, and hear the insects. Through the fence's metal webs he became aware of pale faces watching him. He found the gap, a ragged slit that had been cut with a tool. As he pulled it open, there were shouts and gunfire close at hand. The drops of rain were smacking into his hair and against the earth. An explosion lit up behind him and he felt the heat and flash in his temples as he stepped through. Looking up, there was an outpouring of light from the tops of the trees. The pale faces had disappeared, although he knew they were watching him. Between the rain and fire, he could hear a baby crying. And now Kit was running and stumbling, falling and getting up again, eyes darting from tree to tree, searching out a place of safety in the jungle.